**She had hoped she was done with this scene, but here she was, again walking into harm's way...**

Lana peered in at the casino crowd while surreptitiously tugging at the hem of her skirt—her way-too-short, butt-hugging skirt—worn with the fitted formal tuxedo styled jacket that hit a fraction of an inch below the skirt. It was an intentionally sexy outfit, one she'd worn before with great success.

"I just thought I'd never have to wear it again," she muttered, to herself.

"Pardon?" Adam spoke directly in her ear, proof of the high quality of the discreet head set. Every nuance of his deep voice eased the tension trying to overtake her.

She pulled in a deep breath and centered herself, taking on the persona of the hard-edged party girl, always looking for a good time and a better deal. She searched herself for memories of being alone, feeling friendless, and added those to her character's personality.

Drawing on this persona, she stepped onto the casino floor, not quite wobbling on her ridiculously high heels. Fuck-me pumps. Yeah, right. The feet of the women who wore them certainly got the raw end of the deal. She pushed that opinion to a different compartment. Party Queen Lana was never seen in heels lower than four inches.

"Party Queen Lana is a pain in my ass," she muttered.

No one answered, but she caught the edge of a masculine snicker and almost let herself smile in a non-brittle fashion.

"Here we go," a voice whispered in her ear.

Lana Greene doesn't care that most of the world sees her as avaricious and amoral. All the better for her to stand as a shield against those who would exploit the weaker. Until the day she comes up against a situation too difficult for her to handle on her own, and she has to reach out to her ex-husband, Ty Randolph, owner of Stormhaven Ranch.

Adam Roberts dedicated himself to keeping the world safe—until his efforts took part of a leg and much of his self-worth. Recuperating at Stormhaven—a remote ranch, where the main concern is helping out vets—he jumps at the chance to assist his new friends when Ty asks him to take on an escort mission.

But there is far more at stake than anyone realizes—including a number of innocent lives. And Lana is in way over her head. Now she and Adam must learn to trust themselves—and each other—fast, if they are to have any chance of protecting those innocent lives.

In *A Question of Trust* by Mona Karel, Lana Greene is working undercover to help girls caught in sex trafficking, but she sees something she shouldn't and now she is in over her head. With no one to trust and no one to help, she calls the only one she knows who will help her without hesitation—her ex-husband, Tyler Randolph. He sends an ex-special forces friend to bring Lana to New Mexico and his ranch, Stormhaven, but Adam Roberts has no idea what he is getting into when he agrees to this "simple" escort job. All of his skills and smarts will be needed to get them out of this mess, but will that be enough? Karel has a real talent for creating spicy romantic thrillers that keep you on the edge of your seat, and this is no exception. Very well done. ~ *Taylor Jones, The Review Team of Taylor Jones & Regan Murphy*

*A Question of Trust* by Mona Karel is the story of a woman with a shadowed past who is determined to help the weak among us who are being preyed upon by evil men. When Lana Greene sees a murder of a young woman in Los Vegas and can't get the police to pay any attention to her, she calls the only person she knows who will help her without reservation—Tyler Randolph, her ex-husband and owner of Stormhaven Ranch in New Mexico. Ty sends former special forces operative Adam Roberts to bring Lana from Los Vegas to new Mexico, but what Adam thinks is a simple escort mission turns out to be a fight for their lives. The third book in her Stormhaven Love Story series, *A Question of Trust* is every bit as spicy and exciting as the other two. With a solid and timely plot, marvelous characters that you can't help but root for, and plenty of spicy sex scenes, this is one you won't want to miss. ~ *Regan Murphy, The Review Team of Taylor Jones & Regan Murphy*

OTHER BOOKS BY

MONA KAREL

AND

BLACK OPAL BOOKS

*My Killer, My Love*

*Teach Me to Forget*


The Stormhaven Love Stories Series

*A Question of Honor*

*A Question of Faith*

# A Question

# of Trust

## A Stormhaven Love Story

Mona Karel

*A Black Opal Books Publication*

GENRE: ROMANTIC THRILLER/ROMANTIC SUSPENSE

A QUESTION OF TRUST
Copyright © 2018 by Mona Karel
Cover Design by Jackson Cover Designs
All cover art copyright © 2018
All Rights Reserved
Print ISBN: 978-1-644370-17-9

First Publication: OCTOBER 2018

Published by Black Opal Books **http://www.blackopalbooks.com**

# A Question
# of Trust

# Chapter 1

Lana Greene took one final, deep breath of relatively clean air before shouldering the door open into the high-priced suite at the top of the luxury hotel. Smoke assaulted her nostrils as she entered the room. Exotic, pungent, and difficult to identify—most likely from foreign, possibly illegal sources—the smoke mixed with lust, avarice, and gut-wrenching fear to form a miasma forcing her into taking short, shallow breaths. Preferably through her mouth. The cleaning staff was going to have a rough time making this room habitable again.

She did not allow revulsion to touch her face, though it was difficult to maintain the slightly ditzy sex kitten expression when she wanted more than anything to turn on her narrow heel and escape.

The drapes were closed against the early morning light, shutting off one of the truly lovely views in Las Vegas: the rising sun backlighting mountains with red and orange and gold. It would be another brutally hot summer day.

Too bad no one was taking advantage of the view, nor of the brief, clear cool air. She thought longingly of high mountains and clean air then slipped into the room as gracefully as possible.

"Lana, sweetie, there you are!" The slurred voice called from across the room, grating against her ears and her soul. She turned in the direction, making sure her lips continued the sincere if slight smile.

"Mr. Hoffman, what can I do for you?"

"Ralph. How many times do I have to tell you?" His voice was a drunken slur, but she could hear anger building. Hoffman drunk was even less in control than Hoffman sober.

From the trash and detritus she saw strewn across the room, she had no doubt there was more than high-proof expensive alcohol influencing him and his equally incapacitated friends—if you could call associates in his sort of business friends. Maybe friendly enemies. Maybe even not so friendly, given Hoffman's business practices, which were anything to show a healthy profit—legal, moral, helpful, or not.

"Do you need a meal served, or would you like to have housekeeping come through and pick up for you?"

"We don't want anyone in here. Tony B should have made that clear when he hired you. If you want to show off your Suzie Homemaker skills, go right ahead and straighten up a bit."

His suggestion warranted a baleful glance, complete with raised brows, but she didn't deign a reply. Instead, she turned away, surveying the room.

The men sprawled across fine leather sofas, heels scraping the tops of low inlaid tables, in some instances shifting the delicate inlay. Her ever busy mind automatically totaled the cost to refurbish, and she wondered if she would be able to convince her client to pay up.

"Mr. Bonavides is not my employer. The contract between Make it Work and your group was signed solely by myself. I suggest you reference your copy concerning damages to the property."

Hoffman turned away with a scowl when she made her voice and attitude intentionally mercenary. No matter what the signed contract might say, some people seemed to believe they were far above any consequences of their actions. She ignored the sprawled bodies, the expensive crystal glasses dropped to the thick carpet while full, if the spreading stains were any evidence. The lovely table cover, decorated with handmade lace, was nowhere in sight. Plates of dried leftover food overflowed side tables and piled on the floor, along with discarded bits of clothing. A dark stain smeared across one sharp corner of the table. Bright clothing, what looked like delicate expensive material, trailed along the stained carpet. Not something any of these men would be wearing.

A pile of cream cloth drew her eye to a corner behind one of the couches. Ah, the table cover, no doubt totally ruined. Plus what seemed to be more bits of that bright material along with...a bare foot? Was she seeing a dainty toenail with innocent pink polish? She avoided allowing the frown to form across her forehead while she headed in that direction, buried instincts overcoming her usual control. Until a deep voice, roughened by foreign tones, warned her just before she felt a large hand take hold of her upper arm.

"Ralph might be able to live on vodka and tobacco, but the rest of us need breakfast. Have a meal sent up right away. If you can get it here in ten minutes, there's an extra hundred in it for you."

Lana welcomed the excuse to escape from the fetid room, though she worried about abandoning what looked too much like the form of a girl under that casually discarded cloth—along with a stain trailing along the thick carpet.

Lana avoided looking directly at that sad pile of cloth. Instead, she nodded once, planting a smile on her mouth. She could do nothing for this girl, and if they ever suspected her actions, she would not be able to help any others.

ເ৲১ເ৲১

Fresh baked scones and yeasty donut smells enlivened Lana's nose. Nothing was quite as enticing as a small bakery in the early morning. Especially after the day and night she'd had. Soon her teeth would be biting into a flaky pastry, maybe one with a raspberry filling she could cherish on her tongue before swallowing. She'd learned long ago about the value of little things in her life. A good pastry or two would go a long way toward helping her ignore the bruises and scrapes all over her body, clamoring for her to notice them.

A television screen, discreetly tucked into a niche above the counter, caught her eye, then her whole attention. She turned in that direction instead of leaning over the glass display case. A photo of a delicately lovely young woman—high cheekbones and an exotic slant to her eyes augmenting her beauty—was inset against a dumpster in an alley, with a sheet draped over a sadly diminished body. The sound was turned too low for her to hear the talking head but a text block to the side provided information about "another" tragic death of an unknown female. Except the woman in that picture looked depressingly familiar.

Then the camera showed another picture, another sheet draped body. This time a large man with an angry expression. Then a picture of a hairy arm with a tattoo of a tiger from wrist to elbow.

She'd seen that tattoo, recently, on an arm reaching

for her as she rushed down concrete steps in her ridiculous shoes.

Pastry forgotten, she edged out of the shop and around the corner to an empty seating area with umbrellas opened against the soon to invade bright sun. She automatically looked around while fussing with her hair, her collar, and remembered she'd changed to casual clothes, slim jeans and a loose shirt, and tied a scarf over her head to complete the non-party girl persona.

She dug deep into her old leather backpack and pulled out a phone she hadn't used in a long time. Very little battery showed, but a stashed power cord and an outside plug soon helped her hunt up a number she never thought she'd call again. Desperate times called for desperate measures, and she had not been this desperate for a long time.

The phone rang several times, reaching out across the miles to safety. Until:

"Stormhaven. How can I help you?"

# Chapter 2

Captain Adam Roberts (retired) was as certain as he could be that no one else watched the blonde in the tiny mom-in-law house tucked into a corner of the large, tree-infested back yard of the monstrous, over-grown, pretentious, fake mansion now standing empty, no doubt due to the fact that no one could afford the electric bill to cool or heat it.

No one else was driving past, or watching from a driveway down the street, or even peering through a long range scope at Sydney Starke's damned-near gorgeous sister. The pictures he'd been given had all been of the made-up-perfectly, not-a-single-hair-out-of-place sort of woman who left him cold. This woman, who'd come out of the secluded house when the sun had barely eased through the trees to water a profusion of plants and put out food for the local population of feral cats and gossiping birds, was in full dress-down mode, wearing what looked like thrift-store finds—loose jeans and baggy shirts, with her hair pulled back impatiently into a skewed pony tail.

This woman could make his heart beat in syncopated

time, if he cared about gorgeous women. Wasn't it lucky he knew that gorgeous women were always trouble?

He lifted his phone, snapping a picture of her as she came out to tend the cats, then sent the picture out with *???* in the message.

Within less than a minute the answer came back. *As far as I can tell. You're no Ansel Adams.*

He stifled his snicker in a cough. Working with the group at Stormhaven was more fun than he'd had in a long time. He contemplated sending back something crude but reminded himself he was a professional and this was a job. Plus, he really did like the people he was working with. Most of the time.

So he texted, *Going in, let her know.*

When the blonde tilted her head then dug into a deep pocket and lifted the phone to her ear, he eased himself out of the not-big-enough-even-for-his-frame rental car. Keeping to the available cover as much as possible in the early morning desert hush, he slid along the side of the large front house.

"Ma'am? Ms. Randolph? I'm here from your ex-husband."

⌘⌘⌘

Lana fell against the side of the tiny adobe *casita* where she'd been hiding out. Her heart stuttered almost to a stop before she grabbed enough breath to call out. "Whoever you are, come out where I can see you."

She expected someone built along the lines of her ex-husband and his partner. Big, obviously suited for the work, either as a soldier or a cowboy. When a moderate-sized man slipped out from the shadow of the behemoth wanna-be castle, turning and pulling off his cap so the early light revealed close-cut dark hair and a lean face, she felt her heart jump into flight reaction.

"I have no idea who you are so I suggest you stop right there."

"No problem, ma'am. If you want to snap my picture and send it off to your sister, we can get out of sight all the faster."

Huh? Send his picture to Sydney? Clever.

She followed his advice, lifting the cheap phone, thumbing the camera function. One, two, three clicks. She chose the best of the three to send off to New Mexico and got an immediate answer.

*Yes. Now get back in the house.*

Always bossy, her sister. Lana backed into the house, followed by the man, who continued to keep a space between them. She realized it wasn't only to be polite, he was also keeping himself a safe distance away from her. He lifted his much fancier phone for a couple of quick shots and copied her sending. Then he nodded.

"Looks like Syd has given both of us an okay. You don't look much like the pictures she has of you, so I needed to check."

"What pictures did she have?"

"Formal types mostly. Wedding, that sort of thing." He looked her over and took a breath, as if bracing himself for her reaction. "I think I like this look better."

"I think I agree with you, but there wasn't much choice either way. These were on the mark-down rack at Goodwill, and I only had the cash in my pockets when I got out of there."

"Out of there…" His unusually light-green eyes in a rough-hewn face studied her, then he glanced around the room, no doubt evaluating where she'd been staying.

The whole cottage was small. Cute when you visited for a few hours but restrictive when you had to be here for too long. Lana had already been here long enough.

The quiet, tough man looked as though he was waiting for an answer. *What was the question? Oh.* "Out of the penthouse suite where I heard—I saw—" The memories moved in on her, and she felt the darkness try to take over.

"Easy." He was suddenly closer, taking hold of her arm, his grip impersonal.

Even so, the touch of this man's hand, the strength in his fingers, jolted her. She straightened, started to pull away, then realized he was only supporting her, not trying to move her around, his grip not closing enough to affect the existing bruises. Once she edged away and took a deep breath, he released her and stepped back—giving her space as if he realized she was not comfortable around men who, no doubt, carried weapons and knew how to use them. She wasn't. She hadn't been for a long time. "What's the plan?"

"Getting you out of here first. Getting you someplace safe so you can let people know what it was you heard or saw. Not now." He raised one large hand, palm out. "Right now we need to concentrate on removal. Do you have anything you need to take with you?"

She lifted her heavy tote onto her shoulder then reached for the grip of a soft sided case. He nodded as if approving her ability to travel light. Condescending jerk.

"What about the cats? Will anyone notice they need feeding? Or the plants haven't been watered?"

"The cats are a neighborhood project, greedy little beggars. And the plants pretty much take care of themselves. A caretaker comes by about once a week. I was planning to be gone before he arrived."

"Good. You have wheels?"

She shuddered, remembering her precipitous flight from the high rise and the subsequent escape through the city.

"Not anymore."

His brows met in a quick frown, then he nodded. "Back exit?"

"Yes, through the palm trees. There's a break in the wall, opening onto a small alley."

"I think I saw that road. Can you be there in five minutes?"

She nodded once, her heart racing. He slid out of the house and up the driveway the same silent way he'd shown up.

She'd asked for help and gotten it in spades. But what had asking her ex-husband gotten her into?

 broken ornament

"Just a quick trip," they'd told him. "Out to Nevada and back. Fly into a small airport, drive about an hour, pick up Ty's ex-wife, fly back. Piece of cake."

*Yeah, piece of cake.* Except Ty's ex-wife was nothing like her sister, Sydney. For one, Lana was several inches taller, and all those inches were in the right place. Even dressed down, with no obvious makeup enhancing her thick-lashed chocolate-brown eyes, light hair shining bright in that gloomy room, she had a gloss he bet Syd never had, a way of carrying herself that spoke of fancy restaurants on the arm of rich men, instead of field stripping a weapon while under fire. Sydney Starke was real, solid. Her sister was—

He looked over at the passenger seat. Her sister was sitting very still, staring at his profile. Something she'd been doing a lot of since easing herself into the car. She'd shifted once or twice as though trying, and failing, to find a more comfortable position on the seat.

"Ma'am, are you okay? You weren't hurt when you left that last location were you?"

"Ma'am," she muttered with a small laugh. "No, I wasn't hurt. I'm just not accustomed to running down many flights of stairs or sleeping on a short couch. I need to get out and move around some is all."

"You should be able to do that at the ranch without worrying about who might be watching you."

"Yes, it seemed like a safe place to be. Where are we going and why exactly are you here? Not that I don't appreciate the help."

"We're going to a ranch with a small private airport not too near Vegas. Your—Mr. Randolph's—neighbor offered to give us a lift while he was at a meeting."

"Ah, yes. Kyle Jorden, Ty's obscenely rich neighbor."

"That's the one. Not that many people have their own fleet of planes."

"And he apparently keeps them all busy."

Adam looked in the mirrors, checking constantly for any vehicle that might be following. He kept the window down in spite of the heat. A bit of sweat was a small price to pay for vigilance. Because of this, he heard the distinctive beat of helicopter blades, several times, as if someone was trying to pinpoint a location.

"Ma'am, do you have anything on you from before?"

"What do you mean? I got new clothes, such as they were."

"Purse?"

"Another thrift-store find."

"Shoes, jewelry, watch..."

She slapped her hand over her wrist and looked over at him, guilt in those big brown eyes. Then reluctantly, she unclasped the dainty watch and handed it over. "Do you think—"

"I don't know. But it's kind of odd to have a chopper fly over us twice in five minutes. Hold on."

Adam wrenched the wheel, heading off the road toward a gas station with the questionable promise of "fresh food and cold beer."

"You need to use the bathroom," he stated, not phrasing it as a question.

She grimaced, obviously not thinking good thoughts about the bathrooms in a place that looked so run down.

"We don't need much gas," he continued. "And I doubt either one of us is willing to risk that food. We need a reason to stop for more than a few minutes."

She nodded, and when the car eased up next to the pump, reached for the door handle.

"Hold on." He scanned the parking lot then tilted his head to check overhead. "We might have to ditch the watch here, but I'd rather it kept moving a different direction from where we're headed. Don't be surprised if you see me doing something a little…"

"Illegal? Trust me, there's not much you can do I haven't seen."

With that, she opened the door and swiveled to move her legs out of the car. She stood with the care of someone who'd been sitting too long, and whose body didn't appreciate what it had gone through the last few days.

The interior of the service station lived up to the promise of the exterior, complete with flies, the smell of old grease, and a bored cashier, who nodded without much expression to the back of the building when Lana inquired about a ladies room. Then she straightened, checking out the new man when Adam came in.

ര990

Lana raised her brows while surveying the facilities. At least there was toilet paper and paper towels, though it didn't look like much attention was given to bathroom inspections. She spent what seemed an appropriate amount of time in the room before flushing the toilet then running the water long enough to wash her hands. Adam was at the register, paying for some bottles of cold water while complaining about the "hinky" gas gauge on their rental.

"I swear I'm going to turn that pile of crap rental in if we're here much longer, babe."

"Whatever you think best, hun."

That almost got a reaction from him, but only a quirk at one side of his mouth. An elderly man had come in while she'd been in the back, along with a couple of rowdy teens.

"Y'all can't be buyin' beer here, you know," the cashier called out. "And you can't get anyone to buy it for you, either."

"Yeah, yeah, we know." They went from the large chilled beer displays to the smaller glass fronted water and soda coolers.

Adam gave Lana a minute nod as they navigated past the noisy young men, who smelled like their vehicle air conditioning was on the fritz. It almost hid the dubious perfume of stale cigarette smoke.

Two more vehicles were in the lot, a well maintained older truck, and a newer, large, dusty, dually beyond that. Adam rested his hand in the middle of her back, guiding her away from the building and pointing off toward the smudge on the horizon that was Vegas.

"See what happens when too many people get themselves all squished together? It's no wonder they're always arguin'."

"Not everyone can be as enlightened as your family," she said in as conciliatory tone as she could manage.

This time she got an almost smile and thought she might have heard something along the lines of "cute," under his breath. While they discussed the view, Adam's hand flicked once, and she saw her pretty watch go flying into the over-packed second seat of the truck. She sighed.

"I had to save up a long time to afford that watch, even at a pawn shop."

"You shoulda said something. We could always dig it out of their empty chip bags if it means that much to you."

"Staying alive means just a bit more."

He looked at her over the top of the compact car before sliding behind the wheel.

"Something really spooked you."

"Something would have *had* to spook me, to get me to call my ex-husband for help."

She eased into her seat, bracing herself for the stab of pain. She sensed him looking at her, but after a few deep breaths, he put the vehicle in gear and pulled out.

ෙ෨ෙ෨

What seemed like an eternity of silent driving, punctuated only by the mystery man's deep breaths, was probably only fifteen minutes. His large hands stayed steady on the wheel—no casual one-finger hold for this soldier. In spite of the lack of uniform, she knew he was every inch, every ounce, a soldier. Those lessons she learned early in life tended to stick with her.

She shifted in her seat, looking for that one perfect angle that didn't hurt quite as much—there. At least briefly, the cessation of pain was like a balm. She let herself relax into the back of the seat and managed to draw a deep breath.

"You ready to tell me how bad you're hurt?"

"I told you, I'm just a little sore from running down a ridiculous number of steps instead of using the elevator.

The choice of sleeping on that tiny couch or on the floor didn't do much to help. Not to mention no hot water for the shower."

"All that's inconvenient, but you're in pain, not just inconvenienced."

*Dammit.* She would have to be rescued by the only perceptive man in three states. She didn't realize she'd muttered this out loud instead of in her head until she heard his quiet chuckle.

"Not quite. A team leader who can't tell when one of his people is hurting can get the whole team killed. You think they can keep up, and you end up hauling their sorry asses out of the field. No need to apologize," he added as if he knew what she was going to say next. "Just be straight with me. How many flights of stairs?"

"Twenty? Twenty-three including the sub basements."

"And then?"

"Then they managed to make my car crash, so I got knocked around some. I got lucky there, since the cops had a speed trap set up and were on site immediately."

"Medics show up?"

Not EMTs, or paramedics. Yep, soldier man. Smart soldier man. She wasn't sure he was totally buying the edited version of what had happened. "Pretty fast. They didn't see anything overt—no blood, no broken bones. And they had a real MVA right down the street—bus and bicycle. So I was able to talk them out of taking me in, and I slipped away. Grabbed a cab then a bus then walked to that lovely tribute to bad taste."

"You left the vehicle?"

She shrugged and winced. "Friend's car, kinda old. He's been storing it at the hotel in my extra spot while he's out of town. I grabbed the bag from my car but took his car, hoping to fool anyone following me."

He waited for more information then continued, "How far did you walk?"

"Couple miles? I hit the thrift store first. The emergency bag I kept in my car wasn't enough for more than a couple of days."

"You don't have to pretend with me, Ms. Randolph."

"Greene."

"'Scuse me?"

"I go by my mother's name, or at least her last husband's name. Greene. But I would much prefer you call me Lana."

"Yes, ma'am." His total lack of inflection said more than most men's long speeches. So Adam Roberts didn't think she should have dropped Ty Randolph's last name. Maybe he'd think differently if he knew how little she deserved to carry that name.

The silence extended long enough for her to relax as much as possible into the seat, the empty desert lulling her nearly to sleep. A roar of many engines came up from behind them. She recognized the sound from her years on the road around Vegas.

"Bikers," she said into the silence. "Back a couple of turns."

He nodded and took a quick right off the highway onto a road leading to one of the saddest old buildings she'd ever seen. He guided the car to ease behind the dilapidated structure, risking nail punctures but hiding completely from anyone on the road.

"A lot of the so-called biker gangs around here are pretty innocuous. Once in a while, I have a chance to go out with them. Some are retirees living out their teenage dreams, but instead of riding hogs, they're on shiny purple bikes with big storage sections and sometimes even side cars. I've even seen—"

His upraised hand cut off her forced light-hearted

babble. He eased out of the car, edging around the building until he could see the oncoming group of growling motorcycles.

∾∾

They came in a cloud of dust and noise. Some were definitely purple and oversized, a last-chance dream of freedom. But intermingled were some bad-ass powerful bikes with riders in concealing outfits. All dark. Nothing strange about being covered from head to toe in leather when you're on a motorcycle with nothing else to protect your teeth from bugs, but they sure didn't blend in.

The group swept past, with no obvious demarcation between the retirees and the younger riders. By the time he could figure out if the dark clads on their speed bikes were innocuous or dangerous, he and Ms. Rand—no, Ms. Greene, could be in serious trouble. He slipped back to the car, feeling all sorts of grim.

She had not come out of her seat, not done any of the you've-got-to-be-kidding stupid things too many amateurs did when their lives were in danger. In fact, since he'd taken her out of that house, she'd acted completely contrary to what he'd expected. He filed that away to think about later. Right now they needed to look at some sort of change in plans.

He arranged himself behind the wheel of the getting-smaller-all-the-time car, not yet reaching for the ignition key. She still didn't say anything. Didn't ask any inane questions like "Who was that?" or even "What's next?" She pretty much just sat there in her own little bubble of coping, trying to hide her wince whenever she moved too fast.

"We don't have a lot of time," he said. "They're going to figure out we either turned off or hid somewhere, and it's not like there's a lot of turn-off-or-hide on this road."

"How did they—"

"That chopper was following a small beige sedan. When the tracker moved a different direction, they probably figured out the kid's truck would only be valid if you were in it. There are all sorts of reasons why you would have moved into the truck. No doubt, they either did a drive by or just stopped those kids somewhere. You weren't in it, and the kids didn't know anything about you. So now they're looking around for this car. Dammit."

"You think some of those motorcycles were not retirees living the dream?"

"Hate to say it, but, yeah, I do." He reached for the small phone stashed in the console.

# Chapter 3

Lana reached for the bottle of water. Sipped. Warm but wet, easing into the parched areas of her throat. She let her head fall back on the seat then pivoted her head on her weary neck enough to see the man next to her.

"Time to call the Mother Ship?" Through the fog of pain and fatigue, Lana heard the words come out of her mouth. She winced.

The man's head whipped around fast enough to have Lana pressing hard against the door. "What did you say?"

"Sorry, I guess that was my inner geek coming out." She took a deep breath and forced herself to pay better attention. Wearing comfortable clothes made her too careless.

"Mother ship." He shook his head. "Mother something, that's for sure."

"I wasn't sure if you had anyone watching out, maybe keeping track long distance."

He shook his head, starting to push buttons. "Nope, we're it for now. They have all sorts of fancy equipment at Stormhaven and can access even more. Your sister's a little scary with what information she can grab from the internet."

"That's not the only thing scary about my sister," Lana muttered, suppressing a smile he probably wouldn't understand.

"We're going to have to call with an update anyway. Kyle Jorden will be expecting us back at his place soon." He hit the speed dial and lifted the phone to his ear for a terse discussion then punched off. "So much for that. They're looking for someplace for us to stash right now. Those sharp cross winds are playing sheer hell on the small planes. They won't be able to take off any time soon."

Lana took a deep breath. *Never let them know you're scared. Never let them see you sweat.* She dredged up her polite smile. "As strong as the winds are down here, I bet they're really awful up higher."

He scowled in her direction then put the car into gear, easing back around the building.

"There were buildings and some sign of civilization a few miles back. No doubt, we'll be heading that direction soon enough. It would help to get under cover or around other cars. Top speed for this POS isn't good enough to avoid those bikers once they figure out we're not in front of them." His phone chirped, and he thumbed the button to hear Ty Randolph's voice.

"Best we can come up with is a cabin a few miles away, off the main road. Pretty much abandoned, but Kyle knows the owners, so you'll be okay. It'll get you off the road and under cover. Once the winds die down and the plane can take off, you can head over to where you landed."

"Does this place have furniture?"

"What's that?"

"I don't think Ms. Greene can deal with roughing it another night."

"I'm fine," Lana insisted from the other seat.

"No, ma'am, you aren't. Boss, she's not talking much about it, but I think she hurt herself getting away from that scum."

"Lana? What the hell did you see? What are you running from?" His voice through the phone sounded impatient, maybe even angry.

"Does it matter?" Adam growled. "Whatever it was, she needs medical attention."

"You get to that cabin, we'll get you out."

❡❡❡

"They weren't kidding about this cabin not being much." Lana peered through the dusty windshield at what seemed to be a random collection of old wood with a sagging porch.

"I think that's the first time I've heard you complain. Congratulations."

"Mr. Roberts, I don't think you're very funny."

"Captain Roberts, ma'am. I wasn't trying to be funny. That was meant as a compliment."

"Maybe you should preface compliments with a warning." She stood, using the car door and roof to brace herself.

"I knew you were hurt."

"Seriously, just stiff. Let me walk around a bit, and I'll be fine."

He came around the car, reached out to take her arm.

"I'm *fine*," she said, avoiding his hand. To prove it, she stepped away from him, bracing herself and using the car body for the first few steps. "If you want to help, you could grab my bags."

Once in the cabin, it was obvious the furniture, what little there was, would not be offering much comfort.

Nor was the cabin high on amenities.

"You see any light switches?" he asked.

She shook her head. "You see any lights? I think this cabin defines roughing it."

"Interesting in this day and age. Is there water?"

"Huh. I see a hand pump. I wonder…" She used the water from one of their drinking bottles to prime the pump then started to move the lever. After a time, a reluctant trickle of water came out then something close to a decent amount. "Voila. We have water. Luxury accommodations at our fingertips."

"Luxury?" he repeated, with an even-more-blank look on his face. "What was the name of the horse you took when you left Ty Randolph?"

"What the *hell* are you talking about?"

"Just answer."

He stepped forward, pinning her against the old wooden counter. His hard hands came up to grip her upper arms as if he felt he needed to control her. Gone was the distantly polite former soldier who called her ma'am and avoided anything but the most remote touch.

For the first time, she felt uncomfortable around him. He was wasn't big, like Ty and most of the men on the ranch had been, but he was still bigger than her, with solid muscles. The lean body pressed against hers gave no hope for her to escape. And right now, he had an even-less-civilized look in his eye than any of the men she'd met on the ranch.

"Mosby. His housekeeper is Maria," she said in a rush. "One of his most reliable hands is Jamie, who I think worked with Sydney back in the day. Or maybe he just didn't like me on general principles." She took a deep breath, pushing aside her automatic fear. "Can you ease up a little? That arm's got a bit of a bruise."

As if suddenly aware of how he was restraining her, threatening her, he lifted his hands and moved back. He took a long step with one foot then drew his other foot back as well. This time, their surroundings were quiet enough, and she had enough awareness to hear the faint click.

She looked down at his leg, in spite of her instincts screaming at her not to lose eye contact with the predator. "You're hurt?"

"Not recently."

She processed that slowly then looked back into the stillness of his face. Back into his stoic eyes, with scars surrounding them. Old scars mostly. Scars that looked like… "Shrapnel?"

"Mostly. You pick up all sorts of scars when you're fighting as long as I did."

"A long time," she agreed, her voice soft to keep herself from showing any pity. He would not want pity. "Your leg?"

"That's what took me out of the game. For some reason, the military wants their special ops people to come with all their original parts."

"And I was whining about sleeping on a short bed and falling down some stairs."

His dark eyes sharpened at that. "You fell?"

"I had some help."

"Dammit, woman, you should have told me."

"Well, at least you're not calling me 'ma'am.'" She tried to keep her voice light, even though he was once more looming above her. "Look, it really didn't make much difference. We needed to get away. It was supposed to be a quick car ride then a plane trip so any extra bruises wouldn't have mattered, and I'd be able to recover at Stormhaven. The drugs have just worn off, that's all—if you could see your face! Extra strength ibuprofen, strictly OTC. Plus I don't have my turmeric with me. I couldn't get back to my apartment after—" She looked away from his penetrating stare then turned back to the sink. "I wonder if there's any way to heat up this water."

She felt him pull back as if he was accepting the change of subject without further argument. She heard some rattling, some solid metallic sounds. Heard a sharp snick, smelled a trace of sulfur. Then she felt a blessed waft of warm from the dark corner of the room and looked over her shoulder, squinting to make out his form next to a small round object.

"Wood stove?"

"And some cut wood. Not a lot. We might need to break up some of this furniture if we're staying here for long."

"These priceless antiques? I hope their owner won't be too upset."

This time she almost got a lift from the corner of his mouth.

℮⁊℮⁊

Water warmed in an old metal pot found under the sink helped wash away a day's worth of sweaty grit, then a fresh set of the same nondescript, bland clothes she'd been wearing left her feeling partially refreshed. She first tucked the loose T-shirt into her jeans then pulled it out again, changing the outline of her body even more from the trendy hostess persona so admired by her partner. Former partner. Should-be-dead-if-she-had-anything-to-say-about-it partner. Best-carried-off-by-a-giant-eagle-and-dropped-in-the-ocean partner. She suppressed the growl and grabbed the long-sleeved loose over-shirt to complete her outfit.

In addition to giving her more thickness than she normally showed, it also helped hide the deep bruises on her upper arms where she'd wrenched herself away from angry men.

In the quiet, dim room, the fire offered a point of warmth and at least temporary comfort, especially when Roberts—Captain Roberts—found a couple of old worn quilts to fold up as sitting pallets. Wood smoke scented the air, along with the sweat inevitable in the desert. Masculine sweat untainted by drugs or fear.

"Captain Roberts," she said into the surprisingly comfortable silence.

He turned his head.

"Captain 'who' Roberts?" she asked. "It seems strange to call you by your title when we've been pretty near intimate. Friends generally have first names. Hell, even non-friends use first names."

"It's Adam, ma'am." His voice was level, his delivery deadpan, but she saw the hint of a smile when he turned more in her direction.

"And we're back to ma'am again. Do they train special ops warriors in irritation through words these days?"

"Ma—sorry. But I'm not actually sure what to call you. You don't use Ty Randolph's last name any more, you said something about taking your mother's name, but she was Castleton, not…what was that, Greene?"

"Mom dropped Dad's name faster than she dropped him. Castleton took too long to write, with all the vertical letters. With Greene, she could scribble G then a line for the rest. It just worked out better for me to use that name when I was single. But it would be even easier for you to just call me Lana."

She braced herself for more questions. It was obvious he was brimming over with curiosity, though he continued to keep his expression locked down.

He nodded and went back to contemplating the stove, then he lifted his head, holding out his hand to caution silence. Lana heard it then, a distant sound of powerful rotors. She'd heard that before, when she'd lived near the base. The powerful beat of blades on something that could fly in pretty much anything and land pretty much anywhere. What now?

As the sound drew closer, her tiny throw away phone buzzed, signaling a text. Roberts's—Adam's—phone did the same, bringing them confirmation that the good guys had arrived.

❧❧❧

They weren't able to leave immediately, but Lana was encouraged to settle her aching self on a well-padded gurney, and Adam sat on a camp chair while the energetic crew swarmed around them. The rental car would be returned by a man and a woman who bore a startling resemblance to Adam and Lana, especially when the woman pulled on the shirt Lana had been wearing earlier. Within minutes, the cabin was returned to its pre-visited condition, and the powerful aircraft lifted off at the same time as the nondescript car started down the road.

Lana settled into the padded cot and felt a lightweight cover settle over her. Now it would be back to the place she never thought she'd see again. She'd go to Stormhaven, face her past. Then she'd go after the girls.

# Chapter 4

Leaning her forearms against the large kitchen table, Lana let her eyes drift shut while drawing in the familiar scents around her, feeling them ease the tension that had not left her in so long. The heavy-weight mug felt the same in her cupped hands. Herbs hanging from rustic beams added to the rich-coffee and warm-cinnamon aromas, plus the ever-present odor of horse, man, and outdoors brought up memories she had tried to suppress. She looked around, remembering when she'd sat with Ty and whoever was joining them for meals. Maria still bustled in and out, setting out food and refusing any help. The coffee was different—richer and better brewed. Still coffee but she sipped at it, trying to show appreciation.

"That would be your sister," Ty said, noticing her expression. "She's more of a coffee snob than I am."

"If that's possible," Devin rumbled, his expression no warmer or more welcoming than before. "So, let's go."

Lana set down the mug. "Go?"

"What prompted you to call after all this time?" His

voice offered no compromise, but he'd always been that way toward her.

"Why did I send up the Bat Signal?" Her forced levity brought more frowns than smiles. "Where do I start? There's so much to tell you, so much to explain. But first, I saw a young woman—actually, a girl—killed," Lana said in a matter-of-fact voice.

Everyone sat up straighter. Almost as a single entity, they leaned forward, faces intent—including Rosalind Summerton, the ridiculously gorgeous woman who sat next to Ty.

"Where?"

"Who?"

"Who did you tell?"

"I'm telling you. Now. Because, right now, no one else will listen long enough to believe me. It happened in Vegas. I saw her dead or dying in the room before I was pushed out. The next day she was 'discovered' in a dumpster in an entirely different part of town—either 'the victim of an overdose or slumming,' implying it was her fault, not murder."

"Why do you think it was murder?" Devin again, his tone easing but his golden eyes no less intense.

"Because I saw her in that room the evening before. Passed out but still alive. It doesn't make any sense to kill her since, she was worth so much more alive. They can get upward of seven hundred fifty thousand dollars for the right girls." In her effort to be believed, she forgot to be soft spoken and sweetly feminine.

Sydney leaned forward. "Who are you, and what did you do with my sister?"

Adam straightened. "That's what I want to know," he nearly growled.

Lana pressed herself back into her chair, as if avoiding them. "What do you mean?"

"I was kidding. I think." Sydney half stood. "But now I'm not so sure. You look like my sister." She turned her head slightly. "Ty?"

"Yeah, she looks like Lana. Well, the same face, same body shape. But…"

"Exactly. But."

Lana forced herself to relax. "I think I need to go back farther. A lot farther." She looked around. "Can I have some water? With maybe just a little bit of ice?"

Maria set the glass in front of her, and Lana took a long sip, letting the chilled water ease her dried throat. Then she looked around at the expectant faces. "We actually have to go back to when our parents split up. I was thirteen, Sydney was ten. I wanted desperately to go with our father, but I stayed with Mom. Lucky me. I don't know how much you remember about Mom, but she wasn't quite the fragile flower of femininity she showed the world. She liked money, and she liked men—the more, the merrier—of both. Without Dad to hold her back, she got both in enough quantity to make even her happy. Some of her men were not as honorable as you might want. I learned E and E—escape and evasion—really early." Someone stifled a gasp, and Lana shook her head. "That's in the past, and it helped—" She didn't look up from where her fingers clutched at the glass, the water inside shivering. "—helped me decide what I needed to do with my life. Some friends helped me learn to—project the right image. To put it bluntly—very bluntly—I'm very good at getting people to believe what I need them to believe.

"I learned from our mother that men were not as interested in a woman who could change her own tires and take care of herself. I also learned I could not be that sort of woman. So I learned to take care of myself. I had a great business going, fulfilling people's wishes. You want fairy ponies for your kid's birthday, I could find someone who'd paint the hooves silver and sprinkle glitter in the mane and tail. You want snow in the middle of June, we'd cover your lawn in icy fluff. As long as they had the money for it, I'd find a way to provide it, as long as it was legal and didn't hurt anyone.

"Our mother, on the other hand, was a con artist. We, her daughters, were her longest con. By taking Sydney with him, our father ruined Mom's original plans. She wouldn't let me go, claiming we were both her daughters, but we did not have the same father. Don't worry. I checked that out when I could. I ran DNA on all of us. We're sisters, Syd." Lana noticed the sudden alert expression around the table. "Yes, DNA on file. You can check the 'me' now against the 'me' when I was eighteen. If you found anything like an old hairbrush, you can cross check against the 'me' when I was here."

"When you were here…" Ty asked, obviously fishing for how to frame his question. Probably *questions*— he was bound to have many.

"Was that a con? No. That was me trying to live as normal a life as possible. So maybe a con in some ways since I did not reveal the real me, just the me I thought you'd prefer—"

"That's it!" Sydney blurted out. "That's why you seemed off at your wedding party." She turned to the rest of the table. "Lana taught me how to climb trees and how to booby trap doorways with water buckets. She also knew how to disable a car in thirty seconds, and we sparred whenever our mother wasn't around to stop us." She turned back to Lana. "You were so prim and proper and girly in Santa Fe, I couldn't figure you out."

"This is all fascinating," Adam said, leaning forward. "And I'm sure you have a lot of catching up to do. What about these girls and their value?"

Lana nodded. "When the economy went belly up, luxury businesses such as mine were the first to flop. I was offered a job organizing events by someone I thought was a friend. He said he needed someone with my 'special touch' to satisfy his more discerning clients. And I reminded him, nothing illegal or in poor taste. Unfortunately, his taste wasn't the same as mine. This last time, he wanted a penthouse for a week-long private party. When I realized they were probably dealing in young girls, I tried getting in touch with the local police, but they weren't interested.

"I had to get more proof—names, something I could take to a higher authority. I went to the police when I first suspected these men, and later that day, I barely got away from some unfriendly men.

"The next day, I saw a report of the murdered girl on television. That's when I called the ranch. I knew Sydney worked for a clandestine group that got things done instead of messing around, but I had no idea how to get in touch."

"How much proof did you manage to collect?" Sydney asked, her brow furrowing.

"I realize you don't believe me yet, and that's understandable."

"It not whether we believe you, it's what can we do to stop them."

"Not you, Syd. Not this time." Devin's voice allowed no argument, but he still got the one eyebrow glare.

"Points off to the chest-thumping cowboy," Roz fake whispered then ignored the combined glares from Syd and Devin, instead turning to look closely at Lana. "It doesn't seem like you've had much down time for a few days, and I'm thinking whatever they popped you with in the chopper is wearing off. You want to grab some rest while the deadly duo works out who's going to call Major

Powers? Because I don't think anyone at this table doesn't want to rush to the rescue sooner rather than later."

# Chapter 5

I like her. I didn't expect to, but I do." Roz looked into her coffee cup then at the empty plate where the chocolate cake was now only crumbs.

"Me too," Devin said, leaning against the buffet at the edge of the room. "I didn't think she be like...this."

"She wasn't when she was here. She was meek and quiet. She spent a lot of time just walking around or reading when I was busy," Ty mentioned, reaching for the coffee pot and offering refills. "Which is why the whole Mosby thing was such a mystery."

"We're probably going to find out she had a good reason."

"I, for one, am happy she took off with the horse," Devin said, reaching for an empty mug. "Otherwise, who knows when I would've met Syd?" He sounded matter-of-fact, but there was a flicker of a smile on his face. "For that alone, I feel like I owe her."

"Except it's not about her, or Mosby," Roz said. "It's not about us. It's about young girls being taken and sold. We cannot allow that to keep happening."

"Finally. Someone gets it." The tired voice came

from the hallway, and Lana came through the wide open-ing, still in her thrift-store clothes, moving slowly but not as stiff as before. "We can spend plenty of time playing catch up, answering questions about who and when and why. But we have a chance to do something to help these girls and to stop this game they're being forced to play. *If* we move fast enough."

"Why are you up?" Sydney asked.

"Someone's coming. Kind of a motorcade of big dark gas hogs."

"No chopper? That's odd." Roz rose, heading in to the kitchen.

Lana wondered if she was looking for Maria, or not wanting to be around her lover's former wife.

"It's probably Powers. We've learned to expect the unexpected and get used to him showing up on his own schedule." Devin moved to the window to watch the small motorcade snake up the long drive. "Dang, you must have crazy hearing."

"I wasn't asleep so much as dozing by the window. Even from a distance that didn't look like cattle moving around."

A discreet tone sounded from the monitor on the wall, then Ty and Devin reached for their buzzing phones. "Got it, Jamie, thanks. We're pretty sure it's Powers. Is Roberts at the bunkhouse? Okay, thanks."

Ty slid his phone back into his packet while he turned to the group. "Seems Roberts isn't at the barn apartments. Did he go down to the cabin?"

"He's here." Adam followed his voice into the room.

"Man, I just don't get it. With all your experience, how could you forget the primary rule: When you have a chance to rest, you damned well *rest*." Ty shook his head. "Both of you. You look like something the cat dragged in and refused to cover over."

Lana and Adam looked at Ty, looked at each other, and shrugged.

"Power nap," Adam said, heading for one of the large chairs around the table.

"Dozing in the chair, soaking up sunshine," Lana added, looking around for another empty chair.

Sydney stood. "Take this one. I'm going to let Powers in and take the opportunity to rag on him." She looked around, frowning, until Ty stepped forward with a pillow and shawl. "Thanks. Use these."

Lana lowered herself into the chair. "But I'm not—"

"Trust me. Use them."

Sydney tucked the pillow behind Lana's back then draped the shawl around her. Eyes narrowed, she looked around the room.

"Roberts?"

"No way you're makin' me look overwhelmed."

"I wouldn't dare. Coffee?"

Roz and Maria came in with more mugs and cinnamon rolls to pass around.

"If everyone could please at least take a few bites?" Sidney asked.

"What are you setting the stage for?" Roz asked, evaluating what was happening around the large table.

"Solidarity. I'm not going to let Powers play his divide and conquer games. Dev, if you could take the end chair. You can move when Powers comes in. If you want."

"Clever girl," Ty murmured then looked around the room himself. "Where do you want me and Roz since we were part of Powers's last game?"

"Over here, I think. Roz next to Lana then you. No one does outrage about young girls the way Roz does."

"It's not a game for me, Syd."

"I know. That's what makes it so powerful."

"Where will you sit?"

Sydney indicated a padded chair with a footrest, tucked into a corner of the room.

"That wasn't here before."

"We brought it in when we knew for sure Powers was coming this morning."

They all settled into their seats as car doors slammed outside, then heavy footsteps sounded on the porch steps. Sydney went to the front door, holding up her hand when Devin half-rose. He frowned but acquiesced. They heard her lock the bolt just before someone outside turned the doorknob. After a space of time, they heard a knock on the door. Syd unlocked the bolt as she pulled the door open.

"Trying to walk into a private residence without an invitation is not the way to engender cooperation and good fellowship," she said.

No footsteps entered the house.

"Sorry, ma'am," came a grudging voice.

"Sorry yourself. This time 'sorry' just doesn't help. Major Powers, welcome. You can come in. Your motley crew will stay outside."

"My staff is new since last time, and thoroughly vetted. They have full security clearances."

"Yeah, so did your 'staff' in Georgia. Look where that got us. You—and is that Harry back there? Harry can come in. The rest of you can go wait in the cars. If you want to pet the horses, watch out for the gray stallion. He bites."

Muttering accompanied the shuffling of footsteps off the porch. Then heavier footsteps came in the door, which was shut, and the bolt again locked.

"You can put your coats on the bench out here. It's kind of full inside. How's it going, Harry?"

"Not too bad. Major, let me take that for you."

They came into the room, pausing at the wide entrance while an innocuous, medium-sized, medium-build, medium-colored man in an unassuming suit looked around.

After a moment, he managed a small humorless sound. "Message received."

"Good."

As Sydney stepped farther into the room, Devin rose, indicating his seat at the head of the table for Powers's use. He once more leaned against the buffet, putting himself between Sydney's chair and the rest of the room. As Powers settled himself, Syd moved over to the chair, brushing lightly against her husband on the way. Devin helped settle Sydney, stepping back while Maria bustled in with hot tea and some small snacks.

"Major Powers, I believe you know most of the people here," Ty began, drawing attention to himself. "You met Captain Roberts last time you 'visited,' so the only person who might be a stranger is Lana Greene." He indicated his former wife with no inflection, no indication she was anything more than a guest.

"Ms…Greene, is it? No, I did not have that pleasure while you were in Nevada, nor before when you were in Utah. It's a pleasure to finally meet you." He nodded thanks to Maria for the pot of tea.

His voice stressed the finally, but Lana merely raised her eyebrows. "I believe we have you to thank for the extraction from Nevada," she said politely.

"The crew was fortunately in the area. When they were advised that Captain Roberts needed help, they insisted on coming. In fact, we had far more volunteers than we needed."

Adam shifted, cleared his throat, and reached for his coffee. Devin crossed his arms. "Deal with it, buddy. They just need to give back."

"They're not the only ones," Roz said in a quiet voice meant to carry only to the people around her.

Lana leaned forward to look at this woman who was now sleeping with Ty, but Powers's voice got her attention.

"Yes, well, we need to get through this briefing. Ms. Greene, I believe you have some vital information to share?"

"Vital to me, certainly. I'm not sure if your organization concerns itself with the sexual slave trade."

"We do, absolutely. In fact, we have been attempting to find a way to get someone into those organizations, so far without luck. It seems they are very insular, very cautious."

"They have a lot to lose. Some of the men involved are highly respected in their other lives. They have families, daughters of their own, to protect. Young sons as well."

Powers straightened, becoming, if possible, even more intent. "You have names?"

"Some. Some faces without names. They got used to me wandering through and didn't bother to hide themselves."

"How did you get so close to them?" Sydney asked, leaning forward in her comfortable chair.

Lana looked at her a moment then let her face morph from intense and intelligent to slightly vacuous. It was a matter of just adjusting her eyes a little, making her mouth softer.

"That's...awesome," Roz breathed.

"And a little scary," Devin added.

"Again, a detail we will discuss later," Powers interjected, stopping the conversation. "We will need some sort of validation for what you are about to tell us." Sydney started to speak up, but Powers kept on talking. "I know there have been misconceptions in the past. We need to discuss those and find the actual truth. How did you become involved, what was your level of involvement?"

"I understand," Lana said in a professional voice, allowing her expression to return to something far more intense. "Do I need to go into my background, or is your research accurate?"

Multiple quiet sounds from around the room expressed a lack of faith in the research.

"At one time, I would have had the utmost faith in my research specialists, but we had a slight glitch in the system last year, and we are still investigating how deep the problem went. If it helps, I have your family information up to when Sydney moved out with your father."

"It's a start." Taking a deep breath to compose herself, Lana went quickly through what she had told the others earlier. When she mentioned the DNA typing, Powers shot her a sharp glance but did not interrupt. She got up to her wish-fulfillment business then the association with Tony B, which brought her to the high-rise luxury suite.

"You believe this group was using the suite as a base for their actions?"

"I think it was more of a mini conference, possibly recruiting more people to expand their network. It seemed that young girl was, or could have been, a 'sample,' brought in to show the quality of the goods available."

She took a deep breath and swallowed to hold down the bile. It purely sucked to be talking about this. She felt a warmth along her side.

Adam was leaning in her direction, offering quiet support. Looking across the room, she saw her sister, Sydney, listening with a sympathetic expression on her face. When their eyes met, Syd nodded slightly as if to help her continue.

"You seem remarkably calm about what went on and what could potentially happen in the future."

"You're trying to figure out if I was a part of the system then decided to get out of it, aren't you? What sort of decent woman would ever stick around after she knew what was happening? Why in the world didn't I go to the police or FBI with my concerns?" She looked around at the room, meeting everyone's eyes directly, finishing with Powers. "I realize you don't have the highest opinion of me." She shrugged, reaching for the glass of water. "Some of this we can hash out later, and some is honestly none of your damned business. But the more time you spend trying to point your finger at me and shame me for what I've done, who I've been in the past, the less time we will have to help those girls and shut down this be-damned pipeline. At this point, that's pretty much all I give a rat's hairy hind end about."

She looked down at her lap and realized a large, strong, hand was holding her forearm, gripping slightly in support. She gulped but didn't dare look over into his eyes. Not yet. Not while she was barely holding herself together.

"We're on the clock," she said. "Either you help, or I'm going back by myself. But I will do everything in my power to stop them."

# Chapter 6

Lana held their gazes for as long as she could, then she stood, pushing her chair away from the table. To her surprise, Adam stood with her, as well as Roz and Ty. Sydney started to push herself out of her comfy chair.

"I've got this," Roz said quietly to Sydney as she stepped around Adam to Lana's side. "No, you're not going off alone, Lana. You're not alone anymore."

Lana swayed, absorbing the words through what felt like a heavy wrapping of gauze.

"Bathroom or bedroom?" she heard the tall woman ask. "Are you nauseous or just so tired you want to puke?"

"Yeah, that." Lana let herself be led out of the room while she leaned on two forearms.

Then she felt herself lifted and carried and heard someone say, "It's more efficient this way."

The deep voice rumbled against her arm. A comforting sound.

Within a short span of time, she was on a soft surface, her head propped on blissfully comforting pillows, something cozy laid over her. She heard something about tea later in what sounded like Maria's voice.

Then she slid down into a tunnel of gray.

જ્જ

Lana opened her eyes to what she knew was early evening light. She held herself still, lying on her side curled around a pillow, feeling for her location and situation. She realized she was back at Stormhaven, and she felt the sense of loss that had come to her when she had to leave. Not for the man she thought she could have loved, but for the place itself, and what it might have offered.

She heard a throat clear and realized she was not alone. Tensing, she concentrated, trying to figure out through scent or sound who was in the room with her.

"You're at Stormhaven," a deep voice informed her, speaking in low tones. "It's about five in the evening. You were really tired, nearly passed out, so Roz and I helped you out of the room into here, where you pretty much crashed. You should probably get some more sleep."

She thought longingly of just snuggling back down into the pillow, pulling the covers over her head, and embracing the oblivion of sleep. Then she remembered the girl in the party room and the other girls she'd seen briefly.

"Probably not. There's really too much to do." She yawned, her brain clearing more with the extra oxygen, then sat up, and rotated to swing her legs out of bed, keeping her back to him. Odd that she hadn't noticed him in the room while she slept. Then again, she'd been able to doze in the car while he was driving, as if she knew she could trust him. She rested her hands on either side of her, head down while she tried to dig up some more strength, and looked over her shoulder to see him comfortably ensconced in a reclining chair.

"What are you doing in here?"

"Someone needed to watch, just in case."

"In case I tried to slip out again?"

"In case you woke up disoriented. Since I needed to grab a combat nap, and it was a good way to avoid one of Powers's interrogations, we figured I could stay here as well as anyone. You can turn around if you want. I'm decent."

"You're definitely a decent human being, but I have no idea how I look right now, and I don't want to scare you with the raccoon effect of smeared makeup."

She pushed herself off the bed and headed for the bathroom.

The chair made a whumping sort of noise when the footrest was pushed down, and she heard him stand with a slight click as his leg settled.

"So I should tell them...what? Fifteen minutes?"

"More like thirty. It's going to take a while to get my eyes open all the way."

Finally, he left, and she could take a breath without smelling the man scent of him—nope, she was not going there again. No more making stupid decisions based on what turned out to be a false conviction that a man would be able to solve all her problems.

⌾⌾⌾

They were gathered again at the table when she made it down the hall.

This time Sydney was seated at the table instead of in her padded chair, and she looked as if she had managed to get some rest herself.

"Are you okay?" Lana asked, watching for any signs of illness.

"As much as anyone can be with a parasite taking over their life." But she tempered the flippant words with a slight smile while rubbing her bulging stomach.

"For the next eighteen years, I need to add," Roz said.

"Your day will come, stretch. Then I can mock your morning sickness."

"Morning sickness doesn't run in my family. Good genes."

Powers cleared his throat, and they grinned at each other then at Lana, as if bringing her into the silliness and making her part of their group. She offered a small smile in return, not quite ready to believe.

"We need to track down the head of this group and put them out of business permanently," Powers began.

Lana barely restrained herself from a sarcastic comment, but when she heard, "Well, duh," she thought she'd lost control of her speech. Then she realized the comment came from next to her. Sydney had a professional expression on her face as though she hadn't just mocked her boss.

Powers frowned.

"How do you plan to do this?" Ty asked. "Sir."

"I realize the last time we worked together did not start out so well. As already stated, I have purged those employees and double checked the credentials of those left."

"You're saying it won't happen again?"

"No one can promise that. Greed and foolishness are everywhere. But I'll make every effort not to allow it to happen."

They looked at each other and nodded.

Powers continued. "At the moment, we don't have

much choice. Since the authorities want incontrovertible proof before they'll act—"

"Or they just can't be trusted," Roz added.

"—you'll have to go in and gather information. Find where the girls go, where they come from, and, in particular, where they're held until they're shipped out. It has to be a permanent, safe location, some place they can be well hidden."

"And be trained," Lana said. "I know some of those girls came from small towns and out-of-the-way locations. They had to become indoctrinated, made drug dependent, and learn to be desirable party hostesses. The goal isn't just a prostitute. They want to provide a fully trained, gracious, attractive, girl to decorate your party and your bed, white girls being so popular in other countries."

She spoke in a monotone, keeping herself very still so she could get the information out without bolting. "And it went the other direction as well—girls coming in from 'exotic' locations to be used here. Some of them think they're going to be nursemaids or nannies. Some of them have no idea what's going to happen to them. They've been lied to about a job for good money or else sold by their families, and they're here, not speaking English, having no hope. They disappear into the system, and if they show up at all, it's an unidentified corpse out in the desert."

"There have been task forces—" Powers began.

"Yes, there have been, and there still are. I've tried to contact them. They won't listen to me, won't take my information."

Sydney leaned forward, turning to look at her sister. "Why not?"

Lana laughed, but it was fake and bitter. "Because they're convinced they know I've been in charge of more than one trafficking scheme. They don't trust me or anything I have to say." She saw the glances exchanged between this group of people who were so close. Her sister, her ex-husband, their companions. Brows furrowed, they seemed to be exchanging silent information, while the face of the older man at the head of the table became even more bland. She grimaced. "Go ahead. I know you're dying to ask if it's true."

"Actually," Ty began in a neutral tone. "We're all wondering how you could convince anyone you'd do something like that."

Lana fell back in her chair, breathing deeply to avoid letting the tears fall. "You—why?"

"Probably because they are really smart people," Adam said, once again sitting next to her. "And really smart people recognize the good folk."

"As for me, I don't really know you well enough—yet," Roz said in a contemplative tone. "But I had the same crap thrown at me not long ago. You cared enough to take a chance on calling here, not knowing what sort of reception you'd have because you were fairly certain these guys could help. Smart move, by the way."

A mug of hot tea appeared in front of her, set down by Maria, who took the opportunity to squeeze her shoulder. Lana lifted the cup, using the opportunity to keep her head down and those threatening tears under control.

Powers harrumphed and shuffled papers. "Be that as it may, we need to make plans."

"Major Powers gets uncomfortable around emotions. I think they give him a rash," Sydney revealed in a stage whisper then sat back with an angelic expression on her face before she looked around again. "Okay, boys and girls, what do we know for sure?"

They spent the next hour going over what was known and what was suspected.

"We know the girls come from all over the US," Lana summarized. We know, or suspect, they're not being kept in Vegas since it takes several hours to half a day for one of them to be brought in when requested. We know wherever they're kept has a fairly sophisticated filming room since they've all been 'introduced' in high-quality videos. They're wearing nice clothes, nothing trashy, and are well made up."

"Do you think the differences in time have to do with mode of transportation?" Adam asked.

"That's possible. Car, copter, plane would change the time frame and also the potential distance."

"How did you meet this particular latest group?"

"The person I occasionally partnered with said someone wanted a high-quality penthouse apartment for a week-long seminar. They also wanted nonstop attention, like their own personal concierge. At first, I thought it was just another 'fill the wants' gig until I met them." She suppressed a shudder. "The slime factor was absurdly high."

"What was his name again?" Sydney asked, eyeing her computer screen.

"Antonio Bonavides—Tony B."

"Mr. Bonavides was found dead in Twenty-Nine Palms. Seems he lost control of his car."

"I'd say he wouldn't be caught dead in Twenty-Nine Palms—but, obviously, he was."

"Something to do with a gunshot wound to his head." Sydney looked up at Lana. "I'm betting they'll be looking for you."

"It wouldn't surprise me. Especially since he told everyone I was his honey pot. My taste has never been *that* bad. Does this mean I can't be seen in Vegas?"

Powers shook his head. "I'd say this means you must been seen in Vegas—the sooner, the better. We can fig-

ure out a solid alibi for the last few days that you can take
to the police or to those complicit in the trafficking. Actually, this suspicion might be a plus for you to get back
into that group."

"Okay, I'll bite. What's that solid alibi?"

"Why, sugar," Adam drawled. "You were shacked
up with me in our little love nest out behind that overbuilt
testament to bad taste."

Lana could only gape. She felt the blood drain from
her face, then rush back. "I was…what? Where?"

"You'll wound my ego with that sort of reaction."

"Did you *see* that place?"

"As we speak, a team is making a few changes,"
Powers said. "In addition to furniture, food, and amenities, they're also adding the best possible security system.
According to public records you rented that cottage last
month with the intention of a hideaway. It's all quite legal." He nodded once, and it almost seemed a smile flirt-
ed at the corners of his mouth.

"But…"

Sydney leaned forward. "It makes sense, especially if
anyone finds video of you driving around with Adam.
We're as sure as we can be there's no video of him alone,
and only a few possibilities of you together when you
stopped somewhere. But we don't want that jumping up
to blindside us."

"We thought about having Ty coming to look for
you, but he was seen too much last year with Ms. Summerton. Sydney can't go, obviously."

Sydney sent a scowl in Powers's direction. "You're
really enjoying this, aren't you?"

"Immensely, as a matter of fact."

"Lana, don't let him suck you into his web unless
you really want to be there," Syd argued. "Same for you,
Adam. You can always say no."

Lana sighed, shaking her head. "I really can't. Not this time."

"All right then," Roz said, rubbing her hands together. "Let's get this party started. First of all, we need a name for this caper."

"We do not involve ourselves in capers," Powers intoned.

"Project? Assignment?"

Powers sighed. "Is she ever quiet?"

"Nope." Ty grinned. "Pretty much not."

'I'm thinking Project Goldilocks. That sound good to you?" Roz looked around at the puzzled faces. "Simple. The way I see it, I'm absurdly tall. No, Ty, I am. I always have been, and I'd be silly to think otherwise. Sydney is adorably small."

"Hey!"

"She's right, babe," Devin agreed.

"That would make Lana—"

"Just right," Adam said in a deadpan voice.

Roz nodded. "Therefore: Goldilocks."

Lana shook her head, wondering where all this energy, all this manic support, was coming from. Powers merely heaved another sigh.

# Chapter 7

*G*oldilocks. *Good grief.*

Lana peered in at the casino crowd while surreptitiously tugging at the hem of her skirt—her way-too-short, butt-hugging skirt—worn with the fitted formal tuxedo styled jacket that hit a fraction of an inch below the skirt. It was an intentionally sexy outfit, one she'd worn before with great success.

"I just thought I'd never have to wear it again," she muttered, to herself.

"Pardon?" Adam spoke directly in her ear, proof of the high quality of the discreet head set. Every nuance of his deep voice eased the tension trying to overtake her.

She pulled in a deep breath and centered herself, taking on the persona of the hard-edged party girl, always looking for a good time and a better deal. She searched herself for memories of being alone, feeling friendless, and added those to her character's personality.

Drawing on this persona, she stepped onto the casino floor, not quite wobbling on her ridiculously high heels. Fuck-me pumps. Yeah, right. The feet of the women who wore them certainly got the raw end of the deal. She pushed that opinion to a different compartment. Party Queen Lana was never seen in heels lower than four inches.

"Party Queen Lana is a pain in my ass," she muttered.

No one answered, but she caught the edge of a masculine snicker and almost let herself smile in a non-brittle fashion.

"Here we go," a voice whispered in her ear.

Then from across the room: "Lana, darling! Where have you been? We've been so worried about you!"

Lana turned. It was easy to let a dainty scowl cover her face.

"Mr. Hoffman. I really don't know what you mean. I've been here the whole time."

"We didn't see you here the last few days." His outstretched arm indicated the busy, surrounding casino.

"Not here. In Las Vegas. I've been busy."

"Playing with your latest boy toy?" asked a gravelly voice from behind her.

She pivoted, bracing herself for what she knew she would see. Even if she was supposedly prepared, it was still not easy to meet Ty's scowling, angry face.

"Tyler Randolph. Now, this is a surprise. What brings you to Sin City?"

"Certainly not you. I'm here to help out *my woman.*" He put a special emphasis on the words.

Ty did anger well. Almost too well.

"Hang in there, lady," Adam's voice whispered in her ear. "You need to soothe this savage beast."

"Lucky lady. Is she a rodeo queen?"

"No, she's a writer. I thought it might be a good idea to look for a woman with brains this time."

"Ouch," whispered the voice.

"Ouch," Lana said, with a wide, if not sincere, smile.

"I seem to remember you reading some, maybe you've heard of her? Ross Summers?"

Lana furrowed her brow as if searching for the reference.

"Our Lana, read?" Hoffman chuckled. "Sir, I think you just might be mistaken." He extended a well-manicured hand toward Ty, who took it for a quick, masculine, strong shake. "Ralph Hoffman."

"Ty Randolph."

"Ah, the husband."

"Briefly," Lana interjected. "My geography is so pathetic, I thought near Santa Fe meant twenty minutes, not over two hours." She trilled a lightweight laugh at her ignorance, and Hoffman chuckled along with her.

"That's why you should never leave the city, darling," he said. "You're meant to be a creature of the cities. How in the world can you wear those stunning shoes in the dirt?"

"Precisely," she said, managing to simper.

The sounds of the casino continued around her, desperate cheers from someone who managed a lucky win at the slots, ignoring how many coins they had fed into the greedy machines.

Hostesses floated around the room, feet encased in even higher heels than she wore, supporting the fantasy of nonstop sybaritic delights. Lana dragged her attention back to the smirking man in front of her.

"Were your clients happy with their suite? The last time I was there, they seemed to be satisfied."

The half smile disappeared, and he studied her face, as if trying to decide if she was serious.

Lana kept the slightly impatient expression active. "Last time I checked, the payment had not been deposited. If there is some reason to hold up the payment, I need to know."

"Of course, darling. I'll have my accountant check into that tomorrow."

"Tick Tock. You know I don't work for free. It takes a lot to support my lifestyle, and I have to allocate my energies to clients who pay their bills on time."

She turned away from him to move into the casino, concentrating on giving her stride that extra sway, aided by the unnatural tilt the heels gave her hips. She would be able to see Hoffman's reaction on the video feed, but she could pretty much guarantee he was scowling. He hadn't encountered Greedy Lana for a while. It would do him good to remember she had standards.

Ty had moved off while she was talking with Hoffman, but he returned, joining up with her stalking. "Another sucker you're planning to screw over?"

"Business, Ty. Just business. Something you obviously never understood, with your pathetic little ranch. Beef cattle? In an era of healthy eating? You need to get with the times, cowboy."

She threw the last over her shoulder while she strode away—Queen Lana in full stalk.

Thirty seconds. Forty-five seconds. A full minute.

"Lana, darling, wait up." Hoffman called, sounding a bit desperate.

"Gotcha," she whispered to the voice in her ear.

๛

"That woman is a force of nature," Adam muttered with a slight grin.

"That she is," Ty said. "Same as her sister. This is the first time I've been able to believe they're related." Hands jammed into his pockets, Ty stared at the monitors, watching his ex-wife become an entirely different person than the one he'd married and brought to his ranch. Her cutting words echoed in his head. Though he knew she'd been playing a role, they had still hit him on a visceral level. "Sure didn't seem to have it in her when she was at Stormhaven."

"What's that?" Adam asked, not taking his eyes off the screen.

"Lana. When she was at the ranch, she always acted so meek and mild. Rarely raised her voice, even when I mocked her books."

"The perfect woman?" a neutral-toned voice behind him asked.

He turned. Roz had slipped into the room some time in the last ten minutes. She appeared calm, with a small smile on her full lips. But it seemed brittle.

"I thought so at the time. It's possible I gave her the idea I wanted a meek wife, someone who would agree with whatever I said, and always be there when I came in from the barn."

"So she gave you what you wanted."

"You two want to take this somewhere else? I'm trying to listen here," one of the techs asked.

He scowled in their direction, and Adam looked away from the monitor briefly.

Ty nodded and they closed the door behind them.

They stayed quiet until their suite door closed them into privacy. Roz moved away from him, stepping out of her fancy public author shoes. She wiggled her toes in the deep carpet pile, sighing in relief.

Ty stood by the door, watching her obvious enjoyment, before he stepped fully into the suite. "You sure seem to enjoy kicking off those ankle wreckers."

"It's sheer bliss. My feet were about to go into shut down."

"Why do you wear them?"

"It's part of the package, same as it is for Lana. People want to see the successful author in designer shoes."

"Even when you write kid's books?"

"Young adult—and, yes. Especially if I'm going to let my agent shop the historical, I need to stand out, so people remember me."

"As if anyone could forget you." He moved over to the tiny entertainment nook, filling a large glass with ice, then hesitating, his hand hovering over the drink selection. Water would be a smarter choice than the mind-numbing whiskey.

"I do have the advantage of my height," she said. "But it's a tough gig, getting and keeping the public's attention. Especially when I have my clothes on."

He set down the glass and turned slowly, head tilting a little to see into her face. She was turned away, head down as if concentrating on what she was digging for in her purse. Her voice was still that damned polite tone she'd been using since Lana had come to Stormhaven. She'd been the first person to jump in and say they needed to help.

But—

"Roz? What's up?"

She looked up, frowning. Her normally mobile, open face was remote, that damned half smile staying solid. "I can't find my phone charger. I thought I stuck it in here."

"To hell with the phone charger. What's up? You've been in a different state of mind, a different world since…" He trailed off, contemplating how long she'd been worrying him. "…since we heard Lana was in trouble." He took a sip of his drink. "Don't you think we should be helping her? No matter what she did before, she's Syd's sister, and I was married to her."

"Of course, you should help her. Whatever she did or didn't do, she's not only Syd's sister, she's also a woman alone, surrounded by trouble. I think she's a woman *in* trouble, not a woman *making* trouble. There's a difference."

"I know there is. You were, too, although when I first came after you, I wasn't as sure as I should have been. But you're not answering my question. What's up? Are you upset because I was married to Lana?"

"You were married to her. You slept with her. You cuddled her when it was cold, and you shared little details of your life." She kept her voice steady. "You probably came in limping from the barn and asked her to help pull off your boots when you'd fallen off one of the young horses." She turned away from him, braced her shoulders, and turned back, her head high.

"That's part of marriage or any close relationship." Ty kept his voice quiet, not giving in to the desperation that could come across as anger.

"It's the most important part. It's not about the money, or the rings, or the vows. It's about sharing the little things. The little intimacies. It's about knowing how you grumble when you have to shave after several days of growing scruff. It's about not letting you get into a funk when you're tired—heck it's about doing what I can not to let you get tired." She took a quick breath. "It's not even about the sex. Which, okay, that's nice."

"Nice?"

"It's about being held in the dark. Having the right to insert myself under your arm, to lean on you, or you lean on me. Being able to fix your collar or just reach out and touch you when I need to."

"Intimacy."

"Yes. Sharing. You had that with Lana. She made sure she was what you wanted or what she thought you wanted at the time."

Ty took a long sip of his water, almost wishing for some of that whiskey. "Except we didn't have that—what she was at Stormhaven wasn't real. She was being what she thought I wanted her to be. I look back on it now, it doesn't seem real."

"But now she's so much more. She the strong woman you'd hope to have help with the ranch. And, dammit she's not only beautiful, she so damned noble, helping out the girls, risking her life all this time."

"Whoa, whoa." He set down his glass. Took her by the shoulders and turned her to face him. "You're absolutely right. Lana made herself into what she thought I wanted at the time. It turns out she wasn't June Cleaver or some the-man-is-always-right submissive." He reached up a hand to stroke along the side of her face, pushing her mink brown hair behind her ear. "For whatever reason, she learned how to be whatever she needed to be at the time. I'm sure it helped her get along. Hell, it probably kept her alive more than once. Now she's being the woman she was hiding. She's a lot stronger, and yeah, she's a hell of a lot more interesting than she was."

At this, Roz set her hands on his chest and pushed, trying to pull back. He wouldn't let her, bringing her even closer. "Roz, you're real. You've never pretended to be anything but who you are. When you disappeared to Florida, you tore a chunk out of me because I couldn't equate who I thought you were to someone who'd leave. Lana…" He searched for the words, knowing more than at any other time he needed to get them right. "Lana never fit into my life the way you do." He offered her a smile, his gaze never leaving her face. "She would have never threatened to rip my balls off and glue them to my forehead when I pissed her off."

Roz managed a small giggle. "That was a pretty good threat, wasn't it? But you were being kind of big man/little woman. And I bet she just might say that now."

"She might," he admitted. "But would she say it because she meant it or because she thought I wanted to hear it? When I met her, I think I was still looking for that frilly-aproned, keep-the-house-clean, bring-me-a-drink woman. So that's what she became."

"Now?"

"Now, I realize I was looking for someone who'd look me in the eye and call bullshit when I was getting stupid." He gathered her closer to him, encouraging her to rest against him until, finally, finally, her face snuggled into his neck. They stood that way, absorbing each other. He murmured in her ear, "The sex is 'nice'? You're an award-winning, world-famous author, and that's the best you can come up with?"

He barely avoided the punch to his gut.

# Chapter 8

Lana tilted her hips and crossed her arms, assuming a casual posture that would attract the wrong sort of attention. Sure enough, the beefy jerk in front of her looked down as if wondering what was underneath her long jacket.

She took a deep breath, intentionally inflating her chest while her crossed arms pushed her breasts up for his attention.

Some men were so easy. And she was tired of dealing with them. So very tired.

"What you're saying is you're not sure when your client will be paying me? And I'm supposed to keep on helping them, giving them what they want on trust? Do you think trust will pay my mortgage?"

"I think you're in deeper trouble than you know," a new voice said behind her, deep, with a strong Slavic accent.

Lana turned, recognizing the man she'd seen briefly at the party, just after she'd noticed the girl who later turned up dead. Up this close, under brighter lights, his eyes were even colder, his expression more severe.

"Mr. Novakov, how good to see you again."

"Perhaps. Tell me, what do you know about the girl?"

She felt her heart freeze in her chest and had to remind herself to breathe. How should she play this? In general, the truth worked best, or at least as much truth as she was willing to admit. "Girl? There are so many girls."

"The one, unfortunately, was found dead a few days ago."

She frowned as if still searching her memory. He scowled. "I believe you saw her in your suite the evening before."

"Mr. Hoffman leased that suite. I merely sourced it and made the arrangements, as per the contract." Lana's mind raced while she kept her face remotely pleasant. Did she have a chance to talk her way out of this? She decided the jugular was a good place to start. She stepped forward, getting right up into his face so she could speak intimately.

"That girl? I have to say, after I saw her at the apartment, I wasn't sure if I wanted to have any more dealings with you. How can you stay in business when you treat your merchandise so poorly? She was good for upward of half a mil until your friends ruined her. For pity's sake, if they were looking for some play, you could have found something less valuable for their childish games. You don't dress your little girls up in silk to play in the mud. What kind of an operation are you running? Why would I want to work with someone as careless as you are?"

Hoffman stepped forward, a horrified expression on his greedy face. For a moment Novakov's face was frozen in a vicious expression, then he lifted his eyebrow and allowed his mouth to turn up in what might pass for a smile. "You have courage, silly little woman. I'll grant you that."

"It doesn't take much courage to state simple facts. Nor does it take a lot of experience to recognize an organization out of control. You're implying that you want or need my experience and expertise in setting up or expanding your organization. But you seem to me to be far too careless. I didn't get to where I am by being careless or working with careless people."

He briefly looked as though he contemplated hitting her. She held her ground, lifting her chin to look him more directly in the eye, holding his gaze until his eyes shifted briefly away.

"It's my life as well as my reputation at stake," she continued. "I don't take stupid, careless chances."

He nodded once then turned to Hoffman. "We will discuss this further at Ms. Greene's apartment."

"No. I do not do business in my private quarters. We can meet in an office, or a room in the casino. At a mutually convenient time, but not right now."

"Then we can meet now. Hoffman, find us a room."

"Mutually convenient, and not right now. I need to get some rest."

"You will be staying here."

"I will be staying where I want to stay."

"We will need to be in touch with you, sometimes with very little warning."

"That's why cell phones were invented."

"You were not available several days ago. Where did you go?"

"My work here was done. My private life is just that. Private."

"If you cannot be more cooperative, then we cannot work together." His tone and posture were adamant.

Lana tilted her head to one side then nodded. Both men relaxed. "Fine," she said. "Then I guess we won't be working together."

She turned to stalk away and stepped into the wall of a man's chest. For just a breath, she was scared. Then she caught a whiff of his scent, and she relaxed.

↭

"...I didn't get to where I am by being careless or working with careless people."

Adam breathed a soft curse while allowing himself to admire Lana's words, if not her sanity. She stood up to the large, obviously dangerous, Slavic male with no give in her posture. From here, Adam couldn't see the vulnerable woman who had occasionally surfaced. This woman was strong, tough, and angry.

And also far too likely to get herself into trouble without some back up. He pushed up from the chair and headed for the door. "Going down to the floor," he advised the other man, a computer geek with above average skills.

"Yo. You're on screen and on ear."

Adam waited impatiently for the express elevator to get him to the casino floor then pushed through the crowd toward the small grouping of people. He identified several potential guards and avoided them by taking a seemingly casual route, not appearing to rush but sliding through the excitement junkies with ease. When Lana turned away, he was there to block her. The scent of her rose up to his senses, even under the expensive perfume she'd applied with a light hand. And the feel of her, stepping into him, her breasts flattening against his chest—

He took a deep breath and took hold of her, his large hands gently encircling her upper arms. "Hey, babe, sorry I'm late. You about ready to go?" He stared into her eyes the way a besotted boyfriend might then looked up at the other men. "These guys bothering you?"

က

Lana took a breath, opening her eyes wide, gaze searching his face as if trying to understand why he was there. She moved back half a step, not pulling away from his hold as much as making room between their bodies. If she wanted to stay sane, stay focused on her conversation with the slimy assholes, she'd need not to be so close to the hard, warm surface of his chest, the comfort of his touch.

"Not at all. We were just discussing a business proposition."

Adam looked over at the men, but without the predatory glare she'd seen so often in his hard green eyes. In fact, in his well-tailored suit, carefully groomed hair, and cane, he seemed more like an accountant than a warrior.

Cane?

Sure enough, Adam was holding a dark wood cane with a brass top. She now remembered feeling it against her back when he'd held her arms. Since when did he use a cane? She almost opened her mouth to ask and caught a look from the corner of his eye. Obviously, he did not want to discuss his sudden need for a cane. She gave him a quick nod.

"Mr. Hoffman, Mr. Novakov, Adam Roberts."

"Captain Adam Roberts, US Army, Retired." Adam reached out for a hard, brief handshake. The other two men looked at each other then at Lana, seeming as if they were going to be angry.

"Sorry, I gotta take this gorgeous lady away from you." Adam turned to Lana, bending down to make his next words more intimate. "You know how you feel when you get over tired. Let's go get some rest." He raised his head and narrowed his eyes at the other men. "Gentlemen, she can see you tomorrow."

Adam's right hand settled on her lower back while he used his cane with great effect, displaying to the crowd that the well-groomed, tough-looking man was not at peak performance level.

∽∾∽

Lana stayed quiet as they went through the casino then used one of the private elevators to reach her room level. She kept her mouth shut as they traversed the halls, her heels making no noise on the carpeting. Once she was in her room, away from the ubiquitous eyes of the cameras, she opened her mouth only to feel his rough finger across her lips. A furrowed brow warned her against talking just yet, or at least against talking about anything that mattered.

"You ready to go to the place, babe, or do you need to pack?"

They were definitely going to have a talk about the "babe" appellation.

"I just need to grab a few things, sweetie buns." She moved away from him as she spoke but looked back to see the pained expression on his face, as he stayed near the door. But when she reached for a carry bag, and items to put in the bag, he shook his head.

She sighed, understanding his warning but not liking it. When she reached for a favorite pair of jeans, and some decent shoes, only to once more be warned away, she felt a slow burn of anger. She nodded abruptly and turned to leave.

His attempt to apologize silently didn't make a huge impression, especially not when her feet continued to scream at her.

∽∾∽

Adam eased Lana into the front seat of her car, surprised that she drove something so mundane, and well used, as an old Jeep. He'd received clearance to drive the vehicle so, no doubt, it had either been thoroughly vetted, or they wanted her to be tracked.

He moved around to the driver's door, continuing the appearance of an amputee not comfortable with his condition. He felt her attention on him, and when he opened the door, he saw her brow furrowed. He indicated the need for quiet for at least a few more minutes. Once they were under way, with music playing, it would be safer to talk.

She didn't talk immediately, allowing him to deal with the heavy early-evening traffic. Once they were out of the main thoroughfares, taking a longer circuitous route to the isolated cottage, he cleared his throat.

"We're not positive that everything in your room has been tagged, but enough items were that it didn't seem to be a good idea to take anything from there. I'm told the cottage has sufficient items in your sizes and style preferences." He looked over when he heard a sound from her direction. "Not my words—someone on the team did the shopping."

"That's...encouraging. At least I won't have to wear these damned shoes all night."

"Why do you wear them at all?"

"It's expected." At his quick look, she went on. "Party Girl Lana is always seen in FMPs"

"FMP? Oh, yeah, I know what you mean."

"The story goes her first hard-soled shoes had two-inch heels, and her feet haven't touched the ground since."

"Party Girl Lana?"

"Fun-time chickie. Amoral, always up for a good time, especially when she can turn a healthy profit." She turned her head away, seeming to be watching the moon-lit desert landscape. Her next words were almost whispered. "I had hoped I could leave her behind."

"You have me confused."

"Party Girl Lana was a persona I developed when I was dealing with runaways and the low-life scum who took advantage of them. When this trafficking situation showed up, and I realized the intentions of the group who rented that apartment, she was the easiest one to assume."

"Persona?"

"I've developed a small grouping of identities to use when I'm trying to work a situation. Most of them suit individual situations: Historian, Socialite, Fun-Time Girl. They all have their own wardrobe. Kind of like I'm my own personal dress-up doll."

At a stop sign, he turned to look at her more fully, and she did not turn away. There was little expression to be seen, not even defiance or a forced sincerity. He nodded then shook his head, allowing a small breath of laughter to slide out. "Dress-up doll. Okay."

ⱷↄⱷↄ

Lights showed in the windows of the tiny cottage when they finally pulled up after taking a ridiculously complex route. The lights made the casita look far more cozy than Lana knew it to be. Even so, it was the welcome end, at least temporarily, to her day.

She didn't wait for Adam to come around to her side of the vehicle before she opened her door and slid out. Still, he was at her side before she could close the door. He held the cane in his left hand but didn't set the point to the ground.

She looked down at the cane but didn't ask any of the myriad of questions crowding in her mouth. First things first. She had to get these bedeviled shoes off her feet. Since it made both of them feel better, she let the soldier help her up the steps.

The door opened before she could reach for it, and she stumbled back, pushing into Adam. He'd braced himself, raising the cane in what seemed to be a defensive maneuver. The person silhouetted by the dim light inside the cottage was tall and lean, with short tousled hair.

"Finally!" the tall figure said in a low feminine voice. "I was afraid dinner would go bad, or we'd eat it before you got here. Which would be very embarrassing."

She stepped back until the light touched her face, confirming what Lana had suspected. Ty's girlfriend/ partner was in her house. Lana controlled the strong inclination to be more of a bitch than normal and stepped inside.

Then stopped cold.

"This…" She took a breath. "What happened?"

"We want this to look like a love-nest, sort of secret hideaway. So we, as in Major Powers's mighty band of designers, have gone all out to make it look that way."

The walls were still a utilitarian tan, but artwork, drapes, rugs, and furniture set off that bland color, giving the impression of a jewel box of a small cottage. Through the opening to the tiny kitchen, she saw small appliances and fresh herb pots, plus flowers and plants, that gave the impression of long residency.

"I'm…impressed," Lana said, not moving from her spot at the front door.

"I know. I'm often surprised by what Powers can make happen," Roz said, with a drawl that seemed to underscore her intrinsic lack of respect for the manipulating person. "Anyway, you have clothes in your room, towels in the bathroom, in case you want to at least change, if not wash off the casino stink."

Lana nodded, going through to the small bedroom without further comment.

The magic continued in here, with a large bed covered by a rust and turquoise throw, decorated by jewel toned pillows. The closets and drawers were filled with the kind of clothes she wore when she could—mostly yoga pants, sweats, jeans, and pull overs. A few well-made but plain dresses shared closet space with Southwest-looking full skirts and matching silk blouses.

No suits, bustiers, man-styled jackets. No fuck-me pumps. A covered wardrobe bag probably held the fancier items, but they were not on prominent display. She sighed in bliss. Later, she'd find out who she needed to thank. Right now she was in desperate need of a shower.

When she came out, still toweling her hair dry, she had covered her aching, unhappy feet with thick fuzzy socks and replaced the look-at-me suit with leggings and a slouchy sweater over a camisole with enough support to completely ditch a bra. Her breasts and back thanked her.

Voices came from the kitchen/sitting room section. Adam, Roz and—Ty. Taking a deep breath for strength, Lana followed the sound.

"Here she is. Find everything you need?" Roz's voice was still polite but cool.

"Does it meet with your approval?" Ty began then winced when Roz slapped him, hard, in the upper arm.

"Remember, we are not being judgmental until we know what really happened, and why," she said.

Adam pushed himself out of the comfortable chair as if to step between Lana and the other two people in the room.

Ty gestured for Adam to sit while he stood. "Sit down. I apologize for acting like an ass. Sometimes my own idiocy gets away from me. Anyone want coffee, water, wine, beer?"

"I just might kill for a glass of that nice dark red blend you got," Roz said, moving toward the small kitchen area.

"The boxed stuff?" Ty looked at her, eyebrow raised. "You like that wine?"

"Hey, it's not bad. And it's obviously what Lana drinks, given what they found in her apartment."

Lana grimaced. "Party Girl Lana stocks Chateau de Cardboard. She pours it into a fancy carafe and serves it in fine crystal. She found out a long time ago most so-called wine experts can't tell the difference between boxed wine and the expensive stuff."

"Party Girl Lana?"

"Long story, sorry. Want me to get the wine?" Lana offered, though she just wanted to put her feet up and collapse.

"No, Ty needs to atone for forgetting he's not a total redneck jerk," Roz said as she followed him into the tiny kitchen area. "Don't worry. I'll make sure he gets everything into the right cups. You want some water too?"

"Bless you. I can't seem to stay hydrated in those casinos."

"Dry, cool air, gets to you every time. Adam, what about you?"

"Coffee, black. And water."

"You can have a beer if you want. You're pretty much off duty until the morning."

"Coffee, black. Please." He sat again and lifted his leg onto the ottoman.

Lana sank onto the love seat, set at a clever angle to the well-padded leather chair. All this furniture was new since she had been here…was it only two days ago? Yet it looked like it had been here for years. "Love what you've done with the place," she drawled, settling back into the comfortable seat and tucking her feet under her.

She contemplated the wine, took another small sip, then set it aside and reached for the bottle of water. "I think it might be an excellent idea to address the past before we decide what to do about the present and the future," she said, using her lady-executive voice.

Ty looked over, eyebrows raised as if to question her decision. Then he nodded, once, and seemed to lose some of the cynicism around his mouth.

That might have had something to do with the touch of a long-fingered hand from the woman sitting close to his side.

"Ty asked if I was on a job or project when I was at Stormhaven, and I gave him what was probably a confusing answer. I met him at a rodeo, actually at a bar after a friend of his had won big at the rodeo. When he started describing Stormhaven, it sounded like bliss—a remote ranch, where the main concern was helping out vets. I had hoped I could get away from projects and fake personas and always having to look over my shoulder. The problem is, I heard him talk about wanting to meet and settle down with an old-fashioned girl, the kind who understood their place in life and were always quiet, sweet, and well dressed."

"You didn't," Roz's normally pleasant voice nearly hissed.

Ty winced. "I was drunk. And stupid."

"That's no excuse."

"It wasn't an excuse, for either one of us. I showed him that woman, let him believe I would be the perfect subservient, have dinner waiting, no matter when he came in from the barn, woman. He decided there was no time like the present, and we were married that weekend."

"Vegas," he added. "I was there for the World Champion Roping. And I was—"

"You only have the right to claim drunk once," Roz reminded him.

"I was lonely, dammit. She seemed like everything I wanted in a woman. At least at that time. I've learned a lot since then." He reached out, without looking, to secure her hand, cradling it in his to lift up to his mouth.

"This is what I'd call a no-win situation, Mr. Randolph," Adam drawled from where he sat with his eyes half closed. "No matter what you say next, you're gonna sound pretty bad."

"Not necessarily," Lana said. "Ty never really knew who he was married to. I realized after I'd been at the ranch for a week that I'd made a horrible mistake. But I thought I could bluff it out for long enough to hide out from my life, maybe give me a chance to change. I was even able to meet my sister again after way too many years. Shortly after that, a new man came to Stormhaven. He said he was from another ranch, looking for some day work, and he'd heard Ty was shorthanded. He wasn't a bad hand, from what I was told, but he wasn't there to work. He was there to get a message to me. I was told to drive into Willow Springs one day. He was there, with Mosby in a trailer. Apparently, he'd convinced Ty he was safe to drive Mosby somewhere...I was never sure where."

"Vet clinic, we needed some X-rays from a stronger-than-portable machine. I'd been planning to drive with him, but somehow the new guy was already down the road."

Lana nodded. "I met up with him in Willow Springs, left my car at the grocery store, and got into the truck. He was threatening you, the ranch, the horse, unless I went back to work for Tony B. When I could, I got away from him; dropped off the horse, truck, and trailer; and later called Syd.

Ty looked over, frowning, but without the bitter accusation. "Why didn't you call me?"

"He was ready to rain down all sorts of hell on Stormhaven if I didn't cooperate. Starting with killing Mosby." Lana took a sip of wine then cradled the goblet in her hand. "It took a while to get them to believe I was going to cooperate. Then I found someone who could deal with Mosby, who would take him away until I could get hold of my sister. I knew Syd had kept up with some of Dad's contacts, so she'd be able to help."

"That's not quite how she told it," Ty argued.

"I know. I was having a problem getting a private line." Lana waited for more comments then took a deep breath. "Once Mosby was stashed where I couldn't find him, I had the chance to get away. By then, I was knee deep in their new sex trade game, and I had to work carefully to avoid getting caught up in what they were doing."

"Does Powers know about this?" Ty asked, his voice neutral.

"You don't believe me? I'm not surprised, and I don't think I deserve your trust yet."

"Tell them about your personas," Adam suggested.

# Chapter 9

T hey don't need to know about the personas," Lana snapped.

"I think they do. It seems to me the personas are critical to what you're trying to talk about," Adam stated, not moving from his half reclined position. "When you were at the ranch before, I'm betting you were the sweet, meek housewife."

"Not one of my more successful roles since it's difficult for me to keep up for very long. I've found people like seeing what they think they want, or people want their opinions validated. So they're happiest when I'm what they think I'm going to be whether it's a party girl, a teacher, whatever. The identities I use most often have a complex background, right down to wardrobe, food preferences, you name it."

"Fake identities to fool the suckers." Ty's voice was bitter, his expression judgmental.

Roz spoke over him. "How long have you been working undercover?" she asked in a quiet voice that demanded an honest answer.

The men's heads swiveled in her direction—Ty surprised, Adam nodding as if he agreed.

"I didn't say—"

"You didn't have to," Roz bit back. "No one with your intrinsic sense of honor lets themselves be used the way you have without a good reason. Since I know you aren't a real con artist, you would have some other reason."

Lana felt the warmth of that statement even while she floundered for an answer. "How did you—"

"Because she's scary smart," Ty said, voice flat. "A lot smarter than I was."

"And don't you ever forget that, hot stuff," Roz murmured. "You let your need to play knight in shining armor get in the way of seeing her as she really was. Then I bet your hurt feelings kicked in."

Ty rubbed his hands over his face, stifling the groan. "Like I said, scary smart."

"I'm thinking the really scary smart undercover person is Captain Adam Roberts, Retired," Lana drawled, tilting her head to watch him out of the corner of her eye.

Adam raised his eyebrows, as if to question her sanity, then allowed one corner of his mouth to lift.

Lana directed her attention to the cane propped on the arm of his chair.

"Not many people worry overmuch about a cripple," he stated in a level voice.

"Or a bimbo," she acknowledged.

"Precisely."

Ty scrubbed his palms across his face again. "You've been working for Powers all along?"

"Heavens no. I didn't meet your Major Powers until Sydney's asshole ex found me in Utah—where I was trying to find the people kidnapping young Navajo girls. That project went south fast."

"Who was sending you undercover?"

She sighed, leaning forward, elbows on her knees.

"No one official. I was working off the bad karma of being caught in one of our mother's schemes, even though I told her I wanted no part of it. She disappeared, leaving me holding the bag—in this case, some fake bearer bonds and antique jewelry."

"And they decided to make an example of you?"

"Something like that. Actually, I think one of the agents was embarrassed by Mom constantly getting away from him. When he couldn't catch her, he made do with me." She took a sip of her wine, winced, and set the goblet on the floor.

"I'm not officially on any payroll or working with any unit. So I have to be very careful that I don't run into the wrong people."

"Where was your special contact when you were trying to report this most recent girl?"

"Not available." Such simple words to convey her panic and unrelenting fear.

Adam leaned forward, bracing his forearms on his knees, focusing his attention completely on her. "Do you think that was intentional?"

"I found the timing suspicious. They had never been 'not available' for me, since my information was always good and helped them close a lot of cases." She forced a social smile. "And what's your undercover history or would you have to kill me if you told me?"

"Nothing that exciting. I've always been able to blend in, and I was involved in military intelligence before this." He laid his hand on his thigh, kneading as if it ached. "Once I was discharged and back in more-or-less working condition, a former military buddy got me in touch with someone who didn't see a disability as a reason not to hire me for an active job."

"Powers?"

"Might have been but I took my orders, and paycheck, from someone else. My team got a call for an extraction in some god-forsaken village in the Middle East. That operation eventually led me to Stormhaven, and to Major Powers."

Roz, for once, had no clever remark to fill in the suddenly uncomfortable silence. Ty cleared his throat and nodded as if in thanks.

"Was that you, Roz?" Lana asked, taking in the sudden almost shy attitude of the so far extremely confident woman.

"So I'm told. By the time he carried me out, I wasn't really able to tell."

"Carried you out?" Lana looked at Roz then at the not-as-tall Adam. Not as tall as Roz, not as bulked as Ty. But—she pushed that aside for later. "And were you working undercover?"

"The only undercover I've ever dealt with has been those demon-inspired underwire bras I had to wear to give me cleavage. I was there as a testament to my own ignorance."

Roz stood, gathering mugs, goblets, and water bottles. "And now we're interfering with your rest. I think all of us need a break. The cottage was checked and cleared for listening devices, but there are cameras and some guards outside, so you're safe for now."

Without seeming to hurry, she rushed herself and Ty out into the warm Nevada night before Lana could think about standing up.

∽∾∽

"You carried her out?"

"She didn't weigh much, and she was pretty much

out of it, so it was like carrying a long rug."

"Why do I think there's more to that story?"

"Why do I think there's a lot more to your 'personas,' than you've let me know so far? Neither one of us is in any shape to delve into past or future right now. Let's get some sleep."

Lana looked around, finally admitting to herself what she'd been ignoring.

"One bed."

"Yep. There's one of those fancy air mattresses stuffed in one of the closets."

"Good, I've used those before, they're comfortable."

"You are sleeping on the bed. You need your rest. I'll take the air mattress."

"Not happening. You're too tall to fit on an air mattress, and I'm betting you need room to get comfortable. We both need our rest."

Which was how both of them ended up on the bed.

ఆఛ్ఆ

Adam stifled a groan while he stretched out on the king-size memory-foam-topped mattress. The hot shower, plus the cozy bed, was going to make this night bearable.

He could have tolerated the air mattress, though he doubted Lana would have let him stay there. The little blonde sure showed a spine of steel when she wanted her way.

She acted like she'd fallen asleep immediately at the wall side of the bed, but she was not softening, not relaxing in her sleep. Nor had her breathing changed or eased, though she drew in deep even breaths.

For a woman with a reputation as a party girl ready for a good time, she sure didn't seem comfortable with a

strange man in bed with her. How had she dealt with being Ty Randolph's wife? Given how the handsome
rancher acted around Roz, it sure didn't seem like he
would've been backward in bed with Lana.

Adam shifted, then stiffened when the unwary move
sent a thrill of pain up to his hip. He didn't make a sound.
He knew he didn't make a sound. He'd learned not to react when pain snuck up on him unaware.

A soft voice drifted from across the expanse of bed.
"You okay?" Might as well be a damned ocean between
them.

"Moved wrong."

"Would pillows help? Someone seems to have decided I like a lot of pillows."

He'd seen the pillows, in all shades of bright, tossed
across the bed like an explosion of color. Now he felt
them pushed his direction then felt the bed shift as she sat
up.

"Sorry, I should have thought—is it easier for you to
brace against the wall?"

"I'm okay for now."

She was already moving, sliding toward the foot of
the bed and off, then padding around to the outside. He
edged over, guarding against twisting the wrong way, until his back rested against one of those long body pillows
that was stretched out along the wall.

"You use these body pillows?"

"Only to take up space in the bed."

Her quiet reply held a wealth of information he
didn't have the time or energy to analyze right now. Especially when both of them were in dire need of solid
sleep, encouraged by the soft, dark warmth. He let himself relax against the padded wall, feeling sleep overcome
his bones and joints and...

လ⁓ၑ⁓

Lana heard him sink into deep sleep with the instant ability of babies and warriors. Too bad for her, she was too old for the first and not trained for the second.

Still. Having Adam Roberts on the other side of the bed was...comforting. Probably not something she'd share with him.

In her experience, telling men they were restful didn't appeal to their egos.

Too many men were all about those egos, which was often to her advantage. She pulled a sheet over her body, snuggled into carefully stacked pillows, and prepared to rest. She doubted she'd sleep too deeply. Not with someone she barely knew in the bed. Not with strange breathing so close to her.

လ⁓ၑ⁓

Filtered light woke her. From her time in this house before, she knew it was predawn sneaking through the tough trees surrounding the cottage. Except for the even breathing behind her, there were no sounds.

*No sounds!*

No birds bouncing in the branches, scrounging for seed that had fallen out of the feeders. No rustling of small scurrying creatures. She raised her head slowly, trying not to wake the man sleeping behind her. Too late.

"What's up?" His voice barely carried to her ear.

"No birds."

She sat up all the way and swung her legs off the bed, barely missing the metal prosthetic leg braced against the side of the bed.

"Hold up." A large hand settled over her bare arm, tightening when she tried to pull away. "Just—dammit.

Stop. We have cameras and physical guards. No one can get close who shouldn't be here."

She stiffened against his hold then nodded in acknowledgment. When his hand loosened, she pulled away, standing at the side of the bed but not looking behind her. Dammit. She hated reacting this way. Even so, she found her arms crossing across her chest, her hands reaching out to hold her upper arms. Using the excuse to grab a light robe, she turned away from Adam, not wanting him to see her automatic stress reaction.

"Give me just a minute," his voice growled behind her.

She dashed into the bathroom, taking the opportunity to splash water on her face, brush her hair, and tie the robe more securely. In the mirror, her eyes were huge, her expression dull. Being scared sucked.

&#8736;&#8734;&#8736;

Adam eased himself out the side door and came around to the front. No one stood at the door, but he sensed someone nearby. "You might as well come out."

A form appeared as if coalescing from the bushes. Large, dressed in drab clothing. "Hey, Roberts."

"No one approaches the house without prior approval."

"Hey, it's me. Mike Thompson."

"No one approaches the house without prior approval. As far as I know, you're still on active duty."

"Nope, gave it up a while back. I think right around the time you had that accident." He indicated the prosthesis, now covered by loose sweat pants.

"When you were on active duty, you seemed to understand simple orders. For this operation, the orders cannot be any simpler."

"Well, yeah, but…" Mike trailed off, looking away.

The looking away, the relaxed posture, seemed to indicate someone feeling guilty. The muscle bunching in his jaw let Adam know his former colleague was only pretending to be chastened.

*Interesting.*

By the time Mike swung back, muscles bunching, Adam's gun was out and pointed in his direction.

"Hey, what gives, buddy?"

"I don't know, buddy. What gives? Why are you here?"

"I'm on security detail for Powers."

"When did you start working with Powers?"

"Pretty much right after I left the service. Frank Crowder—you remember Frank? He told me about his interview with Powers and said he was looking for experienced people. The pay is a lot better than anything Uncle Sam had to offer."

All of this was true. And delivered in a sincere, meet-his-eyes-squarely voice.

But…

"I don't remember you having that much trouble following simple directions in the past. Orders, maybe, if they didn't make sense. But not directions."

"Oh, come on. We both decided what jerk rules we'd follow."

Adam felt the air displace at his back as the door opened slightly. He saw Mike's attention waver briefly, then a frown appeared, as if he could not make out why the door had opened.

"I called that first number on your phone," Lana said, her voice low, but not so low it didn't carry to the man in front of them.

"Good."

"Aw, come on, already. You don't trust me?"

"My primary mission is to protect the civilian. I don't trust anyone."

"But we had each other's backs for how many years?"

"We were never on a team together. At most our teams helped each other when necessary. That was the past. This is now."

He heard the footsteps, and the leaves rustling. Which had to be intentional since anyone guarding would be able to move through this brush with no noise.

"Thompson? What the hell are you doing here?" The speaker took in the tableau, Adam's gun holding steady on the intruder, while Mike started to change his face to one of perplexity.

Something still felt off. "Everyone, stop." Adam took a step back until his shoulders touched the wall next to the door. "Lana, you okay?"

"Yes."

"You alone?"

"Yes. Someone tried the back door about a minute ago, but I bolted it after you went out."

Her voice sounded steady, but he caught an undercurrent.

"You." Adam indicated the new person with his chin. "How many men do you have with you?"

"Two others." He tilted his head left and right.

"No one behind the cottage?"

"No, sir."

"Lana, can you come out here?"

In answer, she slipped out through the open door, shutting it behind her. She'd used the extra time to change into jeans and a fleece top, loose and casual, with her hair falling around her shoulders.

"Call your men in. You might send one of them around the cottage."

The man nodded and spoke into his head set. Lana's face had slid into the somewhat vacuous expression of the party girl, not seeming to react to the implied violence or the strange men. He caught a scent of wildflowers, no doubt from her shampoo, along with the very slight trembling and uneven breathing. Nothing anyone else would notice, not when she was giving them the wide brown eyes and tousled-blonde-hair look.

Once the men were assembled, Adam gave them a quick but thorough look. All of them seemed business-like, meeting his eyes directly with no subtext. Except for Mike Thompson.

"Okay, spill."

"This is getting out of hand," Mike began with just a touch of whine in his voice. He rushed on before Adam could say anything. "I just wanted to say hey to my man Adam, that's all. I didn't expect the third degree."

"No approaching the house without prior clearance," the leader of the team said in an even tone.

"Yeah, yeah, I get it. Can't a guy drop in on an old friend?"

Adam shook his head, not believing how Mike was trying to hold on to his story. "Did anyone try the back door?"

"That would be me, sir. Sorry. Since there was a breach, I wanted to be sure your doors were secure."

Adam studied him for a minute then nodded. He lowered his weapon, easing his shoulders. "Mike, it might be a better idea for you to be on the long distance team. We can catch up on old times after the op is finished."

The other man frowned then nodded and turned away. A handgun showed briefly in a waist holster under the loose sweatshirt.

The leader noticed where Adam was looking, and

nodded an affirmative before following.

After everyone had left, fading into the bushes, Adam reached behind him to the door handle and pushed open the door. Lana choked off a brief laugh, turning it into a gurgle. He looked down at her, eyebrow raised.

"Lucky it didn't lock automatically."

*೧ೲ೧*

Later, over coffee, which was much better than the wine that had been stocked for her, Lana studied the dark, fragrant liquid while she considered what to ask. "Any idea what that was all about?"

"It could have been as innocent as he claimed. Old friends catching up."

"You don't think so?"

"I can't be sure. This is the first I've seen or heard from Mike since before my…incident. He said he signed on with Powers because the pay was better. Which it is."

"No doubt it's even better working for Hoffman."

"That's what's worrying me." He took a gulp of coffee. "What's on the agenda for today?"

"I'll need to briefly touch base with Hoffman and Novakov. We left abruptly last night, so I want them to think I'm still willing to work with them, as long as they keep their act together. I'll be poking around some so I can get a feel for what's been going on. And I need to pay some bills." At his quizzical look, she offered a small smile. "Yeah, even we bad actors have to pay rent and keep our credit cards current. Nothing like being in the middle of an op and finding out your card's not up to date."

That brought her a smirk and a quick salute from his coffee cup before he took a deep drink. "Awesome coffee."

"Yeah. They didn't get that quite right. I'm not much of a coffee drinker. I have one of those one cup machines, and I stock up on the special biodegradable pods. It gives people a choice, and makes me seem trendy."

"Ty's kind of a coffee snob. Even the bunkhouse coffee is fancy."

"Yeah, I never quite understood that, but I drank what he served and liked it."

"So he never knew. That's probably why. What do you generally drink?"

"Hot water. I usually don't need a lot of go juice."

"Boxed wine?"

"It's a lot more difficult to judge wine consumption in a box than in bottles. And a drunk bimbo is a safe bimbo."

He hesitated, as if he wanted to ask a question not related to the op, then shook his head.

"In that case, we're going to want to get going. Do you have the right clothes here or do we need to make another stop first?"

"There's enough here for Party Girl Lana. But I'll start out with more business attire. I need to scope out some other places and hit the casino later."

"Other places?"

"Those girls didn't stay in the casinos, or in that apartment penthouse. Someone had to bring them back and forth, and someone had to supply them in the first place. If Hoffman and Novakov want to set up an operation, they're going to be edging out established suppliers. I need to check that out..." She hesitated, searching for the right words.

"You might as well just spit it out," Adam drawled while rinsing out his cup and placing it in the sink. "I hope we're past trying to say things the right way."

She managed a smile and acknowledged his statement with a small nod. "Thank you. Where I'm going, the people I'll be talking with—I might say some things that don't sound so…" She groped for the best word then shrugged. "Nice."

Adam shrugged, offering a tight smile. "Don't worry, I understand undercover talk."

But would he? Only time would tell.

# Chapter 10

So you haven't heard anything about a source for new, more special girls," Lana asked, tilting her head as if the subject was of only casual interest for her.

The aging madam drew deeply on her cigarette, frowning as if searching her memory for any other information. More likely she was trying to figure out if she could use any of this encounter to her advantage.

Suzette was as good as anyone could be who bought and sold lives. She took decent care of her people, but it was more a matter of protecting her merchandise. Something in this woman's past had affected her approach to life, given her this cynical attitude. Which was sad, but at this point, Lana needed whatever information she could pry out.

"So, what's it like?" Suzette's smoke-affected voice grated out. She pointed the half consumed cigarette vaguely in Adam's direction.

"Pardon?"

"What's it like, doing it with a crip?"

Lana turned in her seat, looking over at Adam standing to one side and slightly behind her. His worn jeans fit without being so tight they could impair movement, his crisp white shirt opened at the collar, with sleeves rolled back to display forearms muscled by years of hard usage. His face was professionally remote, the perfect bodyguard. She couldn't say what she wanted to say, couldn't slap the older woman down for rudeness or a lack of humanity. She allowed herself a smile, somewhat predatory, but didn't let it reach her eyes.

"All the important parts work just fine," she purred, with a possessive stroke on his butt.

The older woman smirked in return, stubbing out her cigarette and standing, obviously indicating an end to the discussion. "Sorry I can't help you out, kiddo."

"It was kind of a shot in the dark. If there is a new pipeline, I figured you'd know about it, and maybe cut me in on the action. It never hurts to be a part of what's going on. You never know, I might want to have my own supply available if there's some demand. It won't be cheap, but quality costs."

With a final, empty-minded smile that managed to convey a total lack of ethics, Lana followed the aging madam to the door, Adam close behind. When they reached the door, Adam stepped ahead of her, checking the hall outside before indicating she could proceed.

Suzette's penciled-in eyebrows raised. "I'm impressed."

Lana smiled, conveying sophistication along with ennui. "It never hurts to be too careful. I've found spending for the best is a valuable investment."

She put a touch of swagger in her walk as she preceded him down the apartment hallway toward the elevators.

Adam's left hand hovered near but not on the small of her back. Glancing sideways, she noted his expression remained professional. His right hand hovered near but not on his gun.

This time the tiny grin wasn't for effect as much as humor. She started to make an observation about the distance similarities—until his hand descended that tiny space farther, to rest on the small of her back, heat and strength sinking into her jacket.

"Not yet," he murmured, indicating the corners of the hallway with a quick twist of his head.

She nodded, remembering cameras were a standard feature in hotels and some apartments these days. They bypassed the elevators then paused outside the door to the stairs. He looked down at her shoes

"Can you—"

"No problem," she said, pushing open the heavy door. When she was on the other side, she reached into her capacious carry all, pulling out a pair of soft leather shoes with low heels.

"These fancy shoes are way too expensive to mess up on the stairs," she explained while changing one pair for the other. Once her feet were in the new shoes, she took a moment to just enjoy the sensation before stuffing the higher heels into a cloth bag then into her carry bag. "Not to mention, I just can't walk on my toes for all that long."

He looked down at her feet with a frown.

"You have heels on these shoes. Why did you wear those skyscrapers?"

"Lady-Executive Lana always wears shoes that make her taller, along with the very-tailored suit, so she's taken more seriously." She ran her fingers along the lapels. "But she's very careful to put the shoes away when she's on break, so to speak. She's very careful with valuable items. This reassures potential partners that she's not going to be careless with their valuable merchandise. Besides those damned shoes cost the moon, even on mark down."

"Tough times?"

"Perpetually."

"Working undercover usually helps with the bottom line."

"When you're paid in money, yes."

They hurried down more flights of concrete steps, Adam taking the lead to check at each turning. Apparently, his leg did not bother him during the exercise. Lana took a deep breath to start her apology but was stopped by a quick shake of his head. He mouthed, "Not yet."

Finally, they were in the basement garage. Once he had satisfied himself there was no one watching, he nodded at her.

"I want to tell you—"

His hand came up again, while his head tilted slightly to one side. She heard a click, probably from his minuscule earpiece. Then two clicks. Then a low whistle from behind some parked vans. Adam let out a huff of air as if he found the interruption as irritating as she did.

Ty was crouched behind one of the vans, as if he'd been there for a while. When he saw them, he stood and pulled on a white baseball cap with the logo of a delivery company.

"When we saw 'out of order' signs on the elevators, we thought you might come down this way."

"There weren't any signs on the floor we were visiting," Lana said, feeling her heart rate increase.

"That's kind of what I figured. Roz is moving your SUV down a couple of blocks. We've kept an eye on it, no one's messed with it. Hop in, I can take you over there."

They stayed low, crouched on the floor of the cargo van Ty was driving.

"Sorry we couldn't get a passenger van. You okay back there?"

Lana looked over at Adam. How could it be comfortable for him to be folded up that way?

But he answered with a smile. "Not a problem. Is someone checking out the elevators or letting them think we're oblivious?"

"I'm not sure, but I'm thinking oblivious is better for any long term plans. You're going to meet up with whoever hired these goons at some point. What do you plan to tell them?"

"I hadn't gotten that far," Adam admitted, stretching out his legs until he was more comfortable.

"Security cameras," Lana said.

"Well, yeah, that's why we took the stairs instead of the elevator, but—"

"I wanted to get away from the infernal security cameras," she said, her voice at once harder and with more whine. "I don't particularly want to share my new boy toy with all the perverts who can hack into those freaking cameras."

Ty's head whipped around, then he looked back in time to avoid rear ending the bus in front of them.

Adam nodded, considering the idea. "That would work."

"I really need to tell you," she said in her normal voice.

"No, you don't. Especially not just now."

"Boy toy?" Ty asked, looking at them in the rear view mirror.

"I thought it would be the best explanation for why I have a bodyguard, when I normally don't have anyone hanging around."

"They won't be suspicious, you taking up with a strange male?"

"They think I'm one small step up from brainless bimbo, so not much would surprise them."

"Brainless? Damn, that's good acting on your part. You think you've got them that well confused?"

"For the most part." She thought about Aleksei Novakov, the new man, the one who looked through her, instead of at her. "At least the ones I've known for a while."

"Is there someone you think you might not have confused?"

"This new man, Aleksei Novakov, seems to be Slavic or Middle European—he was at the apartment, and with Hoffman at the casino. He either doesn't think I'm quite as much of a party girl as the others think, or he doesn't hide his opinion as well."

"You don't think you have him buffaloed?"

"I think it's a stupid undercover person who believes their own fake ID. I prefer to err on the side of caution."

"I thought you needed to believe in what you're doing to convince others."

"It's a fine line. A very fine line. One that undercover police have to deal with on a regular basis. That's why my personas are all me, just over emphasizing certain aspects of my own character."

Ty shook his head but didn't say anything else until they pulled into another underground garage. He slid out the door first, nodding to several people spaced around the structure, then looked back at them. "Looks like it's clear. Lana's car is up one level so you can approach it like you've been shopping." He nodded to some bags next to them, prominently labeled with the names of popular fashion stores.

"Oh, goodie. More clothes I can't wear."

"Maybe, maybe not."

She stepped out of the van, changing her shoes before stretching her spine straight and brushing off her suit, took a deep breath, and thought about being a lady executive. Powerful, maybe; ambitious definitely. Damned tired of having to kowtow to the ignorant men around her. Who were they to think they could push her around? When she had the image and attitude in her mind, she opened her eyes.

Both men stood watching her intently. Ty's mouth was slightly open as if in shock, but Adam nodded once, as if in approval, as he grabbed the bags.

"Let me take some of those."

"Not now. You'd expect your boy toy to carry them for you."

"Of course," she said, leading the way to the elevator. "Ty, are the cameras working in this garage?"

"Not on this level, but yeah on the next level. You'll be on visual when you go for your SUV but not on audio. Good luck"

Lana led, putting just the right amount of hip action into her walk, adding a raised hip when she stopped at the elevator. She punched the elevator button with one long finger. "Showtime."

❦

She repeated this under her breath as she put the finishing touches on her make up later that evening: a touch of gold dust glitter on her cheeks, smoky eyes, strong red lipstick.

Party Girl Lana looked back at her from the mirror: a bit sly, a bit sleazy.

"It's all about us, baby," she told her reflection as a reminder of what persona she was planning to work under. "Like pulling on an overcoat," she continued as she went into the main room of the suite.

"What's that?" Adam asked, opening a bottle of her favorite water.

"You have awfully good hearing for someone who's been in combat."

"Good protection. And I also didn't do the ear-buds-blasting music when I was a kid."

"Smart kid." She took the bottle with a murmur of thanks and drank, careful to keep her lipstick intact. When she pulled the bottle from her mouth, for just a moment, she thought she surprised a glitter in his eyes. Then he turned his head away and the moment was gone.

"Do we have an appointment with Hoffman?

"They expect me—us—on the floor tonight. I'm sure they'll be happy to interrogate me."

"And you will tell them?"

"Whatever they want to hear."

∽∾∽∾

"You two have been hounding me to meet with you. I'm not the one who insisted on meeting. Other than collecting my fee, which has still not been deposited in my account, I have no need to see either one of you."

Lana stood, hands on hips, glaring at the angry men. Expensive tailored suits helped to hide their weapons, but nothing could conceal the cold expression, the hooded eyes, and the arrogant twist to Aleksei's mouth.

Hoffman tried hard to look as tough but was failing miserably.

They faced her without any back up, showing their lack of respect for Adam, no doubt due to his apparent disability. He did nothing to disabuse them of this opinion, leaning heavily on his cane while he stood behind her, shifting his weight from time to time.

"Well?" Lana continued. "Nothing to say? It's gonna

be difficult to have a conversation if you won't say anything."

"We are attempting to discern your actual intent," Novakov said in a gravelly voice, his accent more pronounced. "You have been actively working with those who procure young women for the sex trade. Yet there is little to no history of your direct involvement. I would have to be suspicious of your actual motivation."

"I have never been averse to making an easy profit. That's difficult when people don't pay their bills."

"Even so, you seem to disappear from sight after transactions are complete. Along with many of the young women."

"Most of those young women have moved on to their new places of business." She took a deep breath and searched for her best mercenary tone of voice. "Look, I don't have a problem with girls who want to make money from sex instead of giving themselves away to their stupid boyfriends, as long as they want to do it and are treated well. Girls who are drugged and abused and strung out don't bring the same income for me. Once they're out of my direct control, and the bills are paid, they're not my problem anymore. Until then, I want them in the best possible condition."

Novakov showed his disgust with a brief narrowing of his eyes, a slight tightening to one side of his mouth. Sanctimonious bastard. Hypocrite. He was perfectly willing to profit from the bartering of innocent lives but didn't seem to think it was appropriate for a woman to do the same.

*Sanctimonious hypocrite.*

Lana turned her back on him, striding toward one of the casino's less obvious exits. From the corner of her eye, she saw Adam move in behind and to the side of her, using his cane as though he needed it.

A shout from one of the tables caught her attention, and she paused, along with everyone else in the half-crowded room, looking at the happy gambler. A quick glance showed her those who were not as enthralled by someone else's success. She noted who was more interested in their own fortune and who was looking around the same as she was.

She felt Adam's shoulder brush hers, a seeming accidental touch. "We've got some hotel security watching. Most too sunk into their own machines to see anything around them. But there's a few—"

"Off to the entrance to the cave—that's some of Hoffman's 'staff.' They generally hang out for long distance protection, especially around here. Otherwise—I see a couple of wanna-be gangies. Hotel security will keep an eye on them. Those guys in the corner showed up when Novakov did.

"Do you know where he came from?"

"He was presented as a new client. Complete with his own staff and a long list of requirements. All pretty normal. No requests for any sort of companionship, female or male. But my contract is specific: I do not supply companions."

"Never?"

"Nope. It surprises some of my clients the first time around, but they're the ones who didn't read the whole contract, or who thought they could talk me into something else. I provide special places to stay, exotic vehicles to drive. Dancers, musicians, pony rides. It is up to the individuals to get their own entertainment beyond that."

"But apparently some people think—"

"I know." She offered him a quick, tight smile. "Funny how that works."

She turned her back on the celebrating crowd and headed for the elevators. Behind her she heard what seemed to be a low chuckle then the tap of his cane as he followed.

❧❦❧

Once out of sight of the casino inhabitants, Lana made short work of changing her shoes, while Adam adjusted the cane length so he wouldn't be bending over as much. It was a subtle thing that made such a difference.

"Man, I'm going to be for-real crippled if we keep this up."

"Do you really need to—"

"Yeah, I do. Right now, they see me as a broken boy toy, maybe an escort. Not much of a bodyguard. Them underestimating me is to our advantage."

She smirked. "Boy toy?"

"What, you don't see me as your toy?"

"It's the boy part I'm having trouble getting my head around. The toy…" She slanted a look at him, assessing the ascetic face, high cheekbones, sculpted lips—the face of a quintessential warrior that could have been sculpted in marble or cast in bronze. Then his mouth tightened into a flat line, his nostrils flared as if drawing in her scent.

"Sorry," she muttered, turning away abruptly.

"What for?"

"It's not fair for me to take it to another place when you're doing your job."

"Life's not always fair, princess."

His large hand cupped her elbow as he turned her toward the car moving up to their location.

# Chapter 11

Lana came out of the bathroom in yoga pants and a loose-knit shirt, stretching her arms above her head. Thick fuzzy socks on her feet. She bent over, stretching out her back.

"Free at last," she muttered to her feet.

"What's that?"

"My toes. Free at last."

"Why not come over here and park your poor feet up. I can give them a rub."

"What's this 'you rub mine, I'll rub yours'?"

"Just get your feet up here. We can talk later about what you'll be rubbing for me."

He patted the spot next to him on the couch. The ottoman had already been pushed away to make room. She eased into the seat and lifted her feet, using the movement to hide her hot face.

"You really don't need to do that."

"Actually I think I do. It looks like those ridiculous shoes of yours are a critical part of your persona. You need someone to give your feet some TLC so you can stay in character."

"Excuse me?"

"Since Party-Girl Lana and Lady-Executive Lana both insist on wearing toe-damaging shoes, they need to pay attention to said toes. Otherwise, a critical part of their costume can't be worn."

"Are you mocking me?" She attempted to find a severe tone of voice but was stymied by the comfort from his big hands.

"Nope. Just being a good partner and helping you. I figure maybe you can help me too. I do dearly love a good foot rub."

"It seems I'd be getting the better end of this deal since you only have one foot," she said, falling under the spell of those strong hands easing the tensions in her foot. "Unless you're fond of stump rubs."

His hands stilled on her foot, and her words came back to her. He had looked away, shoulders stiff, and she felt her face flame.

"Oh, my god. I don't know why I said that. I am so sorry. I can't imagine why—how—"

His shoulders started to shake as he hunched over her foot, still held in his grasp.

"Adam?"

"St—stump rub?"

"I am so…" She trailed off as he raised his head.

An unholy glee shone in his bright green eyes. "Stump rub? Seriously?"

Then he laughed. His hands tightened on her foot, now held against his stomach. She felt the muscles on his stomach with her toes—and some disturbing other ridges.

"I really didn't mean—

"You have no idea—*no* idea—what it's like to not hear someone trying to tiptoe around what happened. Even the other soldiers. Even Devin and Ty and Powers's men—all of them so careful, even while they're trying to treat me like nothing happened. My family—I have a good supportive family. They helped me with rehab, they visited constantly, had me at home for a while. Didn't stand in my way when I needed to move on. But no one—no one—outside of the rehab facility every mentioned my stump. I was completely perfectly 'normal,' just a little bit 'under the weather.' I lost half a leg, dammitall. I'm not normal. I never will be normal."

"And this bothers you?" she asked in the most level manner she could.

"Hell yes, it bothers me." He searched her face as if her carefully modulated tones made him suspicious. "Social-Worker Lana?"

"Just sharing what's been thrown at me in the past. 'So, Ms. Castleton, how did finding out your father kills people for a living affect you?' Twice a month for a year while my mother tried to turn me against him. It was the single most irritating phrase I've ever encountered."

"Did it?"

"Affect me? Of course, it did. My father left, taking my sister with him. Leaving me with our mother. I don't think he realized how poisonous she could be. Did it turn me against him? Absolutely not. My father was a soldier, even if he didn't march in a national army. He was as good as he could be, given his background. I seriously doubt he'd even think about sneaking into a young girl's bedroom to 'get better acquainted.'"

"Lana…" His large fingers stilled, tightening around her foot.

She looked away abruptly. "Sorry. I usually keep that hidden at the bottom of the swamp."

"Then maybe it's time to come up for air. I meant what I said: it's refreshing for me to hear someone refer to my leg for what it is. And I am honored you feel you can share some of yourself with me. What about your mother?"

"My mother?"

"When men were trying to get into your room?"

"She stopped that." His grip eased, until she continued. "She didn't like the competition. She'd hoped to make me over in her image, but, unfortunately, I wanted to go with my sister and our father. Eventually, Mother farmed me out with some friends in California. They were in theater, and they helped me learn how to hide who I am."

"You couldn't go with your father and sister?"

"Apparently, she didn't know where they were. At least that's what she told me. Nor would she have let me live with him and possibly tell him what had happened. He'd trusted her."

"These friends in California could be trusted?"

"They had no interest in me as a female, just as an apprentice."

"And they taught you to 'hide' yourself?"

"It was necessary. I had no filter between thought and tongue, no matter how hard I worked to put it in place. It wasn't so bad when I played a part. When I played a part, I could 'borrow' the character's mannerisms."

"Party Girl Lana?"

"Yes. I learned to at least fake good social skills." She sighed then groaned when his fingers eased a particularly tight knot. "I usually manage to keep up the persona, but once in a while, I just get…tired, I guess. Plus, I generally don't have to keep the cover going nonstop. I have a small apartment outside town, where I don't have to be anyone else."

"Near here?"

"No, this is a cute little middle class garden apart-

ment. People think I'm a sales representative for an elec-
tronics firm."

"Another persona."

"Yes, but she doesn't interact much, she's mostly
rushing in and out, waving to people, keeping up a small
garden. She pays one of the high school girls to water her
plants when she's not around."

"She."

"Well, yes. She. Me."

"But you don't say *me*, you say *she*."

"Semantics."

He stared at her intently then went back to the foot
rub. "We need to get your feet happy. Ty and Roz will be
by later for a briefing. They've been digging into some of
the rumors of missing girls."

ↄ∙ↄↄ∙ↄ

"Depending on who I spoke with, the question of
girls either missing or strange girls showing up unexpect-
edly ranges from a curiosity to an extreme problem." Roz
sounded matter of fact, her well-modulated voice sharing
information as though she read it from a script. Her eyes
told a different story, and when she paused to take a sip
of wine, Ty reached out to slide his arm around her
shoulders. After a moment, she managed a small smile
and leaned against him.

Lana looked away, taking up a cup of hot water, giving them the moment of private support. Until Roz
straightened and gave Lana a quick nod. "Sorry. It—"

"You have nothing to apologize for. This information is invaluable. These people talked to you—social
workers, councilors, employers, coworkers…"

Roz's smile broadened briefly. "An advantage of being a published writer. People are always willing to talk

about their areas of passion if they think it's for a book. Interestingly, several people recommended I look for Lana Castle. They said she would be my best resource for information."

Lana looked up, frowning.

"What was even more interesting is that some of them think you're part of the solution, some think you're part of the problem. None of them like the agents or cops who used to work the missing-children cases."

Adam leaned forward. "Used to?"

"It seems they're not around anymore. Not at their offices, not working the streets, and not answering phones, or emails, or texts. Vanished."

"That's...disturbing." Lana took a sip of water, mostly to hide the slight tremor in her fingers.

"Definitely odd. Major Powers sent a more formal inquiry and was told either they had never worked for the department, or they were on vacation, depending on who responded."

Ty looked up from his coffee. "Are you sure they were with an agency?"

"Yes." Lana frowned. "I first met them when they were investigating a runaway. I visited them once in their offices, and when I called the agency, they put me through."

"When was that?"

"Two...two and a half years ago."

Roz took a sip of coffee. "When did you start working undercover for them?"

Lana took a sudden interest in their drinks, standing to collect cups and refill glasses. Roz stood also, reaching out to take Lana's forearm in her long fingers. The pressure guided Lana back into her chair. She drew a fortifying breath. "About a year ago." She looked over at Ty. "Right around the time I met you."

Roz released her arm and sat next to her. "Is there a connection?"

"Not really. Although I did think I could hide from them on the ranch, but they found me too fast."

"Why didn't you—" Ty stopped, wincing, then glared at Roz. She offered a small smile and raised eyebrows.

Adam leaned forward to ask. "Since they weren't offering you money, did they threaten you?"

Lana hesitated then nodded.

"Were they threatening violence or exposure?"

She sighed then tried to avoid looking at any of them. After a long silence, she cleared her throat. "Exposure. They found something in a sealed file that could have caused me trouble."

"Can you tell us what was in the file?"

"I'd rather not."

Adam stared at her for a few minutes then took a deep breath. Let it out.

"Okay, I'm good with that."

"But—" Ty said then hesitated. "How can we help if—"

"Not now. Our day started far too early, with someone possibly breaching security. If we're going to have to deal with those two legged snakes tomorrow, we need to do it on more rest."

"Breach?"

"Someone who was in my unit a while back. He's probably okay, but…"

"Does Powers know?"

"I believe so, yes."

"Then let's give you that chance to rest." Roz stood, stepping toward the door.

# Chapter 12

I killed a man."

The words, spoken in the dark, came from the other side of the wide bed. Adam turned his head. She was curled on her side in a near-fetal position, facing him, head tucked down. Hands clasped in front of her. Misery reached out across the space between them to whisper through the barrier he held between himself and the world.

"Was it justified?"

"Oh, yes. He was molesting a girl, a baby really. He liked them soft skinned and downy haired."

"How old were you?"

"Mid-twenties. Far beyond his parameters."

"Were you working undercover or—"

"I'd been putting together a special birthday party. Fairy princesses and ponies with glittery hooves. I came to the house for a last check, and he was there. A friend of the family. I hit him over the head with a brass statue, and he caught the corner of the fireplace on the way down."

"So it was an accident?"

"No, I wanted him dead. That's what I told the police. I wanted his ass dead and his puny brains splattered across the fireplace. However, I did not want that little girl to see something that awful. So I just picked up the statue, cracked him across the neck, and grabbed the girl. Moira took over from there."

"Moira?"

"Goddess of Fate. Celtic Karma."

Her voice seemed calm. Steady. Almost emotionless. Almost.

"Did the police charge you?"

"I was detained, but the final decision was I acted in the best interests of the girl. They didn't even hold me overnight."

"So how did these agents use this information against you?"

"The death, my name, all of it was hidden deep in a sealed file. Not because of my age, but who I killed. Pedophile, but related to some very bad people. I was privately congratulated but publicly chastised. I moved for a while, and it was all forgotten."

"Until these agents showed up?"

"They'd been around for a while. I'd worked with them before. Either they got curious themselves, or someone asked the agents for details, and they handed over my name."

He edged closer to her until he could lay his hand gently on her shoulder. In spite of the warm room, her skin was clammy cold, and faint shivers vibrated under his fingers.

"Lana," he murmured, trying to keep his voice as dispassionate as possible while wanting so desperately to pull her into his arms, cradle her like the children she protected.

She took the decision away from him, turning over

and backing up until she was nestled against him. Her bottom nearly snuggled against his groin, only stopped when he lifted his injured leg, using his thigh to support her while keeping a modicum of distance between them.

She sighed, her breath brushing against his arm, then straightened enough to lift her face. Her head rested on his arm, and the tremors reduced slowly.

"This is nice," she whispered, letting herself relax against him. "I'm so tired."

"You can sleep. You're safe here."

"I'm tired of being—always being someone. It's exhausting to remember who I am."

"Right here, right now, you only have to be yourself. Just Lana. Just be asleep, Lana."

Eventually, the tension slid out of her body, and she gave him the honor of resting against his chest.

ℰↁℰↁ

Lana woke to a dark room. She oriented herself quickly, identifying location—the cottage—day and time—very early morning, on Wednesday—before she'd taken her second breath. What was new, what caused her to hesitate before moving, was the warmth at her back, and the solid object behind her legs. Another thigh, muscular, obviously male. Even through her thin sleeping slacks, she felt the hair roughened surface, matching the arm across her mid-section. Not pinning her in as much as comforting her, completing the connection.

"It's Adam," a voice whispered behind her, breath blowing across her hair, easing against her scalp. He continued to hold her without pulling her closer. "It's early yet, did you want to try for more sleep?"

"I probably won't sleep again, but you sound tired. Maybe you should crash for a little longer."

"You get up, I get up. Bodyguard, remember?"

Oh. Yeah. With his leg, he'd need more sleep. She let herself relax, leaning more weight against his chest. She'd give it maybe fifteen minutes, and he'd be snoring up a storm. Then she could slip out of bed. Just a few minutes…

c∽e∽

The next time she woke, sunlight was filtering through the window coverings, and she was alone in the big, comfortable bed. Adam had obviously managed to slide out of bed without waking her. Something that should not have happened since she was generally very aware of who was around her.

She hadn't slept with a man for years, certainly not with anyone touching her. Yet within a very brief spell of time, she had not only stayed in the bed but had actually slept in his arms. It had felt…safe. Secure.

Shaking her head at herself, she sat, listening for sounds in the cottage. She could smell the coffee, hear the soft clack of computer keys from the kitchen. She decided to head that direction after a detour toward the bathroom.

Adam was staring at his screen, muttering to himself as he reached for his mug, and lifted it to his mouth. Finding it empty, he scowled then transferred that expression in her direction. Fixing a pleasant smile on her face, Lana reached for the cup.

"Oh, no you don't," Adam growled, grabbing her wrist.

Lana froze, not pulling back physically but drawing into herself. Preparing, just in case. Adam cursed steadily under his breath while he took the mug out of her hand then stood to pour out coffee for himself.

"When you're here, when it's just us, you're Lana. Not Hausfrau Lana, not Hostess Lana. Just Lana."

"I was just going to—"

"Get me a cup of coffee. Which I'm perfectly capable of getting for myself. I don't have a problem with you getting the coffee. It's that smile you're using."

"What? I smile. So what?"

"You use this Stepford Wives sort of smile. Like you're here, but you don't really want to be. Or you're here in body only."

"I..." She thought for a minute then shrugged. "Sorry, old habits."

"I understand. It's part of your survival. But you don't need to do it here. Here, you can just be Lana."

She moved toward the counter. "I'm not sure that's possible. 'Just Lana' hasn't been around for a while."

"Maybe we need to invite her to hang around more often." He took a sip of the coffee while crossing back to the table. "In the meantime, apparently someone's been asking around town about you."

She looked up from the electric hot water kettle, eyebrows raised.

"Aaron and Steve?"

"Ah, the missing agents. I wonder where they've been. And what story they've concocted this time to justify looking for me."

"According to what we're hearing, they're worried you aren't around. Asking if anyone's seen you, who you've been talking to."

"None of that's any of their business. I wonder how they're justifying the questions."

"Just friendly inquiries, for the most part, or so they're saying. Once in a while one of them starts to imply you're under suspicion—one of those 'persons of interest' ideas—but they can't come up with any sort of crime."

"So they're still with the agency."

"Or pretending real hard to be. We're going to have someone try to contact them there today. Otherwise, you'll have to figure out when we're going to run into them. Accidentally, of course."

"I'll need to come up with some girls to question them about. It seems several of them went missing just about the time those guys left town last week." She filled her cup with hot water, squeezed in fresh lemon from the refrigerator, then turned toward the table. After a step, she stopped, turned to look at the counter, then at Adam.

"Where did the kettle come from? It wasn't here yesterday."

Adam smiled. "Since you mostly drink hot water, we had someone check out your apartment and pick up your kettle. Don't worry. Your neighbors have no idea."

"You—You didn't have to do that. I could use the microwave."

"As much fancy water as you stocked in that apartment, I couldn't see you happily using the microwave." He looked back at his computer, then up again. "When you're ready, Ty and Roz can come over for a conference."

"Won't it seem suspicious for them to visit so often?"

"Didn't anyone tell you? They rented a wing of that gothic disaster next door. Roz apparently needs it for some kind of research." He shook his head, as if in disbelief. "This writing gig is a great cover story."

❧❧❧

"You're right, it can be a great cover story," Roz said

when he repeated the comment later. "Until you have to produce some sort of writing to prove out your cover."

"That's actually work," Ty added, setting up another pot of coffee. "Or so she says."

"How many hours?" Lana asked, ignoring Ty.

"For me, four to six. I know some writers who can put in a full work day, up to eight or ten hours. My bottom goes numb, and my brain goes on strike. That's actual writing time, not researching on the internet or doing promotional work on social media."

"How much can you write in that length of time?"

"If it's all going well, up to ten manuscript pages. About three thousand words." Roz looked around and smiled. "A novel can run from fifty thousand to one hundred fifty thousand words. My young adult books are between sixty thousand and seventy thousand. The one I'm working on right now will probably end up about a hundred and fifty thousand."

"You can finish a big book in two months?"

Roz laughed, the sound lightening the mood in the kitchen. Ty turned to look at her, the expression on his face one Lana had never seen before. He looked...content. Lana wondered why that didn't bother her more.

"Not hardly," Roz admitted. "If I'm really lucky, I can finish the first draft of one of my young adult books in sixty days. Then I'll be refining and editing several times. The book I'm working on now is taking longer, but I'm writing in fits and starts."

"This project is interfering, isn't it?"

"Not at all. This particular book is just going slower. Why all the questions, are you thinking about writing a book?"

Lana shook her head, trying to stifle the surprised

gasp of laughter. "Not even. That's way beyond my education."

"Anyone who reads as much as you do would already have the mindset to write."

"You did read, didn't you? That wasn't part of your cover when you were at Stormhaven?" Ty's voice was rough, his expression once more grim.

Adam leaned forward and started to put himself between Lana and Ty. Lana rested her hand on his forearm, and Roz turned abruptly toward Ty.

"No, it's okay," Lana said. "He deserves to know. The time at Stormhaven was not one of the finer episodes in my life." She looked across the kitchen, briefly, then back at Ty. "When I met you at that rodeo, you were all hail-fellow, well-met, cheerful, and proud of your entry. You told me about your ranch, about what you were doing for the vets, and in particular how remote it was. It sounded…safe. Right about then, I really needed safe, and I thought it might be perfect for what I needed." She took a sip of the water, realized her mug was empty. Before she could get up, Adam stood, took her mug, and went over to the electric kettle. He poured out a mug full, added the lemon, then refilled the kettle with some of the bottled water on the counter.

Lana watched him, feeling the confusion she had from his actions show up on her face. She smoothed out her expression and turned back to Ty. "I had thought to just ask if I could visit. Somewhere along the way, you insisted on the whole marriage idea, and I realized I could hide better if I wasn't Lana Greene."

Ty looked down at his clenched hands, Roz's fingers covering his as if she needed to support him. "I was drunk," he said. "I know that's never an excuse. I came to Vegas to watch Ben ride, and to see this gray stallion I'd heard so much about. Then I met what I thought was a sweet, innocent, gorgeous woman. She seemed like everything I thought I'd ever wanted. Quiet, demure…how much of it was a lie?"

"A lot of it. I heard you in the bar, expounding on how a good, real woman was helpful and quiet, except in bed, where she was a tiger."

"Ouch. Damn, I must have really been drunk. I don't remember any of that."

"Probably not your finest hour. The agents were closing in on me, threatening to…expose something I'd done. When I approached you, I thought I'd just see if I could visit the ranch. Then—"

"Then I grabbed you and insisted we go to the Hall of Eternal Love?"

"Not quite, but close. You and your friends all gathered around, and I was pretty much hidden until we all left Vegas with the horses and a few things from my apartment."

"Some clothes and boxes of books. Were the books a prop? No, probably not, Sydney told us you'd always read a lot."

"Not specifically a prop. If anyone mentioned a woman coming to Stormhaven, they might have mentioned the books first. As in who would think someone going on her honeymoon would take so blessed many books."

"I burned them."

"Yeah, I heard."

"Sorry." And he even managed to sound contrite. "Knee-jerk reaction. It just seemed like you were more involved in your books than in your marriage." He blew out a breath. "I guess you were."

"Ty…" Lana she leaned across the table, touching his clenched hands. "What if I'd stayed? What if, after we had married, I moved to New Mexico, but no one came after me, so I never left, and Mosby never ended up in a boarding stable in California?"

"I've thought about that a lot recently. Syd would never have taken on Mosby, Devin would not have gone to help her. We wouldn't have met Powers. Roz—" He looked over at the quiet woman and frowned. "Roz would probably never have come to Stormhaven."

"And we would have all been miserable. I would never have been able to help that last batch of girls. And you would not be here to help me out now."

"So you're saying it was all some sort of preordained outcome?"

"No. But sometimes what seems awful for now ends up good after all."

# Chapter 13

Lana stood with Adam at the edge of the casino floor, half hidden by a potted plant. She took several deep breaths, centering herself while she scanned the crowd.

"This is one of their favorite hangouts. They like the smaller casinos, especially when the owners are friendly." She continued to scan the room, then Adam felt a minute stiffening in her body and stepped closer. "*Yesss.* Bear with me, okay?" she whispered.

Adam didn't pull away when she grabbed at his arm, taking an unsteady step in her elegant high heels. Since this was the first time he'd ever seen her waver when walking, he became even more alert, using his cane to brace them both when she staggered.

"'S'okay," she muttered, not quite under her breath. "Got everything under control."

Adam felt himself react when the two men turned at the sound of her not-quite whisper and consciously relaxed. Whatever Lana wanted to portray, whoever she wanted to be, she was going to need his backup.

"Lana! Where the hell have you been, girl?" The

heavier man, thinning blond hair and thickening waist, reached out as he came to Lana's side. She edged closer to Adam, pulling her head back and up.

"I was the one—looking for you two. W—Where have you been?" She spoke marginally slower than normal, with a half breath in between phrases. The two agents looked at her suspiciously.

"We had something come up out of town. Are you okay?"

"Who is this guy?" The shorter, thinner, darker man reached out as if to grab Lana's arm.

Adam turned, putting himself between them and Lana, appearing to lean on his cane as a pivot. Out of the corner of his eye, he saw Lana blink her eyes then shake her head slightly before drawing a deep breath then speaking in a soft voice.

"This is Adam. He's helping me. Adam. This is Steve. And Aaron." Again, she hesitated between sentences, even between words.

"Helping you with what?"

"Are you stoned?"

She frowned. "Stoned? Why would you say that? You know I never use."

"Because you're acting weird."

Adam saw the frown form on her brow and confusion slowly take over her pretty face. She drew in a quick, short breath then breathed out in a puff. He worked overtime to suppress his laughter. The two agents were uncertain, obviously wondering if they should test her, maybe take her in for being under the influence.

"I was trying to find you. Remember that girl we placed? Pretty, dark hair, mole on her upper lip?"

The agents looked briefly shocked, but it was so brief Adam would have missed it if he hadn't been watching. From the tension in Lana's hand, she'd also caught their reaction. She swayed on her feet, leaning on his arm just a little more.

"Name was Anne or Annie or Angie…"

"Angela. Yeah, we put her on a bus home to Idaho."

"You sent her off alone?" She frowned more then looked at the ceiling, as if a better answer was in the chandeliers. Then she did the rapid-blinking-and-head-jerking again. "Did you confirm she got home?"

"Of course, we did. We know our jobs. Been doing them long enough."

Lana raised her hand to her forehead, rubbing her long elegant fingers across her face and down. Then she jerked her head again as if she was trying to stay awake.

"You don't look so good, sweetheart. Maybe we should—"

The other agent nudged him. "We should get over to the Golden Nugget. Remember, Cory was going to meet us for a drink?"

"Oh, yeah. You take care of yourself, Lana. We'll be watching for you, now that you're back."

They turned away but looked back over their shoulders. Lana continued shifting from foot to foot and clinging to Adam's arm. She even added a few head nods as if she was listening to a personal sound track. Then she turned her attention to another part of the casino, near one of the hallways, and took on the stillness of a prey animal near a pack of wolves.

Adam looked into the mirror next to them, seeing a tall man in the shadows who seemed to be staring at Lana.

"You okay?"

"Fine," she answered automatically, her voice crisp and eyes focused. "Let's get out of here."

∽∾∽

In the mirror, Aleksei Novakov looked at her with disgust obvious on his face. He had briefly watched the two agents hurry away, then his eyes focused on something…someone, maybe…on the other side of the casino. Then his attention turned back to her. There was no doubt he had believed her zoned-out performance. Since he'd never shown much respect for her at any time, this wasn't a complete surprise.

Adam urged her into the hallway a few steps away while leaning heavily on his cane. Once they were out of sight of anyone in the crowded casino, he straightened up and increased his pace, his free hand taking a strong grasp on her upper arm. She straightened as well, concentrating on not tripping in the higher-than-usual heels.

"Damned fancy boots," she muttered.

"They got the job done. Sorry, you'll still need some protection for your feet."

"I know. And I didn't bring a big enough purse to stash flats."

A door closed down the darkened hallway to their right, and a muffled curse sounded before footsteps came their way. Adam pushed her sideways, into a swinging door. Bathroom, by the smell of cleaners and deodorizers. He pushed back against the door to avoid any swinging then leaned against the wall next to it. Lana turned her face away while she tried to control her breathing. The footsteps shuffled past, no more voices but heavy breathing, and no hesitation.

A deep, but young, voice sounded outside the door. "You think Coach is gonna realize we ducked out of that lame show?"

"Who knows? We can tell him we wanted to see that glass stuff over at Caesar's. I'm an art major, why not?"

They chuckled in the way of half-inebriated young people everywhere. Lana let herself relax, just a little.

After a moment, Adam eased the door open and looked out.

"Clear." He slipped out of the doorway, bringing her along with him, and turned in the direction the boys had come from. "They were coming from one of the underground passageways. How are your feet holding up?"

"These boots are not made for walking, but I'm good for a bit longer."

"Sorry they're not comfortable. They do look good on you."

Lana glanced over, but he was concentrating on the area ahead of and behind them. His quiet words had sounded sincere, but he'd never said much about her appearance before, especially not her more extreme outfits.

"Okay," he muttered, and she realized he'd activated his ear bud. "We're coming out the lower level on the northeast side."

They traversed the dimly lit corridor until it spilled into a parking garage, half empty, with mostly older vehicles.

"Probably staff parking," Adam mentioned.

"You do know the niftiest places to take a girl."

He only smiled, while trying to look in every direction at the same time.

"Aleksei—that's the grim gentleman watching from the hallway upstairs—has at least a few of his home boys with him. Middle European, maybe Slavic. Short on conversation, big on muscle." She shuddered, remembering the flat eyes, nearly devoid of personality.

"Have you had a run in with them?"

"No, just talked to some of them, saw them hanging around. That was enough."

His hand briefly tightened on her arm then loosened as he directed her toward a large vehicle coming down the ramp.

"That looks like our—" His words were cut off as the vehicle accelerated, seeming to aim directly toward them.

Lana started to dodge before Adam could push her to the side, moving behind a pillar, aiming for the wall. Maybe a car could help protect them.

"You don't want to get between a vehicle and the wall. They could use it as a weapon." He looked around quickly then spotted something a few yards away. "This way."

It was a setback in the wall, containing some valves and heavy pipes. He ducked in then pulled her down to a crouch, while the behemoth of a vehicle screeched past, sliding as the driver tried a maneuver more suited to a much smaller vehicle. While it crashed into a pillar then a truck, Adam pulled her along the corridor opening between vehicles and the wall, sprinting while staying bent over. Lana grabbed for air while she did her best to keep up with him, knowing his support was the only thing keeping her moving forward at more than a stumble.

They made it around a corner into a darker area, putting more pillars between them and the screeching banging. She heard doors opening and slamming behind them, and curses muttered in guttural voices.

"Shit, they're on foot now," she whispered between gasps.

Adam continued to scan the dark, looking for an advantage, then urged her toward a pass through from their level to what looked like an outer access.

She moved in that direction, ignoring her feet as best she could. "I get out of this, I burn these damned boots."

He looked her direction, and it almost seemed like he was grinning.

"You're enjoying this?"

His response was a quick shushing sound. Then he

tilted his head, seeming to listen, and nodded. "This way." He put her in front of him, aiming for that pass through, as a van, lights dimmed, came up the ramp. "This one."

The doors slid open while the van kept moving slowly, and he lifted her into the space, following immediately after and sliding the door almost shut.

"Go, go, go!"

They increased speed smoothly without turning on the headlights. There were no seats in the back of the van so Lana braced herself as best she could when they went around a corner.

"How the hell did they know—" She shook her head and blew out a breath. "If there's another tracker on me, I hope it's in these be-damned boots.

"More than likely around your collar, when Agent Short put his hand on you."

"That makes sense. I noticed they were eager to leave right after that stumble. And Aleksei contacted some of his goons, at least one of them, in the room. I thought he was having Steve and Aaron followed."

"It would be somewhere in your scarf." Adam accepted a scanner from the person in the passenger seat, which soon emitted a low tone and a brief flash of light. "Got it. Hold on." he continued passing the scanner over her, down her legs and around the boots with no other indications.

"Sorry, you have to keep the boots."

"Actually, I don't. They can go to my favorite thrift store any minute now. As soon as I can find something else to wear. What about the scarf?" She started unwinding it, being careful not to interfere with the tiny transmitter.

The agent in the passenger seat took the scarf with the same care. At the next stoplight, they pulled up next to a boat on a trailer. She stepped out long enough to slide the scarf under the boat cover, making sure the elastic would hold, then jumped back into the van.

"If you're looking to dump those boots, I wouldn't turn them down," the female agent said. "We might wear close to the same shoe size."

Lana hesitated. Tempting offer. "They might be a bit too distinctive, and I wouldn't want you targeted. Ask me later." She caught Adam's expression out of the corner of her eye, his smile not much more than a quirk of his lips and a narrowing of his eyes. Approving her decision and agreeing with her.

"Stashing the scarf probably won't save us much time," Adam said. "We tried that trick before."

"It's a classic, because it does work," the female agent disagreed. "We'll be shifting to a different vehicle ourselves in a few minutes, so if someone is following this van, they still won't find us."

"And it's not like white panel vans stand out much," added the driver.

⌘⌘⌘

Soon they were in a small luxury car. Lana sank into the soft leather seat, stifling a groan as she let some of the tension leave her body.

"Feel better?" Adam asked while he checked mirrors and set his own seat to a more comfortable position.

"Anything would feel better than the floor of a delivery van. I think I have a brand new collection of bruises."

He eased into traffic, his face half turned away, but she could see the smirk pulling at his lips. "It got the job done."

Lana shrugged, bringing her ankle up to her knee so she could pull off the slouchy boot, then setting that foot down, and doing the same to the other boot. She let her toes expand while she dug her fingers into her arch. "That's the last time I wear standing-around boots when I know I might need to be moving a lot."

"Why did you?"

"They fit the profile of a slightly-dizzy, maybe-not-completely-in-control person. Someone more interested in fashion than comfort. That would get the agents' attention since they know I'm about comfort as well as fashion."

"Confusing them?"

"Or making them think I'm out of control. These are also extremely expensive boots, obviously new, and I made no bones about having to be frugal, especially since working for them cut into my business."

"That was a clever observation about the letting that agent have the boots. I thought you'd be ready to chuck them the first chance you got."

"I had a thought of them attracting attention, which could have put her in danger, but also of someone using them for proof—of life, of death, whatever."

"You thought she might have done that?"

"I don't know her at all, so I have no way to tell, or to trust her."

"You don't trust too many people do you?"

"If you think about it, I only know two people in this situation directly: my sister and Ty Randolph."

"Directly?"

"My personal knowledge gained through experience. I know Devin indirectly through Syd, and she's an excellent judge of character. Roz through Ty. I met both of them recently."

He didn't say anything, and she continued.

"You, I met on the recommendation of my sister, and Ty, but they only knew of you recently."

"Major Powers?"

"I knew about him peripherally after Syd's ex-husband attacked me."

"You categorize trust?"

"I see it this way: we trust or don't trust, according to our own experiences as well as how well we know the person involved. In my experience, most people are more concerned with their own needs. When their needs coincide with mine, then they're more trustworthy, at least for a time. I've had little experience with automatically trusting people and not being screwed over. I've learned to be more cautious."

"I supposed I can understand that, given how those agents have treated you. Was the man you killed related to Aleksei?"

The question seemed to come out of left field. Lana turned her head to look at him more fully. His attention was completely on the road, eyes forward, both hands on the wheel. "I don't think so," she said. "That man was Hispanic, from Central America. Aleksei is from some sort of Slavic country."

"So much for that theory."

"As far as I know, no one has connected me with that crime."

"Not a crime. At most justice."

"A man died."

"A pedophile. Are you sure they're really human?"

"Maybe a sub species. Unfortunately, even killing a sub species can be considered a homicide. More to the point, when, or if, his family finds out, they won't care what precipitated his death. Only that he's dead." She frowned and looked away. "I never met Aleksei until this last job with Hoffman."

"Was it a legitimate job?"

"I thought so, but when Hoffman didn't pay me, I had to wonder. He's always paid promptly, even when he complains about the billing." She pulled a corner of her lips between her teeth. "No, before then. When I saw that girl passed out in the main room. Aleksei noticed me, watched me. He was always watching me, no matter what I was doing."

"You're worth watching."

"Not like that. He never looked me over like he wanted a free sample. This was more predatory, as if he'd already decided I was guilty of something, and he was going to make me pay."

"And no idea what?"

"No. I tried to get some information out of Hoffman, but he would just say to deal with it, Aleksei was a new partner and was going to make all of us rich. Something about new sources, new opportunities."

"You thought new girls coming in?"

"That's what it sounded like. Which was the only reason I kept working with them, since Aleksei's goons set my teeth on edge. Aleksei himself rarely made the effort to talk to me directly. When I tried to get a closer look at that girl at the penthouse, he got in the way."

Adam blew out a breath, slowing at a stop sign then powering through when he didn't see traffic.

"We need to see if Powers has gotten any more information on Aleksei. Something's not adding up." He hesitated, then glanced over at her, his face revealed then in shadow from the street lights. "Do you want Ty and Roz to take over?"

"Take over?"

"You need to be with people you can trust. According to you, they're the only ones you can trust."

She frowned, sorting through the earlier discussion. Oh, that. "When this started, the only people I knew were my sister and Ty. I met Roz, got to know her, so that expanded the trust."

"Right, you trust Ty and Roz."

"And you, Adam, I trust you."

# Chapter 14

*A* *nd you, Adam, I trust you.'*
Adam heard those words in his head again as he
looked at himself in the steamy bathroom mirror,
seeing the scars, the suspicious eyes, the mouth tight
from random pain. But not as tight. Not as suspicious.
Not, somehow, as lonely or withdrawn. That quiet statement, in a low voice, across the dark of the car, had
somehow soothed so many of the savagely broken corners of his mind.

She hadn't looked away from him immediately but
hadn't said anything else the rest of the drive. Once at the
house, she'd slipped out of the car, stepping nimbly
across the gravel pathway to disappear into the house for
her evening ritual of washing off the casino stench.

Once she was out of the now-steamy bathroom, he'd
gone in, for pretty much the same reason. Not only washing away the smell but also washing away the person he
had to be while he was with her at the casino. No more
fancy suit, styled hair, cane-using man. Just plain Adam.
Scary.

He'd asked Lana to be herself, he could do no less.

ᚼᚼᚼ

Stupid, stupid, stupid. Why did she lose control of her mouth around this man? He'd been unfailingly polite, had been a perfect partner, falling in with all of her hare-brained ideas. So what did she do? Make some kind of a declaration about being comfortable working with him. Then ran away before he could respond. If he had wanted to respond.

Lana set up the coffee, pulled out plates for the mini muffins someone had stocked in the refrigerator. And refused to let herself be any more sidetracked. Letting herself get upset was not a good path to success.

"Are we expecting company?"

The deep, soft voice cut through her self-recriminations. She stopped short of dropping coffee mugs but could not control the quick indraw of breath. Giving herself a moment to collect, she turned, slowly, to face the man at the kitchen entrance.

He'd showered and changed the slick hair and suit for old sweats and jeans, his dark hair barely towel dried. She chastised herself for noticing he looked even more appealing.

"Some sort of gathering to exchange information. Powers still doesn't trust any of the communication devices."

"That makes sense. This whole action has been pretty rushed."

"Have you been involved in something like this before?"

"Undercover? Many times. Mostly before my injury, and usually overseas. We spent as much time preparing as possible, especially if we planned to interact with the public on a regular basis."

"That must be why—" She hesitated, and busied herself with setting down the mugs then turning to the refrigerator.

Adam was already there, reaching for the cream and the lemon.

"—You don't need to do that."

"Working together means sharing work," he said. "Why what?"

"Why what—oh, your experience must be why you're so good at picking up what has to be done without being told several times."

"Somewhat, but you're the one who is dynamite at letting me know what you need without trying to feed me ridiculous lame clues."

That stopped her cold, next to a chair where she dropped her hand to brace herself. "I am? No one ever said—"

"Bet they told you they couldn't figure out what the hell you needed them to do after they botched an assignment."

"Well, yes."

"Bet they said women could never get these things right, you didn't have enough training, and to leave it to the professionals."

She could only stare.

"Bet it was Tweedledum and Tweedledumber."

"How did you—"

"I've worked with way too many arrogant, clueless blowhards not to recognize the sub species. You probably blew them out of the water a time or two, got their supervisors looking too closely at their work records. So they started to chip away at your self-confidence and then threatened you. Or was it the other way around?"

"About the same time," she answered in a monotone. She was focused too much on Adam's voice, what Adam was saying, to notice the door opening behind her. The change in air pressure alerted her, but Adam's lack of re-action, beyond a slight smile, kept her from turning.

"Par for the course. Women like you scare men like them."

"Women like me?"

"Independent, tough, and scary smart."

"See, I told you he was super perceptive." The new voice—female, with an undertone of humor—brought Lana around, turning quickly, and almost slipping in her stockinged feet.

"Steady there." Adam reached out to brace her. "Maybe you need to change back into those killer boots."

"Never again. No matter how hot they looked. Hey, Roz, Ty. Ready for some coffee? And it looks like some-one raided a bakery, was that you?"

"Guilty as charged. We might have Powers over here later, if he can get away from his current time-sucking meeting. Since we don't have Maria's cinnamon rolls here, we need some other good bribe."

"Are we doing something we need a bribe for?"

"You never know."

Roz grabbed herself a cup of coffee and brought the carafe to the table where she poured out for the rest of them. Adam had already poured out Lana's water.

"You know, Adam, you could give the rest of us a serious complex." Ty nodded at the mug of hot water, accompanied by a lemon in a small dish.

"To be fair, I never drank hot water at the ranch. At least not where you could see."

"Tea sometimes, right? Why not just drink the wa-ter?"

"Probably because she was trying to fit in," Roz pointed out, and Ty frowned.

"But—"

"Before you beat yourself up any more, or we get into useless bickering, there's something you need to see." Adam brought his tablet to the table. "I got this from the casino feed."

He set it on the table and touched the start. They all saw Lana in her obviously expensive, almost-revealing dress, standing just at the edge of the camera pick up. She turned her head toward Adam then took an unsteady step forward. They watched through to the end, seeing her almost, but not quite, appearing out of control, without any obvious overt actions.

"I knew you were good, but—" Ty looked over at Lana, frowning, then back at the still picture at the end of video. "—this is amazing."

"Why in the world aren't you on the stage?" Roz asked.

"Too many people, and too much else to do with myself."

This time they all heard the footsteps outside. One of the interchangeable bodyguards entered first, looked around the small cottage, nodded, and stepped back out. Powers came in next, as innocuous as every other time she'd seen him. The fussing over seats, drinks, pastries took up some time, until he was ensconced in the most comfortable chair, sipping at fresh tea, and reaching for his pipe. When Lana frowned at him, he put the pipe away.

Powers nodded toward Adam's tablet, still showing the video feed from the casino. "Excellent job. Were you attempting to be arrested?"

"I was hoping to irritate them enough for them to try to take me in on suspicion of drug use. Any test would have embarrassed them."

"It almost worked. The smaller one was really tempted," Adam said.

"I was playing off their suspicions. Once someone

has a preconceived notion of what I'm like, it's not difficult to convince them I'm all sorts of depraved."

"Or demure, or subdued," Roz interjected.

"Or a wild and crazy party girl. Most people tend to
see what they think they're going to see, especially after
the first impression. The only difficulty is when two people expect disparate Lanas, based on their own precon-
ceptions."

"Has that been much of a problem?"

"Not really, which is fascinating. It seems people see
what they want to see."

"Is this little scene being played out for my benefit?"
Ty asked, frowning. Roz laid her hand over his.

"Not precisely, Mr. Randolph," Powers said. "I
wanted to view a current example of Ms. Randolph's ac-
tivities. I'd heard about how she operated but had not
seen it firsthand. Most impressive."

"Ms. Greene."

"Ah, yes. Very well." He reached again toward his
pocket then subsided. "As she pointed out, people see
what they think they want to see in many situations. Here,
she gave the appearance—very subtle—of a woman attempting not to look overcome by drugs or alcohol. Aided, no doubt, by the agents' negative opinion of her."

"And when she was at Stormhaven, she was the perfect demure wife, because that was how I wanted to see
her?"

"Precisely. I need to inform you, we have researched
the doctor who offered you that flu remedy. He is not
presently licensed to practice, nor was he at that time. But
we found no connection between him, and Ms. Greene."

Lana looked up abruptly. "You thought—" Then she
nodded. "That would make sense in some circumstanc-
es."

"I never thought—" Ty said.

"You wouldn't since you didn't realize you were given a mixture, including mild hallucinogens. Some of which would have stayed in your system for a while."

Lana leaned forward. "Even without being re-administered?"

"No need for that," Ty bit off. "He gave me enough to 'really take over' the fever. Couple of weeks' worth."

"Did you take them all?"

"Nah, I never do. Yeah, I know, bad habit. After the first few days, maybe a week, I didn't feel so bad. Then I felt better and tossed the rest."

"You threw them away?"

"Probably stuck them in a bathroom drawer or cabinet." Ty frowned. "Bet you need them."

"We could have them analyzed, just in case. If you could call your partner?"

Ty flashed a quick grin. "You don't want to call Sydney?"

Powers ignored the comment. "Retrieving the pills could be of some help. Thank you."

Lana shook her head. "You're saying Ty was under the influence when we married."

"Most likely. And for that first week or two of your marriage."

"Do you think this means we could have been followed from the beginning?"

"More than likely it was coincidental. Simply very poor timing."

"But you don't believe in coincidence?"

"Not generally, no."

"Was this 'doctor' known to treat young females?" Lana asked, eyes on the table top, her mug of water, anything but the rest of the people present.

A quick tension took over the table.

"Not to my knowledge. We are attempting to find a

connection between him and others who do treat young people. But, Ms. Greene—" He leaned forward and waited until she raised her chin. "—none of this was your fault. Any connection between this doctor and the agents would have occurred after your move to New Mexico. Not before. The question is if traces of drugs found in that young woman's body would be the same as what was forced on Mr. Randolph."

"The girl at the party?"

"Yes. There were a few unusual components not generally seen. Some of the others we questioned observed her disorientation, similar to your actions this evening. Not unusual in cases of drugging, but we did not want to ignore any possibilities."

Lana scrubbed her hands over her face, happy for the lack of makeup. "Gah. What a mess. Ty..." She hesitated, not sure what she was going to say.

He held up his hand. "We can talk about it later." He glanced at Adam, who was sitting back, observing, with little expression on his face. "Maybe."

"You think this doctor hooked up with the agents after I met Ty?"

"It seems most likely. It's very likely the agents used some sort of pressure on the doctor to acquire his formula, or his source."

"That does seem to be a standard procedure for them."

Powers merely cleared his throat, shuffling through some files.

Lana stood abruptly, needing to move, needing to...run? She took a deep breath and turned to the refrigerator. "Protein anyone? Sandwiches? Or do the yummies work for you?"

She heard enough grunts in the affirmative to bring out packages of good sliced meat, cheeses, condiments, and spread them on the counter with necessary knives and plates.

An assortment of sandwiches and snacks soon covered the available space at the small table. She ended up with a plate of beef and cheese rolled up together, along with some pickles. Plus a fresh mug of hot water; Adam nodded when she smiled her thanks.

While they were assembling their own snacks, Powers was finishing his muffin. When they were seated, he set down his fork.

"We need to discuss how to move forward from this point. It would seem we have two parties to consider: the agents, and this Aleksei Novakov."

"Have your researchers found any more information?" Adam asked then bit into his thick sandwich.

"They have tracked him to a healthy business in Ukraine. No obvious connections to crime or those suspected of criminal behavior. He was in this country briefly two years ago and returned six months ago." Powers took a sip of his coffee, set down the mug, then dabbed at his mouth with a napkin. "He was here two years ago to identify the remains of his younger sister." He held up the head shot of an attractive brunette whose vivacious personality shone out of the photo.

Lana sat back in her chair, letting the rare roast beef and havarti cheese fall out of her slack fingers. "Oh, crap. Dee Dee."

"You knew her?"

"Yes. Oh, yes. She's partially why the agents have been on my ass. Now it all makes some sort of sick sense." She reached for the photo, holding it by the edges, tilting it until the light showed every detail. "She wanted to be an actress. I hired her as one of the fairy princesses for this little girl's birthday party. She was good, really good. And tough. You wouldn't know it by looking at this picture, but she could more than hold her own. She'd been raised in one of the state athletic schools…skating, I think. After the ponies left, the party dispersed pretty fast. I can't remember her ever coming back for her check. Considering how she was found, that didn't surprise me much."

"She was found in the woods, dropped under a tree. Badly damaged prior to her death." Powers's voice held little emotion, but his eyes narrowed.

"Do you know what the tox screen said?"

"We're looking into it."

"Because if she had that same strange mix in her system, then I did bring trouble to Stormhaven, and I did help kill that last girl."

"Not. Your. Fault," Adam said evenly.

"I have to—sorry, but I have to—" Lana pushed herself away from the table and fled to the bathroom. Once in there, she held back the bile, taking deep slow breaths to calm herself. After a few minutes, she turned on the cold water to splash her face then rub a washcloth over the back of her neck. A soft knock at the door brought her head up, and she stared at the woman in the mirror. Her mask was beginning to fade. How long was this going to keep going on?

"Lana?"

She'd expected Roz to come check, being the only other female and at least seeming to be compassionate. But it was Adam's voice at the door. Adam. Not Roz. Lana murmured an acknowledgment, and the door eased open.

In the mirror, Adam's face showed the usual lack of expression, but his intense light green eyes met her in the mirror, showing…softening? Concern?

"I'm fine," she managed to say, while dredging up some control over her own expression.

"No, you're not. But that's okay. You don't need to be 'fine' right now. Let yourself be upset and concerned. Be scared. You have every right. Just don't be hiding yourself. Remember, here, you can just be Lana."

She took a shallow breath. Let it out. "With you, I think I can."

He almost spoke, his mouth starting to open. Then he allowed himself a tiny quirk to his lips and nodded. "Thank you," he murmured. "I think there are a few others you can trust. Are you ready to come out now? We have more to discuss before we can get some sleep."

# Chapter 15

Adam stepped back to let Lana precede him into the room. The three people around the table looked up, then away.

Except for Roz, who held her gaze steady. "Are you okay?" she asked in a low, soothing voice.

"I will be, thanks." Lana settled into her chair, noticing that the water in her mug was hot. She sent a quick smile toward Adam when he settled into his own chair.

"It may be too dangerous for Ms. Greene to stay around the casinos at the moment."

"Because of Marten?"

"That has been resolved."

"Who's Marten?"

"The young man Ms. Greene killed."

Ty and Roz turned toward Powers, shock obvious on their faces. Then they turned to look at Lana, who was sitting very still.

"Yes, Ms. Greene killed a man," Powers continued. "To be more precise, she eradicated a lower life form. Far from putting her at risk, or causing an international incident, she will no doubt receive a commendation, once the paperwork goes through. His family will not be a problem for you. The true details have been explained to them, and they are, if not relieved, at least understanding of what he had been doing when he died. They had no idea he had degenerated to that extent, or so they claim. Unfortunately, at the same time, the young lady disappeared and was not found immediately. In the interim, Ms. Greene met and married Mr. Randolph and left Las Vegas."

"Leaving the agents, Heckle and Jeckle, free to commit every possible level of mayhem with my reputation. Later using the threat of his family to gain my cooperation."

"So it would seem."

"They must have approached me after Dee Dee was identified by her brother. I'd done a few jobs for them, pretty simple for starters, and I was glad to help them since I thought they were watching out for lost kids. They got greedy in short order then tried to get me involved in some shady deals. The pressure picked up pretty soon after that."

"It seems they are back to applying pressure again, using your recent 'under the influence' meeting to try to block you from working with children."

"That would hurt my business. The theme birthday parties are a big hit."

"You don't sound overly upset."

"I like my business, but I've mostly stayed with it to keep contact with young people and also keep an eye out for some of the predators."

"You going to need to stay away from the agents and the casinos for a while. For your own safety."

"I can take care of myself."

"You've had hand-to-hand combat training?" Adam asked, his tone casual.

"I have a black belt in 'mouth.'"

"You also have killer boots," he said. "That's not much protection against a gun. These people play for keeps."

"Especially Aleksei Novakov's 'staff,'" Powers interjected.

"Has something come up?"

"Just some minor incidents so far. Bullying, being belligerent. They're on a watch list with some of the casinos. We've increased the coverage around Ms. Greene."

"I'm going to have to ask—who is footing the bill for all this protection? Not that I don't appreciate your help."

"You don't need to worry about that," Ty said.

"What, I don't need to 'worry my pretty little head'?"

Roz cleared her throat, and when Ty looked over at her, she raised one eyebrow and gave him a serious look.

"What?"

"You seem to be reverting to Neanderthal and condescending, kind of suddenly," she said in an even, cool voice that held some threads of warning.

"I am?" He looked over at the others. "I am?"

Adam nodded. "You are. It seems to be a default mode when you're confused or feeling out of control."

"Shit. Sorry. I didn't mean it to sound that way."

Powers broke in. "Ms. Greene, your safety is directly related to the safety of young people, both citizens and immigrants. We don't have an unlimited budget, but we do have sufficient funds to keep you safe, as long as you don't try anything too foolish."

"We had an incident here a few mornings ago—" Lana started then looked at Adam. Had he wanted to keep this information private?

He shrugged. "One of the perimeter detail came up

to the house. It seems he figured since we'd been deployed together, I would want to see him."

"Yes, the team leader informed me. That man has been moved to another job."

"Since there have been some staffing issues in the past," Ty said. "I'm sure you can understand questions about your current workers."

"That issue has been resolved," Powers said in a tone of infinite patience.

Roz leaned over to explain to Lana. "Major Powers and Ty are talking about a disgruntled senior staff member who thought he deserved Sydney's promotion. He interfered wherever he could, including poor research and lack of cooperation. Then he joined up with the wanna-be terrorists who were going to try to blow up a national park."

"They have been dealt with. But your concerns have some merit. After your morning meeting, I had team leaders examine their people more closely and reassign those who might have proven inefficient. Including the young woman who wanted your boots, by the way. It turned out she has become friendly with your agents."

"Good catch," Adam murmured to Lana.

She managed a brief smile. "This does not address the real reason we're here, which is finding the new source of young people." Lana held her voice steady. "Who's keeping them, and where are they being kept? I've talked to everyone I know here, and no one has heard as much as a whisper of anything new."

"Other than the agents," Adam reminded her.

"Precisely. And I have to wonder—I knew they were snakes, but…"

Roz raised her eyebrows as if in shock. "You wonder if they're the source of the young people?"

"Or the source of the rumors—in particular, the ones

that paint you as a soulless dealer in young people?" Adam interjected.

"It would make sense. I think they've been dipping their toes into the stream, grabbing up what they can siphon off without getting caught. Deirdre was here legitimately, and she had a good support system. Her loss is more likely a tragic coincidence, which the agents used to paint me black. It might even have given them ideas on how to proceed, using me as a cover. This latest girl—"

"The one you saw at that party?"

"Yes. She seemed out of it from the beginning. I tried to talk to her, but she always had one of the men around her. And Aleksei—I don't think I ever saw him with the girl, just standing back and watching me around her. In fact, I think he showed up after the girl did."

Powers pulled out a small note pad, found a page, then looked up. "Why was this group meeting being held, and how did you get involved?"

"My business provides what people want, whether it's a dream vacation, a special party, or a totally discreet meeting place for an international group. Hoffman came to me with their request, and I put it together with a penthouse I knew would be available for a few months. I have restrictions, especially for groups wanting to meet privately," she went on, seeing the questions rising around her. "Nothing illegal. No drugs, No underage, even if they claim to have proof it's all in the family. Hoffman knew that."

"Hoffman made the arrangements for this job?"

"That was our usual deal. He made the arrangements and subcontracted some requests to me. I gave him my fee, he tacked on whatever he wanted to make, then paid me after he was paid."

"Have you been paid for this event?"

"Not so far. I probably won't be. Hoffman was playing in really rough water, I'm not sure we'll hear from him again anytime soon. I made a point of demanding my money from him, in front of Aleksei, reinforcing my mercenary reputation. If Hoffman told Aleksei the girl was from my 'stable,' that won't make our Ukrainian friend happy."

"All the more reason for you to lay low for a while. Just consider it, would you?" Ty's tone was reasonable.

"Okay, okay, I get it. No more Nancy Drew, at least not for now. Besides, I really need to get some rest."

The tension around the table eased as they all sat back. Powers arranged his paperwork, reaching for his briefcase, and his guards stepped forward.

"Will you be staying here?" he asked.

"For tonight."

"After that?"

She only smiled, almost but not quite giving in to the childish taunt: *That's for me to know and you to find out.*

☙❧

"Are you staying here?"

Adam's voice in the dark. Smooth, rich, enticing without attempting to overwhelm or influence her. Just there, a solid presence. She took in a breath, letting his scent soothe her, and remembered she needed to answer.

"I haven't decided. If I'm not doing any good in my primary goal, there won't be much reason for the guards. At that point, how safe will this house be?" She scowled in the dark. "And I need to learn how to protect myself."

"We haven't had live guards since the first few days while they finished setting up the perimeter cameras. Those can be reset to feed into my tablet so we'd still have some control of who shows up."

"We?"

"Bodyguard, remember?"

"But that's for the duration of the job. What about after Powers pulls back?"

"Bodyguard until the job is done, and you're safe."

"Then what?"

"Then I'm not your bodyguard. I don't have to be around."

She felt her heart sink and chastised herself. Stupid reaction when he'd been in her life such a short time. She could not stifle the quick breath. "Then you aren't around?"

"No, then I'm not around because I have to be, I'm around because I want to be. Or you want me to be."

ꞇꞆꞇ

Silence. She almost thought he wasn't breathing. She knew she wasn't. And she realized how much courage it had taken for this private man to admit such a thing. She turned, peering in the dim light, trying to find his expression.

"Will—will you want to be?" she asked.

"More to the point, will you want me to be?"

"I'm not sure that is the point. You're the one who's putting himself between me and danger. How can I not want to be safe?"

"When it's not about your physical safety?"

"What's—oh. When it's about emotional safety?"

"Or not about your safety. Just about you."

"I'm not sure. There—there hasn't been a me. Not for a long time. I've always been about what I can do to help. What I can get done to atone for—"

"For some kind of a bullshit thought that you need to make up for something your mother did? Or someone else did?"

"For what I did not stop from happening. Which is pretty much the same as doing it myself."

"You're really doing a number on yourself, aren't you?"

"What do you mean?"

"You carry around this load of bogus guilt everywhere you go. So you can't see any value in yourself."

"Don't be ridiculous. And don't change the subject. Let's get back to what happens after this job is over."

"Once I don't have to worry about your physical safety? Then I can let myself notice what your butt looks like when you walk away in those ridiculous shoes. I can let myself be attracted to your very female scent and even let myself think what it would be like to sleep in the same bed without having to keep myself on the other side. I might actually get some sleep."

"You—"

"Yep, blue balls. Every morning, every night."

"Adam—"

"Nothing to feel guilty about. My balls, my problem."

"But—"

"Just thought you might want to know not everyone thinks you're shallow and plastic and worthless. Mind you, we can't do anything about it until the op is over."

"You thought I needed to know this—now?"

"That, and I thought it might be fair for you not to be able to sleep well either." He turned over to face the wall, letting her look at his sleek, muscled back. "Good night, Lana."

☙☙☙

If ever a moment called for coffee, it would be this one. Lana staggered into the kitchen, ignoring the cheerfully bubbling water kettle, and reached for the coffee pot. Adam had obviously come in while she was in the shower and somehow managed to avoid her while they changed places. The water ran in the background for his own brief shower. Funny how she knew more about this man after a week than she knew about Ty after the entire span of their admittedly short marriage. She'd also slept with Adam more than she had with Ty. Although until last night, she hadn't thought of him as more than a warm body in the night. Stupid of her, she admitted.

The aromatic coffee was dark and hot, and she took in a deep breath. Wonderful smell. Too bad she didn't much care for the taste. But still. She sipped at it then shook her head. How did people worship such a bitter brew? Although this was better than most, it was still…coffee. She shuddered and took another sip, moving to the table to collapse into a chair.

It was just too early to be up, but she'd only managed spotty sleep and finally gave up entirely when she heard Adam's breathing deepen and level out as he eased into sleep. She tried not to be jealous of his ability to sleep whenever there was an opportunity.

"You're drinking coffee."

His quiet voice grabbed her attention, and she barely refrained from jumping out of her skin. She should have heard the shower go off.

"I do once in a while. I enjoy the aroma and appreciate the caffeine. I've just never been enthralled by the taste."

"Have you tried it doctored up? Cream, spices, flavors?"

"It's supposed to be coffee, not dessert."

"You could give yourself, and the beans, a break."

She shook her head, trying to pull sense from his words. With a small quirk to one side of his mouth, he grabbed her coffee mug, poured out the half-drunk liquid, then busied himself at the counter with his back turned toward her. After a minute, he pivoted back, handing her a mug of fresh hot coffee, the scent even more aromatic.

"Try this." He set the mug in front of her with his usual lack of expression in his face or voice. No pressure.

She sipped cautiously then nodded.

"Better. Still not my drink of choice. What did you put in it?"

"Some spices from the cupboard, mostly cinnamon and nutmeg. You might want to add some sugar or honey."

"No, this is fine. Where did you learn about doctoring coffee?"

"I worked as a barista for a while. Let me know if you need more. You didn't get a lot of sleep last night, and you'll need some energy if you plan to leave this morning."

She frowned and found herself chewing at the corner of her lip. It was difficult putting how she felt into words.

"It's just...a feeling I have here. Like I'm in a fish bowl with people watching or listening to everything I do or say."

"There are no active cameras in here."

"But there are cameras?"

"For security when no one is here."

"And what about sound?"

"Again, here but inactive."

"Are you sure? Are you absolutely, positively sure?"

He stared at her, face completely immobile, eyes piercing while she could almost see thoughts racing behind them. Bending over, he pulled a thermos out of the cupboard.

"You need to pack a bag, at least three days' worth of casual clothes and the sturdiest footwear you have. I'll get the food pulled together then pack my own."

She hesitated, head tilted, trying to fathom his words.

"Hurry. We need to be on the way as soon as possible."

❧❧❧

"Why the rush?" Lana asked ten minutes later as they eased away from the cottage, melding with the night in a small van she'd never seen before. "And whose vehicle is this?"

"Ours, for the moment." He looked over at her as they paused at a four-way stop. "Courtesy of Rent-A-Wreck. I had Ty pick it up for us yesterday."

"You already had this trip planned?"

"Not specifically. I just hoped you'd take advantage of an opportunity to get out of the spotlight for a day or two." His eyes gleamed briefly in a street lamp illumination before he turned his attention back to the road. "You're not sleeping well, and barely eating. As much as you talk about Party Girl Lana, she's wearing you out."

"I'm—"

"You're also not resting in the house we thought would help you feel comfortable. We didn't—I didn't—realize you spent so much time alone, away from your apartment in the casino."

"Why would you know that?"

"A major part of good undercover is research. I made too many assumptions without asking." He glanced at her again then back to the dark highway. "I'm sorry for that."

"I should have said something."

"I'm also sorry I didn't realize how much the surveillance around the house would bother you. You're a private sort of person, I should have realized that and made adjustments."

"It's not your responsibility."

"I'm in charge in the field. I should have paid more attention."

She leaned back in her seat, looking out at the moon-lit desert rushing past them. "I didn't think it would bother me, since I know there are cameras pretty much all over the casinos and a lot of Vegas. And it's not like anything was turned on when we were in the cottage."

"But you were never alone, and you're used to being alone a lot. It showed up in how you were reacting."

"You're taking me somewhere different for the sake of the operation." It made sense. Didn't make her happy, but it made sense.

"I'm taking you somewhere different for your sake."

He turned his attention back to driving, reaching over to flick on the radio to an easy-listening station. A combination of the soft music, warm interior, and tires racing across the road soon had her dozing.

# Chapter 16

Lana set down the bags Adam had handed her to bring in and looked around the cabin, lit by the moonlight edging through the windows. It was small but what she could see of the construction seemed so efficiently planned the sense of space pleased her.

Adam left a lit kerosene lantern on a large, blocky, flat surface while he finished unloading the vehicle then busied himself in that corner, kneeling on a thick mat to maneuver some levers, then striking a match. Lana edged closer, squinting a little to try to understand what he was working on, recognizing the smells of a struck match, then fire transferring to another surface. After a few minutes, he leaned back, head tilted while he listened, then nodded once.

"That should do it. We'll be warming up soon."

He braced a hand on the blocky structure to stand then tossed a quick look in her direction. "You want a tour?"

"Seems like I can see most everything from here." She turned in a slow circle, noting the obvious kitchen area, bedroom, and...

"It's through this door." He indicated a shadowed door next to the blocky structure. "The stove helps with water heat when or if I use up the solar warmed water."

"Stove?"

He indicated the blocky structure. "Here."

"That's a stove?"

"Bio-mass rocket stove," he said with some pride in his voice.

"Is that something experimental?"

"It's been used in other countries for a long time. Just getting started here, mostly by off the grid livers."

"You built it," she said, interpreting the tone of his voice as well as the tension in his body.

"Yep. When I first got out of rehab, I wanted somewhere I could live easily, in spite of the injury. Off the grid but not without basic amenities."

"This is your place." She heard her words, her tone, and tossed him an apologetic smile. "Obviously."

He nodded.

"Does anyone else know about it?"

"The basic structure has been in my family for a long while. It was hand built a while back, maybe a hundred or so years. Some friends, mostly from my unit, helped with the initial remodel, as a sort of project in between training. Some of my buddies came by after rehab to help with the extra upgrades. No one local knows when I'm here, unless I want them to know. This stove doesn't send out much wood smoke smell, and there's not much line of sight." He turned to face her, tilting his head to look directly into her eyes. "You're safe here, Lana. You can relax."

"No cameras?"

"No cameras. No microphones. Well, except for the ones in my work kit but they're to use on someone else. Not you."

She felt that tight band around her chest relax, and she nodded. "Good." She drew in what seemed like the first deep breath she'd taken for a long time. "Thank you."

"No need to thank me. It's my pleasure."

The stock answer seemed much more sincere in his quiet, even tones.

"No one knows we're here?"

"They know you're with me. Well, Ty and Roz know you're with me. Powers knows we're not at the cottage." He looked away then back at her. "No one knows specifically where we are. No one can drop by for a chat. No one will show up to help out. Not unless we call them and tell them where we are."

"No one?" She didn't mean for her voice to come out so soft but her throat was closing up on her.

"No one. Unless we call them."

"How did you know?" In the dim light, she saw his small frown. "How did you know how much it bothered me?

"Like I said earlier, you're not resting, you're not comfortable." He looked like he wanted to add something, gave her that one sided smile, and turned to the stacked bags and boxes he'd brought in earlier. "There are sheets on the bed, and I packed that great air mattress so we'll have plenty of room."

"But you—"

"We can talk about who sleeps where later. For now, you need to get some good rest. Another reason I wanted us out here was so we could work on your self-defense skills."

"You remembered—" Her throat closed up when he gave her another one of those quiet, intense looks. "Of course, you did. You remember everything. Another perk of having a highly skilled bodyguard."

This time he looked away. Taking a step sideways, he picked up her backpack. "Here. Get yourself comfortable. I need to put some things away. Then we'll get to work."

예예

"Now I understand how you carried Roz out of that place," Lana muttered, looking up at Adam in the gathering daylight. In the way of the desert, the air was still cool, softly caressing her damp skin with a promise of later, intense dry heat. The ground underneath her was more of an unyielding surface, especially after she fell on it. Numerous times.

"How's that?"

Adam didn't have the decency to pretend to be breathing hard. Looming above her, he braced himself easily, his outline more clear now than it had been ten minutes before.

She still could not pick out his features to confirm the smile she knew had to be on his face. He was enjoying this far too much.

"You tossed her into the air and ran underneath her the whole way." Leaning up until she was on her butt instead of her back, she tilted her head, peering up and— yes, a smile tugged at one corner of that mouth. "On that springy leg." She indicated the metal blade which he'd put on to replace the normal-shoe ending for his prosthesis.

"That would have been difficult, even though this leg is better for athletics. It was nearly five miles to the extraction point." Voice dry, he looked out at the nearby bluffs, as though comparing this desert to that one.

"Five miles?" She looked away, gathering her energy. "Well, don't I feel like a slacker?"

"It's what I trained for ever since I entered the service. Five miles is a short sprint, and in that group, I was the most logical choice to carry her."

"You were the strongest?"

He eased down onto the ground near her, legs pulled up, wrists resting on his knees, hands loose, then looked over at her. "At that time, the weakest. Not my leg, my eyes."

From this distance, she could see his face more clearly, his eyes glittering in the increasing light. A faint silver gleam on one arm caught her eye while she waited for him to continue.

"I'd taken a piece of debris in one eye the week before, and my vision wasn't up to par. Since we didn't want to bring anyone else into the mission, I was elected to carry while the rest of the team provided security."

She looked away, mulling over his words. "You hiked five miles in, five miles out with a burden when you only had partial vision?"

He shrugged. "It was the job. We were happy when we found her. She was in pretty bad shape."

"Hero material, absolutely." She said it lightly, but her heart clenched. "I'm betting Roz feels the same way. Not to mention Ty."

"No doubt." He shrugged again. "I could say it's just a day in the life, but we did feel extra good being able to pull her out in time." He looked over at her, eyes solemn. "I'm sure Ty would have been as happy if you were the person rescued."

"Don't kid yourself." She straightened, aiming for an impersonal air. "Ty would have been pleased that anyone was rescued from what sounds like a hell hole, but the events following brought him together with Roz and changed his life." She sighed then nodded. "For the better." She pushed up, bringing her feet under her body.

Adam rose smoothly, reaching down to help her. The silver gleam seemed to be an armlet, with some etching and copper accents. She tried to concentrate on the design, but his fingers waggled. "Break's over, we need to get some more sparring in before it's too hot to breathe out here."

"Yes, I definitely do not want sand in my sweat." She accepted his hand, giving a quick, secret glance at his groin area. As she continued to observe, there was no change in that area. Either Adam had impossible control, or he didn't find her fascinating enough for his body to show any interest. She had not decided which mattered more.

She expected Adam to release her hand and step away into one of the fighting forms he'd shown her. Instead, he held her hand loosely until she tried to pull away, then he resisted.

"You just checked me out—again." He spoke in his usual even tones, the Southern barely heard under his calm voice.

Lana mentally cursed his perceptiveness and decided to brazen it out. "You must know you're worth checking out."

"You also checked out Hoffman, the agents, and Aleksei."

She shrugged, looking away. "Occupational hazard."

"You did not check out Ty or Devin."

"Goodness, you must have something better to do than to watch me at work."

He reached his other hand up to cup her shoulder then gave her a gentle shake. "Not now. Not Party Girl Lana or Good Times Lana. Not now, not here. Here it's Just Lana. I don't think you're checking out men for the usual reasons."

"Which reasons? You mean so I can calculate how much influence I have on them?"

"Not quite." He didn't elaborate, just stood, watching her, his hand on her shoulder supporting more than confining.

Lana drew a breath and stepped into the abyss. "I learned...I found out..." She shrugged, leaning her head back in frustration to stare at the lightening sky while trying to vocalize what she'd taught herself to do instinctively. "When a man is interested, especially if it's just physical, his attention isn't always on finer details of a discussion, He only wants to..."

"Think with the little head?"

"He wants to do what comes naturally, so he can claim his instincts overrode his common sense. Thereby blaming it all on the female, as has been done so many times in the past."

Adam slid his hand from her shoulder to cup her neck, leaning down far enough to look into her eyes. "You learned this at a very early age, didn't you?"

She shrugged, leaning against his large calloused hand, trusting him to take her weight. "Being observant is sometimes the key to survival."

"Agreed, no matter what you're trying to do. How old?"

"Pardon?"

"You know what I'm asking. How old were you when you learned how to check out the bulge in a man's pants?"

She tried to look away. When he didn't let her, she closed her eyes against his piercing green scrutiny. "Maybe twelve? When my mother's friends started to notice me? It doesn't matter." She opened her eyes to face his anger. "Seriously, it does not matter since it helped make me better at my job—at reading men and making them think they were doing what they wanted to do, not what I wanted them to do." She brought her free hand up to touch his wrist, hoping to ease the tension she felt there, and forced a smile. "Don't think I haven't noticed how you so adroitly avoided your original question."

He raised his brows, and almost let himself smile. "What's that?"

"You were asking me why I was checking you out. It was not, my bodyguard, an attempt to decide how I could best manipulate you. I was mostly wondering if you had any more reaction to me now than you've had before." She shrugged. "I can see that you do not."

"You don't see a damned thing." The harshness in his voice stopped any desire to tease. "I've noticed you from that first moment I saw you on that porch," he continued, "scared spitless but still taking care of the birds. Sleeping in the same house, hearing you breathe while you sleep, has been torture."

She glanced down automatically and frowned.

"Control, babe. More control than I've ever needed, even when I was fighting to stay awake after that blast ripped off half my leg. It's the only thing that's helped me stay professional when I needed distance to protect you. Damned hard, especially when I was on the same damned bed with you."

"But—why?"

"If I let the little head take over, I lose the edge I need to keep you safe. You needed to trust me to take care of you, not take advantage of you."

"You don't think I should have had some say in that decision?"

"That decision? It had to be my decision. Before we could discuss the decision, I wanted to be sure you were safe, and no one else could interfere."

"Just because it's 'your' little head, doesn't mean you get to make all the decisions."

He pulled at her neck until their foreheads met, and she could feel his body shaking. "Naturally, you'd say something that made no sense whatsoever." Laughter erupted and continued to shudder through him. "You're definitely going to drive me nuts."

"Insanity. Just one more service provided by Make It Work. No additional charge."

"Will power, control, and a really strong jock strap."

She frowned at what seemed to be a non sequitur. "Doesn't that hurt?"

"You have no idea."

"I just might. I wore those damned boots and a push up bra."

"Want to compare bruises? I sincerely doubt your push—" He took a deep breath. It was his turn to look up at the sky as if to try to erase any thought of her underwear.

"There's no way to compare, since I doubt any of my bras would fit you—any part of you."

"I'm not so sure this is a good time for humor. Laughing is seriously not doing me much good."

"I'm not trying to be funny." She blew out a breath. "I am trying my damnedest to get you out of that jock strap from hell and into bed. With me." She did her best to come across as strong and determined. For the most part, she succeeded.

"Just Lana?"

"As long as it's Just Lana and Just Adam. Not Adam the super warrior or Adam the bodyguard."

"I think we can manage that. Once I can walk again. You pretty much destroyed my control."

"It's about damned time."

"You wouldn't be so cheerful if you were wearing

those shoes and that bra you talked about—you're not, are you?" He gazed down her body.

"How dumb do you think I am? Of course not." She looked at him in return, this time not hiding her perusal of his groin. "But you are, aren't you?" She let her grin loose. "Jock strap from hell, huh?"

"I don't think you can claim no binding on your body." His gaze had settled on her chest.

"Sports bra, of course. Minimize bounce and give support."

"Also minimize any accidental display?"

"Without overly restricting movement, yes."

"You wear restrictive undergarments all the time?"

"Whenever it's possible someone might see me, yes."

"Again, for much of your life." He shook his head then gestured to the small house. "Best get inside before the sun starts to bake us."

ೕೕೕ

Once inside the relative coolness, Lana accepted a damp towel to pat at the sweat on her face while she turned to narrow her eyes at Adam, doing the same.

"You wore something to restrain your erection? You have to know I'm restraining an overabundance of in-poor-taste remarks. Such as how hard that must have been for you. What a hard job for that piece of equipment. I have more."

"I have no doubt you do. Don't restrain yourself on my account."

"That's just it. You did restrain yourself." Banter gone, she leaned against the counter. "Why? Was it the equivalent of a hair shirt?"

"When I first saw you—" He saw the immediate denial on her face, the shutting down, starting to turn away. "You have to know what you look like, Lana. I was prepared to meet a woman so beautiful she made Tyler Randolph, a highly intelligent, experienced operative, act like a blithering idiot. So I was ready for a blast from that level of sexual allure. Instead, I saw a woman who had been scared enough to call the ex-husband she knew had to hate her guts. Not for herself, but for girls at risk. Here's this woman, dressed down to street level, worrying about the birds having enough to eat and drink. Sure, that could have been part of your cover, but in that case, you would have been dressed to impress, not just to cover up enough to step out onto a private porch." He laid the towel across the back of a worn wooden chair. "I could have resisted that first Lana, no problem. But after thirty seconds of talking to you, I knew if I didn't do something to remind myself I was at work, then I'd blow the operation and put you, those girls, the people I've learned to respect, in jeopardy."

"You've obviously used this apparatus before."

"Yep. Once when I was undercover as a monk, and it would have been a really bad thing if I got an erection at an inopportune time." She looked as if she were holding in a gut-busting laugh, and he had to grin. "Nope, not all that much temptation, but we had to take every precaution."

"I imagine it's also extra protection for the area," she said in a voice that attempted to be sober. "Can't have the manly equipment in danger."

"You're absolutely on target there." He spoke as seriously as possible. He knew his face revealed nothing. It never had.

"To suppress and protect?" she suggested, arching one of her perfect eyebrows.

"Oh, damn don't make me laugh!" Hunching over,

he eased himself into the bathroom, enjoying the burble of her giggle behind him.

❦

Adam reveled in the feeling of water soaking into his skin, knowing he would dry as soon as he stepped from the small shower. He had to admit to a feeling of freedom when he pulled on his lightweight shorts, not even adding underwear. Now if he could just exert his legendary control and avoid pointing in Lana's direction without raising his hands.

Fat chance. He turned when he heard Lana come into the kitchen area, humidity from the shower gathering around both of them. Dark dampness held the loose T-shirt to her body, cradling then lifting away from her unfettered breasts. She took a step forward, and her breasts swayed, just enough to rub her nipples against the cloth. He felt his liberated cock rising in response.

Lana's lips turned up in that little smile she used when she wasn't trying to impress anyone, just express her own amusement. Her soft brown eyes glinted amusement as she pointedly did not look at his groin area, instead reaching for the kettle on the stove, pouring herself a mug of hot water.

"This might not have been such a great idea," she murmured before taking a sip.

"Why's that?"

"If your goal is to get in more work today, I'm thinking you need to do something to keep from distracting me."

"Me distracting you? Seriously?" He gestured now, a controlled movement to indicate her tousled hair, her far too attractive breasts. "You look like you just stepped out of bed after a night of hot sex."

"We all know how deceiving looks can be." She hid her frown in the large mug. "How long since we've slept more than a couple hours?"

Now he looked more closely at her face, and the wash of guilt had the predictable effect, as he felt the pressure let up on his shorts.

Dark smudges under her eyes spoke to the lack of decent sleep, not to mention various bruises along her upper arm, showing below the loose short sleeves of her oversized shirt. The shorts below were equally loose, and revealed red marks on her thighs that no doubt would become dark bruises soon.

"Damn. When did you—"

"Just Lana means no makeup, no concealer. Anywhere. Unfortunately, lack of sleep shows up on my face way too fast. I've become a master at concealing."

"In more ways than one, I'd say. That's it, you need some rest."

"I'm not the only one, tough guy." She set the mug on the counter, almost controlling the trembling in her delicate fingers. "You've been carrying the lion's share of the work this last week, and I know you're not as tough as you pretend to be."

He started to protest, to insist he could go another week without sleep. But his body pulled at him, reminded him that he was no longer insanely young. "It's a foolish warrior who does not rest when given the opportunity."

"Rest." She drew in a breath, as if scenting the subtle smells of drying air, dust, desire. And regret. It showed on her face, along with…relief?

"Lana, are you afraid of me?"

"Why would I be afraid of you when you've done everything you can to protect me?"

"That's why I'm asking. You almost seem…relieved that I'm not pushing you for—"

"Sex? You're too noble to push me for sex."

"Nobility went out the window long ago." He reached out to touch the bruise on her arm as lightly as he could, feeling the delicate skin against his calloused fingertips. "I did that, hustling you out of the casino."

"Saving my life," she pointed out.

"Doing my job," he said with controlled anger.

*೧೫೧*

Lana hesitated at the harshness of his voice. "You've done your job. Masterfully, I might add."

"And you're thinking now you need to pay me back somehow?"

She turned away, drawing in a breath to speak, then shaking her head. Her loose blonde hair shimmered in the dim light, falling forward to hide her expression. But not fast enough to hide the hurt in her eyes.

"Ah, crap. That sounded pretty bad, didn't it?" He hesitated when she shrugged then turned her face far enough in his direction to reveal her not-so-sincere smile.

"I've lived in a world of payback long enough to learn truth might hurt, but it's still true."

"The last damned thing I want to do is hurt you in any way." He reached out again to touch her arm, not missing the tension under her skin. "Why don't we revisit this discussion after we've both had some sleep?"

She glanced at him, the bedroom, the couch.

"Bed's big enough for both of us. You've managed to restrain yourself so far from attacking me in my sleep. I think I'm safe enough for now."

This surprised a giggle, quickly suppressed. Then another one while the tension slid out from under her skin. "I'll make every effort to continue to restrain myself," she promised in a solemn voice.

‹›‹›‹›

"How long have you been afraid of sex?"

The question, in a low controlled voice as warm as the air around her, filled the darkened room. Lana was in that twilight world of not quite asleep but not awake enough for deep thought, until the question cut through the haze. Her heart stuttered before she could manage to say, in a tone of world-weary derision. "You're kidding, right?"

"I don't think so," he rumbled, seeming to be on the verge of sleep himself. "You're really good at the subtle flirting, at letting men think you're gonna be more than they could ever handle in bed. But you keep this…wall…around you, a barrier you slip behind whenever someone seems to be getting too close, too intimate. You go from Marilyn Monroe to Grace Kelly in a breath."

"Grace Kelly?" Even through her increasing distress, she felt a glimmer of amusement. She turned her head, starting to face him. A hard hand rested on her shoulder, keeping her in place. The feeling of his warm strength jolted through her body, and she found herself clinging to the edge of the bed.

"Just stay there for now. You haven't been physically afraid of me for a while, there's no need to start now."

"Afraid of you? Why would I be…" She realized his hand was more comforting than restraining, and she stilled, though keeping herself ready to bolt.

"Like that. You're trying to make me believe you're all in for whatever I might want. But you're also ready to be out of here like a sprinter from the blocks. If you lean any farther over the side of the bed, you'll be on the floor."

She acknowledged the truth of his words and eased

back enough that she no longer had to brace herself away from the edge of the bed.

"That's better. If it helps, remember my prosthesis is at your side of the bed, up next to the night stand. I'm not going to lie, I can get around without it, but I'm much faster and more efficient with two legs."

She felt a gurgle of laughter, possibly hysteria, try to push its way out of her throat at the image of a fully armed warrior hopping across the desert. To attack or rescue…she couldn't quite decide. His fingers tightened briefly, then he slid his hand down her arm to rest on her waist. No farther. No threatening to sneak a feel of her hip under the loose shorts, no sliding to the front to urge her to ease back closer to his chest. Just his warm palm, staying connected to her. Letting her know he was there while she slid into sleep.

⌘⌘⌘

She woke later, refreshed but very warm. Somehow she'd slid into the middle of the bed, and her rear rested against—she stiffened and thought about moving away before—

"Yeah, I'm hard. I think I mentioned I've been at least semi hard around you from the beginning. No, we're not going to do anything about it until you don't wake up afraid of my getting hard against you." His voice rumbled even lower than normal.

She thought to reassure him. "But I'm—"

"You're not accustomed to sleeping with a man. I get that. I haven't slept with a woman since…well, a while." He nestled closer, his erection nudging almost politely against her. She flexed minutely. "Oh, now that's just not fair, Goldilocks."

This surprised a…was that a giggle? Surely not.

His hand now rested on her ribs, just below her breast. So close, yet, she realized, not close enough. Not close enough at all.

"What's not close enough?"

Oops. "I must be sleep talking."

"Nope, not getting out of it that way. What's—"

A buzz, low but insistent, caught their attention.

"Mine, I think." Damn phones. "I thought reception wouldn't be good out here." She edged toward the side of the bed, immediately missing the feel of him behind her.

Lana peered at the display in the dim light and sighed before accepting the call. "This is Lana, what can Make it Work do for—"

"Where the hell are you?"

She jerked the phone away from her ear "Excuse me?"

"This is Steve Short. Where the hell are you shacked up with that crip?"

She felt Adam stiffen behind her before she disconnected then turned her head to speak over her shoulder. "I'm so—"

"You never apologize for someone else's ignorance, Lana. Bet he'll call—"

Sure enough, her phone buzzed again. "If you cannot act in a professional manner, I will not converse with you any further."

"Sorry, this is Aaron. Steve was worried for you."

"I sincerely doubt that. You haven't been worried for me since you set me up with that pedophile in Tonopah." She felt Adam's hand tighten briefly on her waist. Then his phone buzzed quietly, and he rolled away. She told herself she didn't miss him. The person at the other end of her phone connection continued to mumble.

"You'll have to say that again, I didn't hear you."

"That boyfriend of yours is too much of a distraction. We found—we have a line on—you need to get away from him. We found those girls without your help. He's too much of a distraction."

"I do not work for you, and you do not have any right to tell me what to do, where to do it, or with whom."

"He's dangerous."

"Well, of course, he's dangerous. Our government made sure he was well trained."

"Not like that. He's…" The voice trailed off, and she heard some rumbling, as if the speaker held his hand over the phone. "Is he there now?"

"Go back to what I said before. None. Of. Your. Business."

"He's holding a gun on you, isn't he? Lana, you have to get away from him."

The panic seemed too forced. She dropped her voice into a low, sultry purr. "Oh, Agent Temple, don't you realize how much more exciting it can be when there's such a possibility of danger?" She heard the suppressed snort behind her as Adam answered his own phone.

 లుౡ

Adam felt his lips stretch into a smile as he hit the button on his phone to accept the call from Ty. "You know your timing really sucks, don't you, Randolph?" When Ty didn't come back with an immediate quip, Adam sat up. Lana looked over her shoulder, eyebrow raised, her face showing nothing of the sex kitten phrases coming out of her mouth.

"It's about Lana," Ty began.

"Of course it's about Lana. This entire operation is about Lana."

"It's about stories spread, about how unstable Lana

is, how many children she's harmed. They say they're planning a rescue, and she's being mentioned as the person who put the girls in that place."

"Sounds like we've managed to set someone off. She's on the phone now with those agents, learning how unstable I am."

"Yeah, we heard that one too. Looks like the vacation's over. Let us know when you're on the move."

Adam punched off, holding back the irritation, thinking about how close Lana had come to trust, her sweet rear snuggled against him, an honest reaction instead of an image maintained to hide or protect her. In the dim light, he could see the impatience on her face, which she allowed to show in her voice.

"No, I do not need to come scurrying in. I don't work for you, I don't report to you. Not anymore. I'll get there when I get there." Then her finger moved to disconnect the call. "Crap," she whispered, rolling over to sit on the side of the bed. Her head bowed, hair falling forward to obscure her face until she took a deep breath and stood. "Guess play time's over, boys and girls."

"Nah," he said. "It's just a brief delay of game."

She turned, a bright question in her deep brown eyes.

"You can bet on it."

"Well, it is Nevada, after all."

# Chapter 17

Light edged the mountains behind them as they drove back to Las Vegas, the car alone on the narrow road, a bubble of privacy. Lana knew she should be trying for more rest since she'd been too long without adequate sleep. Too much had happened, too fast, and when she tried to order her thoughts, she found only chaos. Closing her eyes didn't help since she was then inundated with the feel and scent of the man sitting next to her. She forced her eyes open, working hard not to squirm.

"Lana," his voice rumbled in the dark. "You need to stop wriggling over there. I'm barely holding on as it is."

That got her attention and brought her back to staring over at his profile in the early dawn. He was concentrating on the road, his posture relaxed but upright. She glanced discreetly down.

"None of that. We have to get back into work mode."

"You back to the jock strap from hell?"

"Nope. That was for your benefit, so you wouldn't feel uncomfortable. That doesn't mean we can take time out to explore. Not right now, anyway."

She opened her mouth to pout, to complain, then

closed it again. This was not the time to play any of her coy Lana roles. He took a moment for a longer look then nodded.

"We'll work it out," he said in a lower voice.

"Right. Job first." It helped to hear *his* sigh echoed from the other side of the car.

☙❧☙

"I can't believe I wore these shoes before and sur-vived," Lana muttered, scanning the cacophonous room, lights blaring at her from every direction, while she tried to stretch her toes inside the fashionably uncomfortable heels. Funny how she'd been able to wear them for hours before.

Roz's mellow voice slipped into Lana's grumbling. "Let a girl get out in the country, and she never wants to come back to the bright lights."

"Isn't that supposed to be the other way around?" Ty muttered.

"Not for the smart women of the world," Adam pointed out.

"It would be nice if everyone would get out of my ear." Lana barely moved her lips while she looked out over the casino floor, working to pull her persona around her like the shield it was meant to be. Today she was Con-Woman Lana—amoral, devious, and willing to do anything to succeed. She'd used this persona often enough that the veneer pulled on like a well-fitting dress, but today it was not near as comfortable. Having the chat-ter filter through her inconspicuous earpiece helped more than she might have ever thought it would.

"Quiet on the set," came Adam's steady voice again. "Stooges alert at two o'clock. That's under the flashing neon signs for those who are positionally challenged."

"Did Roberts just make a joke?" Ty whispered.

Roz came back with, "Maybe that desert interlude did them both some good."

Lana suppressed the smirk trying to escape and schooled her expression for maximum effect. The agents spotted her and bore down with little regard for the people at the slots and wandering across the room.

"Where have you—" Agent Short growled—actually growled—reaching out to grab her arm.

"Are you all right, Lana?" his partner cut in, moving between them and blocking the grab.

This brought him closer to her than she preferred, and she took a deliberate step back. "I think you might have your hearing checked since I have said several times now, my location was none of your business."

Short reached around his partner and finally grabbed her arm, his fingers digging in. "Let's not get uppity, missy."

Lana let her brows raise when what she wanted to do was use the pointy toes on her shoes in his groin.

"He did *not* just say that," Roz whispered, outrage in every word.

"Special Agent Short, you will release my arm immediately, or I will contact security. Although I probably do not need to bother, since there are cameras on every inch of this floor."

"They won't—"

The burly security officer moved in from behind the two agents. "Problem, Ms. Greene?"

"Nothing to concern you," Special Agent Short snarled.

The guard stolidly ignored the two agents. "Ma'am?"

"Not at the moment, thank you. But if you could check back?" She offered a quick smile and calm demeanor.

The guard nodded, gave the two agents a warning glare, and stepped back to stand at the wall, obviously not intending to move.

"That's not necessary, Lana."

"From where I stand, it's very necessary.

"You don't know what you're playing with."

"Why don't you fill me in?" She lifted her brow and let a slight smirk emphasize her question.

He reached for her elbow again. "Not here."

"Right here. In plain sight of enough people and cameras so nothing can be misinterpreted. No recordings can be lost, no chance I'll end up in a ditch somewhere." She took a short breath and raised the other eyebrow, going for an arch look. "So, if it's all the same to you, we can just stay right here."

"I don't know where you get those ridiculous ideas. Are you into fantasy games these days?"

"If it pays, I'm into it. But we all know there's little fantasy to what's been happening."

"About that. We need to talk."

"So talk. I'm listening."

"That man—the crip?"

Lana took a step back, preparing to wheel around and leave in a huff.

"Sorry. The vet. He's not right."

"Define not right. My experiences with him have all been quite positive."

"I'm not talking about how good he—" Short grunted when Temple jabbed an elbow.

"We don't mean how he is privately. Captain Roberts's records show that he's not completely stable."

"He's a war veteran, a damned hero who was injured protecting the rights of weenie little bastards like—"

"He's a damned psycho. He can't be trusted in public, that's why he was shoved out of the service."

"Hang in there, hot stuff, you're doing great."

The calm, quiet voice in her ear stopped Lana from the scathing reply she wanted to use. Instead, she pulled up an enigmatic smile and let the agents see her professionally calm face. "He's not so bad, once you get to know him. However, I doubt you actually sent such a frantic message just to try to warn me about Captain Roberts."

"You need to stay away from—"

"I got it. I'm not completely stupid. Roberts is a loose cannon. What. Else?"

"It's about the girl."

"What girl?"

"The girl you saw at that party."

"What—party?" She bit out the words, letting some of her frustration and impatience show. Enough to let them know she wanted answers now.

"That last one you set up in the penthouse."

"Oh, yeah, the one I haven't been paid for yet. I wonder if I can file charges against that little pissant for defrauding me."

"Aleksei Novakov?"

"No, Hoffman set it up. He's responsible for getting money into my account. The rest are just bit players."

"I don't give a damn about your payment."

"Well, that's where we really part ways, because I don't care about much of anything else. I'm a businesswoman, Special Agent Short. Plain and simple."

"Yeah, and we know all about your *business*, don't we?"

"Actually, I don't think you do." She looked around the half-crowded casino, her attention drawn by a slot payout customer. Rare happy customer. If they were smart, they'd scoop those winnings up and go home. Sadly, most people weren't that smart. She turned back to the

agents who were barely containing their impatience.
"Okay, you've delivered your so-called information. You
have some questions, ask them. I have better things to do
today, particularly since Hoffman has not paid his bill."

"It's not like you're hurting financially."

"Snooping again? So much for cooperation and dis-
cretion. How fortunate I trust you as much as you trust
me." She allowed herself an eye roll. "Being self-
employed means I don't have an automatic pension, re-
tirement plan, or paid leave."

"You saying your little trip out of town cost you?"

"Agent, one day you'll learn that some things are beyond price." This time the slight smile she allowed herself was not forced.

Special Agent Temple tilted his head, watching her
intently. "It seems like your trip was beneficial."

"How so?"

"You seem...more clear. Less confused."

Lana pushed her eyebrows up again. "Stress can
make any of us seem confused. But thank you for your
concern."

Hands in his pocket, Temple continued to study her.
"We need to talk, privately. Will you come with us?"

"No, I will not come with you. I will meet you. At
your office or a public location of mutual agreement."
Rage showed briefly in Short's eyes...and perhaps a
touch of fear? Lana turned on the be-damned heels and
tossed over her shoulder. "You have my contact information. If you call the main number, you will be for-
warded."

"We need to—"

"I did not get to where I am by being stupid or foolish, nor by working with stupid or foolish people. Your
office, during normal working hours, or a public location."

She turned fully away and stormed out, allowing her anger to show.

ൟ

Around the corner, in one of the service hallways, Adam leaned against the wall, checking his phone. She could read the tension in his shoulders, see the preparedness in his stance—weight balanced so he could explode in any direction.

When she entered the hall, he looked up, his polite smile lifting the corners of his mouth while he put the phone away and stepped forward, emphasizing his use of the cane. Just in case someone would be watching and note his disability. As she passed, he set his hand in the small of her back. Supporting, as always. Formal, remote, non-intimate. Even so, the most authentic touch she'd felt for hours.

She realized she was done with fake and remote and always playing to an audience. She let her spine relax, just enough to press back into his palm while she continued to stride forward, her heels tapping in time to her increasing heartbeat. Did she dare too much? Did she care how he reacted? Yes, she did care, but she knew she had to be the one to take that one small step toward letting him know how she felt. Here, away from the fantasy refuges. Here, where she'd had to guard every move, every expression. Every emotion.

For the briefest instant, he hesitated, then his hand rested against her, the heat penetrating to her skin. His palm flattened to cover more of her back, and his fingers flexed just enough to let her know how much he'd been restraining himself. Heat flooded through her, every inch of her skin warming, sensitizing, letting her know she wanted—needed—more. She tilted her head far enough to glimpse his face, set in the same remote expression. But those fingers continued infinitely tiny strokes, pressing and lifting, caressing her back and her heart.

When she opened her mouth to speak, not quite sure what she was going to say, he gave her a minute head shake. "Not now." Then he corrected himself. "Not yet." His attention seemed to be on the corridor around them, looking to the front, glancing behind, never meeting her eyes. But the pressure on her back increased enough to let her know he had not shut her out, only delayed what would inevitably happen. Soon.

The casino sounds faded away behind them while they turned into a corridor she'd never seen before. Even more remote than the passages to private casino parking. They turned another corner, revealing only blank walls and doors with signs indicating storage. Adam looked up at the ceiling then back behind them as he guided her around this last corner. His cane rattled to the floor, and he used that hand to touch her face then cup her cheek while the hand at her back moved her around to face him.

Lana lifted her face to his, searching, hoping, for something more than his normally stoic expression. Except now, she saw softening around his eyes which almost glowed with intense light. A corner of his mouth lifted beyond his usual quirk as he studied her face in return.

"Just a minute. Maybe even a few seconds. I just needed—" His hand slid into her hair, tilting her head at an angle, pulling her closer. "We can't—not here, not yet." Instead of his lips pressing over hers, alleviating the ache she felt in hers, he eased his cheek next to hers. The shudder in his body matched the trembling in hers, and she slid her arms around his back, reaching up to cup his shoulders and pull him even closer.

She felt his broad palm stroke lower on her back. Not

quite to her rear, where again she anticipated the more intimate touch edging down her spine, and she eased herself forward to—yes. There was no doubt about his involvement in the embrace. His honest involvement, both of them trembling slightly while they skirted the edges of danger.

"Not here. Not now," she whispered against his ear. "Dammit."

She felt the chuckle sneak up from his diaphragm, not quite making its way out his mouth but somehow softening the edge shared between them. She nestled just a little closer, reveling in the hardness against her stomach, the iron hard arms encompassing her, promising safety and more. For once, she knew this was a man who could deliver on such a promise.

"Guys?" the voice squawked in her ear. "You're off cameras. You okay?"

Adam pulled her even closer then eased back. "Yeah, we're fine. Just checking out a hallway we hadn't seen before." His voice betrayed none of the tension in his body, but when he loosened his hold enough to look at her face, she could still the passion, the strain, in his face. "You okay?" he asked in the barest of whispers then allowed a wider smile when she nodded. "Let's get out of here."

With a deep breath, he resumed the professional expression on his face, nodding when she did the same. When they stepped back into the hallway where the cameras would once more reveal their movements, they would be seen only as partners. Professionals, getting the job done as best they could.

For now, the memory of his body against hers would need to stay in a very secret place.

෴

The unobtrusive escort met them near the hallway to the parking area, falling into loose formation, one in front, one behind. Adam continued his surveillance, never looking too long at one place, eyes always alert, body balanced. Anyone watching would see what had been seen every time before: an impersonal bodyguard serious about his assignment. Only the continued flex of his palm and fingers against her back told her this was no longer impersonal with him, and she schooled herself to maintain the illusion of a professional relationship.

"Which vehicle?" he muttered to their watchers.

"The SUV. Red one, third level."

Adam waited until they were strapped in to advise their listeners. "We'll be taking a brief detour." They'd varied the routes to the cottage, driving several similar vehicles to add a level of confusion for anyone trying to follow.

"Necessary detour?" That was Ty's voice asking.

Adam took on an air of patience. "Can never be too cautious."

Ty's answering grunt seemed to imply far more than agreement. Lana found herself wondering about the sub-vocal language shared by some men.

"Something funny over there?"

She looked over to see the corner of Adam's mouth lifting—what would be a full out grin on most men—before they passed the public illumination for the darker streets of a business complex area. "Just contemplating universal male non-verbal communication skills."

He glanced at her quickly before concentrating on the route he was taking through a dark parking lot. "You're thinking grunt means the same everywhere?"

"I've observed many iterations of said grunt."

He nodded, face still serious, but she thought she saw a glint in his shadowed eyes. Then he pulled to a stop in a deeper shadow under some shade trees. "This should do," he murmured, pushing the gear shift over and leaning down to ease his seat back.

"What—" was all she managed to get out of her mouth before he reached down to release both their seat belts. His large hand encompassed the back of her neck, pulling her forward to meet him in the middle of the car.

She expected, and braced herself for, an onslaught. They had teetered on the edge of frustration for far too long. Instead, she felt his mouth brush hers, then his lips nibble up her cheek while his hot breath caressed her skin. She managed an inarticulate sound, and he pulled back.

Before he could ask, before he could study her face in mute concern, she reached up to slide her fingers around his neck, mirroring the hold he had on her, and pulled his mouth back where it belonged.

There. Lips touching, opening. Tongues stroking and mutual groans when that first taste burst upon them. He sucked her gasp into himself, answering with a groan, and a shift to position their mouths into a seamless entity. But his hands remained chastely above her shoulders.

With a final swipe of his tongue into her mouth, he pulled back enough to rest his forehead against hers. "Sorry—had to—couldn't wait—"

She couldn't form thoughts into words any better and had to be happy with taking deep gulps of air filled with his unique scent. When he didn't move on with the seduction, she leaned forward, silently asking for his touch lower—on her breast, on her waist, on her hips. Lower. More.

"Not here."

She held back her sigh. "Not now," she agreed. "It seems non-verbal communication can be also successful between sexes."

Quiet shared laughter filled the small interior, reducing the tension, if only briefly.

Adam recovered first. "We can't go dark for too much longer. They'll start tracking."

"What if we had them spending their night trying to track us down?" she suggested as innocently as she could.

"Sounds entertaining, but...we can save that for another time." He eased back, reluctance in every stroke of his long, rough fingers against her face, reached across to secure her belt without touching her. "Let's get ourselves to then and there."

He settled back behind the wheel, repositioning his seat and securing his own belt. Lana subdued her frustration, pulling her remote persona around herself in false comfort. Until his hand reached out to hers, enclosing it in warmth, then pulling it over to rest her palm on his thigh. Only then, did he reach forward to move the gear shift.

⁊⁊⁊

The cottage looked the same, set off to the side of the large, dark main house. No one waited at the door, but the interior lights were on, the water kettle was hot, the ceiling fans turned to make a welcoming cool environment. Lights shone just bright enough to see while soothing her eyes from the glare of the casino. Air clean—which she definitely was not.

Adam obviously noticed the stench. "All the smoking restrictions in the world won't make those places smell any better."

She bent over to loosen and step out of her foot-torturing shoes. Funny how much more difficult they had become to wear. "The bigger casinos are better regulated. Shame the people we need to deal with fit better into lesser facilities." Catching the fine shoe back-straps, she straightened, stepping onto the plush rug with a happy sigh. "Better. Much better."

"You want to get your shower, and I can check what's around for a snack?"

"You don't want to—" She looked back at him, standing so still, face in the shadows by the door. Hands held loose and seeming relaxed. No sign of the fierce lover who'd grabbed and held her for a scorching kiss.

"You go ahead. You always feel better after a shower." He turned away, reaching for his phone while looking around, checking for...what?

"Something you're not sharing with me?" She worked to keep her voice professional, not allowing any insecurity to show. Wild, rampant, ridiculous insecurity.

Her reward was a slight smile. "You go ahead. I need to check in."

She tried to hold his gaze then turned away. Shoulders straight, steps secure. Head high. Never, never let them see you react. Never.

Once in the privacy of the closet, she reached under her arm to unzip the form fitting top, hanging it up to air before putting it away. Same with the skirt. Light from the bathroom showed her in the mirror. Midnight blue against her pale skin, the damned torturing bra looked good, no matter how painful. Matching panties, chosen to entice, to tempt. Too bad no one else would see—

"Keep going," he whispered from the doorway. "No, don't turn around."

His image was at the very corner of the mirror, backlit by the dim kitchen lights, leaning against the doorjamb, thumbs in his pockets. Even in the gloom, she could see the glitter in his eyes.

"Leave the stockings on."

She reached behind her back, searching out the fastening, arched her back, and angled to show more in the mirror, feeling suddenly wanton and sexier than ever before. The hooks released, and she allowed herself a small groan of relief as her liberated breasts fell forward. In the mirror, they bounced a little as her nipples rose, hardened from the freedom and the gaze of the man behind her. Holding the bra by one strap, she eased her other hand up her torso to rub at the wire indentations, dropped the bra to one side to cup both breasts for a quick massage.

She reached to hook fingers in her panties, and he was there before she saw him move. Hard chest covered by soft shirt warm against her back, dark hands reaching to cup her breasts. "Leave them." His warm breath, scented with coffee and mint, caressed her ear while his fingers stroked along the bra marks then plucked at her nipples until he flattened his hands, cupping her in his palms.

She leaned her head back. "I smell like—"

"We both do. We can take care of that later." He pulled his hands away far enough to rub against her nipples, setting up a soft friction that had her trembling.

Lana twisted, taking him off guard as she grabbed at his shirt. "Off."

He pulled, she pushed, then they were chest to chest, sensitive breasts nestling in wiry chest hair. She reached around and up, reveling in the lean muscles and hot skin, pressing against him for a modicum of relief before she slid her hands down to his slacks.

"Nope." He pivoted, lifted her enough to push her back against, then onto, the edge of the bed, sliding her panties off along the way. "Not yet. Gonna taste—"

"Later, dammit." She twisted against his hands on her thighs to open the bedside table, grabbing for the box of condoms, fumbling for a packet. Or two. Or three.

She grabbed a handful and pushed them his direction, slapping them against his chest, which vibrated with laughter.

"Impatient, are we?"

She lightly scraped her nails down his back, reaching for the waistband of his dress slacks. Her thoughts bounced around her head. Wrong thing for him to wear.

"What should I wear?" His voice came out with another explosion of laughter.

"Oops. Didn't mean to say that out loud." She drew a deep breath, trying to calm herself. Gave up. "Nothing. You should be wearing nothing. Now."

She pushed at the belt buckle cutting into her skin. "Ouch. Off."

He raised up immediately. "Damn. Sorry."

Then he worked at the belt, at the fastening, hampered or helped—who could tell?—by her fingers. Pushed down slacks and boxer briefs far enough. Grabbed one of the condoms stuck to his chest with sweat. Then—

"Yesss," from both their mouths. He pushed the slacks down more, perhaps to avoid zipper damage on her thighs, before he pulled out, thrust in again. Braced his elbows along her sides and leaned in for a kiss.

Then another kiss, mouths melding, tongues tangling, until he had to move again in a harder, faster, stronger rhythm. Until their worlds imploded.

*ಊಲ*

Lana felt Adam at her back as they entered the observation room at the casino. She knew her face was in the severe getting-the-job-done expression as his would be as well. He walked on her right side, one step behind and to her side, not touching. Both projecting consummate professionalism.

Roz looked up as they came in, glancing between the two of them. The tentative smile on her wide mouth spread, and she had a gleam in her eye. "You have a good night?"

"Got some sleep," Lana agreed, not looking over to see the expression on Adam's face. Something had grabbed Roz's attention

Lana had woken to deep breaths, not quite snores, accompanying the warm pillow rising and falling under her face, and held very still to allow Adam as much time asleep as possible.

They'd had their shower, a gentle frolic in the small area. She'd been introduced to his prosthesis, helping to remove it and giving him the promised stump rub, leading to another delay in showering.

Then sleep. The deepest, most profound sleep she could ever remember. Waking content and, for the moment, at peace with the world. A very brief moment.

Surely none of that showed on their faces. Or did it? Roz offered another enigmatic smile then a shrug as if apologizing in advance for something. "Adam, you had a phone call."

He automatically reached for his own phone then frowned.

"On one of the team phones. They asked me to get a message to you." She shrugged. "When I asked them why not call you directly, they just said Reynolds needs to see you."

Lana saw his muscles stiffen then droop as his head fell forward. "Reynolds?" she mouthed.

He took a composing breath and sent one quick glance at her. "History."

"Person or code?"

This time, Adam looked at her directly, and she could see approval in his normally stoic expression.

"A little bit of both," he said in an undertone. He looked back at Roz. "Did they leave a number?"

"A message number, yes. You call them, they'll call back."

He took the piece of paper she handed him. "I'll need to check out one of those empty offices." Lana followed his hold on her hand.

Once in the small dimly lit office, Adam reached out to cup her jaw in his large hands, the rough fingers sliding through her hair, tilting her face up until she had to meet his eyes.

"I will probably have to go. My team—my teammates—need me. At least that was the code."

"Of course, you do. I'll be okay."

He shook his head, pulled her closer. "Something feels off, but I can't put my finger on it. Maybe it's the timing. The agents say they found those girls, supposedly they can break this ring for now. And I have to leave. To leave you alone."

"I've been alone before." She gulped then braced herself. "I've been alone for a long time. I will be fine."

Adam shook his head, still not shifting his gaze from hers. "I've worked undercover for a while. Been whoever I needed to be to succeed at the job. Established relationships, lived with women as their friend or lover. Whatever I had to do."

"You don't have to tell me this."

"Yeah, I do. At the end of the job, no matter how long I was with the woman, I just packed up and—walked away. No muss, no fuss. I never went so far as to be engaged, never promised any happily ever afters. I just walked away."

"You're warning me all things come to an end? We knew at the start, once this is resolved and we figure out how to find these girls and keep them safe, you'll be walking away?" She steeled herself to continue to seem remote. "I should be grateful you're giving me some warning."

"I'm telling you—" He grabbed her hands, not letting her pull away. "This time, I can't. I can't walk away. When we're done, when we've figured this out—" He released one hand to pull off the heavy silver armlet and slide it onto her arm, above the elbow. "You keep this for me. I will come back. I won't be able to walk away."

She met his gaze, did not look away. "That's a relief because I'm not sure I could let you."

∾∾∾

The staccato rasp of her heels against the tile floor echoed back from the hallway. No carpet here to muffle the sound and interfere with the Southwestern theme of stucco walls and what looked like high-quality original art. She stepped closer to one of the displays. Perhaps not quite original but certainly a high-quality pretense. She wondered if the owner knew the difference.

She knew she was most likely under surveillance, so she maintained the executive-bitch persona, not allowing any expression on her face beyond a slight eyebrow raise. Behind the mask, scenes from this morning threatened her composure while warming her. Adam, risking emotional intimacy while explaining where he had to go and why. Promising to return. For once, she believed. She wanted to believe.

"Ms. Greene?" The cultured voice brought her back to the present, and the reality of an obsessively young woman. "Mr. Winfield will see you now."

Lana followed the mincing steps and tight skirt to a well-furnished, if not exciting, office. The man coming around the desk was equally bland, but the other one—

"Aleksei, what a pleasant surprise to see you here."

His expression held no pleasure, though his voice was pleasant. "No surprise. I am in this country to develop new trade contacts. Mr. Winfield is proving to be an excellent source of...information."

He was letting her fill in the blanks, no doubt feeling very clever.

Lana had spent too many hours dealing with this sort of game. She ignored him, turning to Winfield. "Your message seemed urgent. What can Make It Work do for you?"

Aleksei broke in before Winfield could reply. "Where is your shadow?"

Eyebrows raised, Lana looked over with a bored expression. "Excuse me?"

"The bodyguard. He is not with you?"

"I had no idea I needed a bodyguard to visit a long time client." She turned back to Winfield. "That's right, isn't it?"

Winfield shifted in his chair, not quite meeting her eyes.

"What aren't you telling me?"

"We have always been friends. But Aleksei—"

"Selling me out? What was your thirty pieces of silver?"

"No, nothing like that."

"I think, everything like that. Mr. Novakov is so obviously not a fan of mine. Why, I do not know since I have only met him recently."

At this, Aleksei stiffened as if he was having difficulty restraining himself. Then he obviously gave up the effort.

"We have only met recently, but you have harmed my family beyond measure."

The chill in his voice, the sudden tension in his body,

and Lana wished for the strength of Adam at her back. At least there were no bodyguards in the room.

"You mean Dee Dee."

"Her name was Deirdre."

"She wanted to be called Dee Dee. She wanted to be an actress, but she took other jobs in the meantime. Her agency sent her over when I put out a request for energetic young women."

"And pretty," he sneered.

"Pretty was a plus, but I needed them to keep up with mobs of children at upscale birthday parties. The costumes were princesses and fairies. We had ponies and small castles and multiple tables for tea parties." She sighed, remembering the energy, the fun, of dozens of laughing little girls all dressed in their fanciest. "Dee Dee was an obvious choice since she was not only enthusiastic and energetic, she understood the ponies and got along with everyone. I hired her several times, and she was always a favorite."

She turned away, pacing to the window. Mindful of Adam's cautions, she stood to the side to look out. Another bright Nevada day. Of course. But she was not seeing the pavement and billboards.

"This party was a huge deal. Fancy mansion, lots of little girls. Lots of obvious wealth. Too much green for the desert, but this person didn't have a problem with extravagance. He told me money was no object for his daughter's party, and he meant it." She turned to face them. "It didn't hurt that he was trying to impress his new business partners. What he forgot to mention was that his new partner's cousin, also attending, was a sexual predator of the worst sort. Or maybe he didn't know. I found the partner stalking a little girl who could not get away since she was in a wheelchair." She heard gasps from the two men, peripherally noticed them taking a step forward.

"I hit him with what was at hand, in this instance a brass ornament. My only thought was to distract him until help came, but he stumbled and banged his head on the fireplace. It didn't help that he was high on something nasty and had no balance."

She wrapped her arms around her middle, grabbing for her elbows, stroking the silver armlet. "The police came, and everyone agreed it didn't need to be made public. At least everyone who talked with me. I was assured the information would remain private. It was hours before I could leave that place, and I thought all my helpers had cleaned up and gone home." Now she looked directly at Aleksei. "In the confusion, Dee Dee disappeared. Her roommate called me that night, so we could report it and start to look. I called the client, just in case she had stayed there for whatever reason, and the man said he'd take care of it. They found her fairly quickly, but I don't think she was in that part of town on her own. When I tried to ask questions, I was told to keep my mouth shut, or they would tell the predator's family what really happened."

"'They' being the man who hired you, who was obviously a part of organized crime," Aleksei stated with a sneer.

"'They' being FBI Special Agents Short and Temple, duly hired officers of the law. In exchange for their silence and protection, I helped them close down predators and kidnappers. Stupid for them to do it that way, since I'd been working on this by myself for several years already."

"This is not what they told me."

"I'm sure it's not."

"They told me they had been investigating your involvement in the sex trade."

"That's essentially accurate since my involvement in the sex trade consisted of trying to find the common denominator behind so many of the disappearances and kidnappings. I knew they were involved, but I wasn't sure how deeply, and I couldn't go to the authorities without strong evidence."

"They wouldn't believe you?"

She allowed a small, bitter smile. "It seems I worked too hard over the years to convince them I was not a good person."

"Why would you do that?"

"A good person isn't approached to help transport sex victims. A good person can't wiggle their way into organizations where young lives are considered a financially valuable commodity."

Aleksei's frown deepened. "So all this—the clothing, the attitude—it's fake?"

She shrugged. "I do what has to be done."

"The bodyguard?"

"When I saw that young girl at Hoffman's party, I knew I would need more help. I contacted someone who was not involved with anyone local, and they sent Captain Roberts to assist."

"He is not with you now?"

"He is handling another matter. Plus, some people are convinced the immediate danger is over since so many young women were found and helped."

"So I understand. These young women were found without your help." His tone and expression let her know how he felt about her help.

"That's what you were told? Interesting."

"You don't believe that?"

"Let's just say I'm skeptical about the timing." She looked at her watch. "And speaking of time, I have somewhere else to be. I squeezed you into the schedule. If you need me—truly need me—let me know. Mr. Winfield has my number."

Aleksei drew a breath as if he needed to say something else then shrugged and turned away. She wondered briefly about the flash of expression she'd seen on his face, seeming more like guilt than anger.

She didn't have much time to ponder this meeting, nor the sudden phone call bringing her here. Her heels tapped down the hallway toward the exit until two men stepped into the light from the glass entry door. Crap. Adam had told her not to go anywhere alone. Fine time for him to be proven right.

"Ms. Greene?"

The voice sounded familiar. Then both men turned enough to step out of the backlighting. She recognized the leader of the early surveillance team—and the guard who had gone around the cottage. She let herself relax. Unless—

"Why are you here?"

"You need someone with you. And a driver." His face held more than a public stoicism As if he had to—

"What happened?"

"You need to come with us." When he saw her hesitate, he reached out his hand. "Now. Please."

# Chapter 18

Lana cursed her ridiculous shoes as she hurried down the hallway, flanked by the team members. The door guards stepped out of her way, opening the final door as she approached. Those inside turned to defend then stilled and stepped back to reveal Ty's back then the woman in his arms. Roz leaned against him, watching the man in front of her. One of Adam's crew held out something metallic. Lana strengthened her spine as she approached.

Roz looked up, blinking away the tears as she stepped away from Ty. "It's his, isn't it?"

Lana had no trouble identifying Adam's metal prosthetic leg. She took it from the man, fingers gone numb. Yes, there was the mark on the cup that fit over his thigh. The metal joint replacing his knee. A picture flashed of her stroking the leg that slid into the cup, and the memory of his groan of pleasure. She nodded. "It's the one he wears when he's more active."

"It was found near the crash." The man who spoke looked as if he'd been in a wreck himself.

"What crash?"

"We think a chopper. At least it looked like a crash from a distance—same kind of light display. Some of the guys split off to check once we found—" He nodded at the prosthesis in her arms. "—I came in to report and gather some more help. Maybe get some extra eyes on the scene."

"You couldn't call?"

He frowned as if searching for words. "I'm not completely convinced about our phones. Even the 'project' phones."

"You think there's a problem with Major Powers's equipment?"

Ty grimaced. "Wouldn't be the first time."

"Maybe not what Powers supplied as much as what actually came into our hands. Mike Thompson was in charge of some of the procurement."

"His name keeps coming up. You think he's involved." Lana's level voice made it a statement of fact.

"I know we saw him in that group with the captain this morning. I'd like to think our past involvement would make him more loyal, more likely to be helping than harming but—" He shook his head once. "I'm not making assumptions."

"Where?"

"Out in the desert north of town."

She took a deep breath then looked closer at the prosthesis. New gouges cut into the metal and traces of what could be blood were on the cup. "How did it get off?" she said almost to herself.

"What do you mean?"

"The connection is pretty secure, it doesn't slide off easily. Unless—" Her mind gave her pictures of a crash impact so violent it could— "Did they find a body?"

"No bodies yet. This was on the ground near the crash site."

Lana looked over at the speaker, lean and hard bodied, dressed down in camouflage. "Crash site?"

"We had a report of a helo downed by what seems to be a missile, probably shoulder load. Surface to Air."

She looked closer, recognized more of his face when he turned his head. "You were with the team that—"

"Yes, ma'am, the extraction last week."

"Wasn't Captain Roberts working with you?"

"That's what's so puzzling. We had a code word message to meet him, but when we arrived he was already gone."

She looked around the room. "We?"

She heard several quiet acknowledgments.

One of the men toward the back stepped forward. "I got to the meeting point before anyone else and saw the captain with some tough-looking dudes, like Slavic?" When she nodded, he went on. "And I coulda sworn I saw Mike Thompson, or someone who looked a lot like him."

"Mike Thompson?" Lana said through tight lips.

"Yeah, you know him?"

"He was on the first security team at the cottage. The team leader moved him away when he tried to approach Adam." She indicated with her head the man who stood behind her.

"You say Adam called you?" Roz broke in, sitting up and leaning forward

"Yes, ma'am."

"Did you talk with him directly?"

"No, ma'am, through a message. But the message had the code words, so I knew it was him."

"That's what Adam said," Lana mused. "He wouldn't have left except whoever called 'had the code.' Was the code the same for everyone on that team?"

"It was different for some of us."

"Was all of that old team with you?"

He looked around. "As many as were in the area. I haven't seen some of them for a few years."

"Who outside the team would know those codes?"

"No one, ma'am. It was all pretty hush hush."

"What about Mike Thompson?"

"No, he was on another team."

"That's what Adam said to him. Their teams worked together, but they were never on the same team." Lana started to pace, realized she was wearing the decorative shoes. She toed them off, leaned over, grabbed them,, and threw them against the wall as hard as she could.

"Lana—" Ty took a step toward her then stopped when she pivoted on her bare heel.

"That damned Russian asshole. I need some clothes." She looked around the room as if deciding whose rough gear would fit her.

"You need to take a breath."

"I need to get out of these damned stupid clothes."

Roz stepped forward, shrugging out of her casual over-shirt.

"Not even. I need something I can run in. Your clothes will just trip me."

"I'd think the bigger, the better. You're about to get naked in a roomful of strangers, sweetie."

Lana looked around, bit back a laugh that might have been a sob. Someone stepped up behind her, and she felt the warmth of a hand approaching her shoulder. She twisted away, bringing up her fist in a defensive move, utilizing skills drilled into her by recent sparring.

Ty stepped back, hands raised. "Sorry." His expression was strained, and he glanced over at Roz then back to Lana. "What can we do to help?"

"Find me some damned clothes. Take me to this so-called crash site, after I talk to that damned Russian."

"Aleksei? Why?"

"Something he said just now. I think he was talking with Short and Temple and believed he had correct information." She took a deep breath then closed her eyes, trying to dredge up his exact words, trying to hold herself together. "Hearing that some of his men might have been in that group—"

"Take a minute, or ten," Ty said.

"He doesn't have a minute."

⁕⁕⁕

This time when Lana's heels hit the hallway tiles, there was little sound, and she was not alone. Roz and Ty flanked her with Adam's friends behind them. Her new clothing—jeans and a comfortable shirt—registered as a background to the thoughts she refused to let overcome her. The clothes were mostly retrieved from her apartment the week before and kept safe in the observation rooms. As if Adam had known she would need—no, she would not go there. Not yet.

She clutched the prosthesis in her hand like a weapon as they blew past the perky receptionist, ready to slam open the doors. Before they could do some damage that might make her feel better, the doors opened, revealing Aleksei and Winfield, standing in the center of the room. An arm moved in front of her—two arms, one from each side—Ty and one of Adam's men, stopping her before she could storm in.

"Hold up. Someone opened those doors."

At a nod from Winfield, a man stepped into sight then another one from the other side. They pushed the doors completely against the wall then crossed to stand behind Aleksei. Lana strode into the room.

"What did you mean?"

Aleksei frowned at her, obviously confused by the question. "I do not understand."

"You said your men were not available. What did you mean?"

"They are not my men."

"They travel with you, follow your directives, stay around you. Whose men are they?"

"They came with me, yes. I knew I would need...what you call muscle...to deal with—" He waved his hand in her direction.

"With who? Me? I'm hardly your weight, much less a trained fighter."

"But I was led to believe—" The expression of shame and confusion on his face might have been laughable.

"What, 'the agents' spun you a fairy tale, so you went to Rent-A-Thug?"

"They were loaned to me in exchange for information concerning my sister." He shrugged. "I am a businessman, not a crime lord. These people came to me with information and assistance."

"You brought mob enforcers with you—snuck them into the country? And now you've lost control of them?"

He nodded, not meeting her eyes. "They grew bored and received an offer from someone else for a short-term job."

"Short term. Kidnap the person who was helping reveal a human trafficking ring? Good job, Aleksei. Way to honor your sister's memory."

He looked up, rage pulling at his face, then blanched when she raised the prosthesis.

"This is what they left of Captain Roberts."

Before she could follow through on her desire to smash Aleksei in the face, Roz took a grip on her forearm.

Lana nodded. "You're right. He's—Adam's—going to need this."

Aleksei never took his gaze off the prosthesis. "What are you saying?"

"We found Captain Roberts's leg at what seems like a crash site," Adam's team member bit off the words. "Looks like someone took down a chopper with a SAM, but we didn't find any bodies. Your thugs fond of setting up fake crash sites?"

"They are not *my* thugs."

"Evidence proves otherwise. Why did you ask me earlier about my bodyguard?" Lana spoke almost casually.

"A matter of curiosity. Every time I had seen you before he was at your side, protecting you, guarding you." He smirked. "A mercenary, protecting you. No doubt being paid with favors."

She took a step forward, raising the leg.

A deep voice spoke behind her. "Mercenary?" One of the team moved in front of her. "Captain Roberts served his country for over a decade, decorated more than once for gallantry above and beyond. He lost his leg, and nearly his life, attempting to protect the rest of his unit, engaged at that time in defending a village school in a country we still cannot name. He is the reason my kids and wife have someone coming home to them. What have *you* done that's remotely as worthy of attention?"

Aleksei blanched. "I had no idea. I was told—"

Lana glared at him. "It seems you were told, and you believed, many things that were not true. Have you ever thought about fact checking?"

"They were government workers, helping to protect the innocent."

"Government workers, yes. Protecting? Or keeping themselves in touch with those they could use and abuse?" She blew out a breath then turned her back on him.

დაფი

The cold rage took her back down the hallway, into the glaring sun and busy streets.

"You're going back out. I'm going with you."

His "Ma'am" conflicted with Ty's "No, you're not."

She ignored Ty, focusing on the edgy man in front of her. "I'm either going with you, or I'll go alone and risk blowing the scene. Neither one of us want that."

"Lana, you can't. It's too dangerous."

Roz's mellow voice broke in, a thread of steel under the humor. "That's not a decision you make for her." She put her hand on Ty's arm, fingers pressing in while she looked over at Lana. "Anything you need from us?"

Lana shook her head but nodded to the soldier. After a moment, his shoulders sagged before he spoke to the rest of his team. "We need someone here on communications. And some leathers for Ms. Greene. We're taking bikes."

დაფი

Pink. They had found a pink motorcycle for her, with matching helmet and pink stripes on the black leather jacket. "You have got to be kidding."

"Best we could do in the timeframe." They'd borrowed the bike, and the outfit, from one of the show girls who spent her off time on the road. The bike might be girly on the outside, but the engine gave a satisfactory roar. "You're sure you know how to ride?"

"Well enough to know the basic controls." She glanced over as he straddled his own well-used cycle. "Yours, or borrowed?"

"Mine. There's almost enough open road out here to help me relax." He fiddled with the controls, with the saddle bags. "And yeah, the pink bike keeps up well enough."

Lana nodded. "Thank her for her generosity."

❧❦❧

There was a definite feeling of freedom, racing down the road with nothing between her and freedom but a helmet and some leather clothing. Lana pushed away any hesitation, and doubts, and let the evening air flow around her. As they slipped through the sky-filling early sunset, she let possible outcomes drift through her mind until she had to push them away and only remember Adam's last words before they parted:

*'I'm telling you, this time, I can't. I can't walk away. When we're done, when we've figured this out, I will come back. I won't be able to walk away.'*

Nor could she let him. "Hold on, Adam. We're coming."

❧❦❧

They gathered with some of the other searchers at a rest area with at least minimal cover. Lana took the opportunity to avail herself of the restroom, almost shivering in the chilled air. The leader was waiting when she came out, the water she'd splashed against her face already dry.

"You don't fully realize how hot and dry it is when you're in a car."

"No, ma'am. It's one of the reasons I like tearing up the roads on my bike. It keeps me just a little closer to reality."

She drew in a breath of air that felt almost cool. The evening light tinted low scrub bushes, darker lines showing a myriad of depressions and arroyos. "Some reality." He could be in one of those cracks in the ground, hiding from the day's brutal heat and not found soon enough. A small pained whimper escaped her, and she felt the man's hand rest reassuringly on her shoulder.

"The captain's always been tough, ma'am. Lately, he seems even more focused than normal."

"But he's—" She gulped the words back, appalled she'd allow that much emotion out in front of a stranger. Still… "He's missing—"

"That's never slowed him down." He rested his hands on her upper arms, turning her to face him. "I've known the captain a long time, and I have never seen him like this. You've become the most important thing in his world. If he has to crawl out of that desert, Captain Roberts will come back to you."

She gasped then stopped another near sob. No time for drama, not now while Adam was—

Dredging up a sincere smile, she nodded her thanks. After a moment, he dropped his hands and stepped away. "You ready to move on, ma'am?"

Lana allowed herself to show impatience. "Tell me, does your biker chick let you call her ma'am."

A bright white smile flashed across his bearded face. "Yes, ma'am, she does. Sometimes. But she always gets even."

Lana felt a bubble of laughter rise up and squelched it. Obviously not fast enough.

"Don't feel bad about laughing. It's a natural reflex. Dark humor, maybe, but it helps ease the constant strain and lets us think better."

They were about to get back on the bikes, back to searching through the night, when a radio crackled. The faint voice that emerged carried an undercurrent of stress. "Sir? I think there's someone you need to talk to. Bring Ms. Greene."

ᛞᏜᛞ

The man was almost a caricature. Leaned down to essentials covered by skin dried dark. Battered hat. Stained shirt, torn jeans, both washed almost white. A hint of beard, but not as if he forgot to shave. More like he didn't bother. The small diner was the same as its counterparts across the country, floor swept clear of dust, metal napkin holders on old tables, and a pervasive odor of always-brewed coffee. The old man straightened when he saw the pink biker leathers and stood when Lana pulled off the scarf she'd tied over her hair. Before he could talk, the young team member made introductions. "Can you tell Ms. Greene what you said earlier, please?"

"I run a horse rescue. Mostly what we get from the sales but also dumps from people who abandon their horses."

They nodded, but Lana wondered why she'd been brought here to listen to him. She restrained her restless movement.

"Last night, night before, some asshole blew out one of our fences then hazed the horses. Poor things, some of them are barely able to walk, but they ran every which way. Took most of the day to get them back."

*Get to the point*, Lana nearly growled, blood pounding in her head.

"Finally got all of them back 'cept for this mare we brought in last week. Dumped on the side of the road and obviously abused before then. Skinny as could be. Took a while to find her." He took a gulp of his coffee, wiped off his mouth.

Lana realized he was enjoying the stage. "Can you get to the point? Please?"

He peered at her through narrowed eyes as if thinking to chastise her impatience. Then he smiled. "Damnedest thing I ever did see. That spooky old mare was creeping across the desert with a man hangin' on her side. He'd stumble, and she'd step over to support him. He sorta tried to get on her back but couldn't quite make it."

Lana stepped closer.

"Not surprising, seein' as how he was as beat up as she was and missing a leg."

❧

"No, you are not driving the bike. Or a car. Or anything else. You will let one of us drive you."

Lana pulled her arm away from him, tensing to escape his restraint. The men formed a ring around her. "You're holding up the parade. Let me go so we can get to the hospital."

"More of a clinic," the old timer said as if apologizing.

"Better, probably. Harder to find him. We still don't want to waste any more time. Ms. Greene, please."

Lana looked at the key ring in her hand, noticing how the pink crystal balls knocked against each other. "Sorry. Of course." She handed the keys over to one of the men, moved to the waiting dusty SUV. A truck roared up, slid to a stop. The men all turned, crouching. Then standing when Roz rolled down the window. "Hop in."

Lana let the soldiers boost her into the high rise truck while Roz kept talking, sharing information that helped to soothe nerves.

"We got a message probably the same time you did.

Still not sure what phones are safe, but we had one of the new ones."

"You know where he is?" Lana grabbed at the seat belt and strapped in while Ty waited before he tested the truck's acceleration. Motorcycles surrounded them, escorting them from the rough restaurant parking lot then down the paved road.

"More or less. Guess the old timer finally blabbed just before you got there. He was holding out until he was sure it was safe to tell. One of the guys must have mentioned your name, or Ty's."

Ty spoke but didn't take his eyes off the road or the escort. "It's a small clinic, which is good. But we don't know who else might have sussed this out. So until we're there…" When they got to the clinic, he kept up his comforting chatter as they hurried down the hall. "Last time I did this was in Georgia. Devin was half wild until he got to Sydney. She was having some false labor pains, cramps, something. Roz was in another room, some yahoo scared her."

"Told me Sydney hadn't made it." Roz's voice was grim, her long legs eating up the hallway, but still not keeping up with Lana, who realized they were nattering on, trying to keep her relaxed until they reached the curtain at the end of the hallway, offering her comfort and a place in their lives.

Two of Adam's men were already there, on guard. They nodded at Lana but narrowed their eyes at Ty and Roz. During the standoff, Lana slipped through the curtain.

There were no machines helping him breathe, just a small tube slipped under his nose—cannula, her mind defined it—to offer more oxygen. A single bag of what looked like plain fluids led to another tube, snaking down to tape on his arm. His darker than before arm showed bruises even darker in so many places she was afraid to reach out, to touch him and convince herself he was there. He lay very still, with his eyes tightly shut, the lines in the skin deeply etched as though he was holding in the pain. His eyes slid open, shut, then opened wider, green sharpening as he focused on her face. "Hey there, Goldilocks." Barely a whisper but his mouth twitched, and his finger beckoned.

Lana stepped forward, extending her arm, then her hand, until she could touch that finger. She still stood, keeping her back straight, not quite touching her knees to the bed. His finger immediately hooked behind hers, and he pulled at her relentlessly until she fell to her knees next to the bed where she could hide her face against the sheets. His finger released hers, and she felt it touch the top of her head.

"I never wanted to care for anyone this way. It's messy, and it's scary—" he said. She heard him take a shallow breath. "—but I'm finding out it's part of being alive. Really alive."

"I didn't want it either. Caring this much—it makes me vulnerable."

"But it's worth it?" His voice rasped, barely above a whisper.

She gulped and took a chance. "Oh, yeah. So worth it." And she edged a little closer until she could nestle her face against his body and take a deeper breath, filling herself with Adam. Stealing a brief span of time for them. Until a recognizable voice growled from the other side of the curtain. "We could have used you guys in Georgia."

"Flattery will get you nowhere." The reply was polite but firm. "Sir."

Roz laughed, the rich bawdy sound bringing a gentle movement under Lana's face. No doubt as much of a chuckle as Adam could manage.

His strained whisper wasn't much louder. "That floor's got to be cold and hard under your knees, Goldilocks. And I don't think my guys can keep out the crowd for much longer." He accompanied his words with a nudge to her shoulder.

Lana used her hands against the mattress to push herself up, wincing as a myriad of bruises made themselves known—including, she noticed, on her thighs and rear. She pulled over a stool and eased onto it, wincing, while Adam kept a hold on her fingers.

He leaned his head back against the pillow, but that smile slid back onto his lips. "Is that actually a pink cycle suit?"

"Long story. I'll tell you later." She looked over at the curtains, assessing the increasing volume of comments. "You ready?"

He closed his eyes but nodded. "As I'll ever be."

# Chapter 19

The room became even smaller as Ty and Roz crowded in. Adam's men looked into the room then stepped back, once more taking up protection positions. Questions tumbled over each other.

"How are you feeling?"

"How did you get here?"

Lana held up her free hand. "Hold up, is Powers coming? Adam shouldn't have to tell this more than once."

"He's aware," Ty said. "But we're not sure how far behind he is."

"I'm not sure how long Adam can talk—" Lana began then looked down at the pressure on her fingers.

"I'm good for now," he said in that low raspy tone. "You'll have to share with Powers."

Ty pulled in another stool for Roz then leaned against the wall near the hospital bed. "That works for us."

Lana offered Adam the cup with a straw, and he leaned forward to suck in some water then eased back. "How much do you know already?"

"If it helps, we know you went to what you thought was a gathering of some of your old team. But you ended up with Aleksei's goons." Lana's voice sounded calm, even to her own ears. She knew her expression was anything but calm. "There was a crash." She stopped to gulp air.

"It's okay." He squeezed her fingers. "You need to sit down." Once she was on the rolling stool, he started to speak in short sentences. "Yeah, total set up. Shoulda known when I saw Mike Thompson there. They overpowered me, took off flying low. Dumped me on the way out. Pulled off my leg first." He looked up at Lana.

"We have it. Some of your team went looking as soon as they realized you'd left the gathering point before they got there." Her throat tightened up with the memory.

"I don't remember a lot. I woke up with something rubbing my face. Turns out it was a horse. Nothing like any of Ty's. Kinda scrawny, but it gave me something to grab onto and lean on."

"Old guy mentioned he went looking for the horse and found you."

"He dragged me into his truck's back seat. Full of stuff. I kinda ended up on the floor, so doubt anyone saw me. Dropped me off here, said he needed to get back to the horse." Adam started coughing, and Lana reached for the water cup.

"This patient needs to rest." The authoritative voice belonged to a middle-aged man with a tired face and a clean lab coat over faded jeans. His name tag read Sommers.

Ty swiveled his head to look over at the doctor. "How bad was he?"

"Another day, even a half day out there without water, he wouldn't have made it. At best, he would have risked severe kidney damage. He'll be okay now if he takes it easy a few days."

Someone outside the curtains snorted.

"That's what I thought." The doctor managed a small smile. "*Try* to take it easy. Lots of fluids, of course. I'll have a few prescriptions for you."

Lana stood and stepped forward. "You're saying if we'd been a little later, he'd be dead?"

"Or so severely compromised he'd need extensive critical care for an extended period of time. Kidney complications, just for starters."

"Right now, only the people in this room know he was found in time?" Roz asked as if only mildly interested.

Ty straightened from leaning against the wall to rest his hand on her shoulder. It hadn't been all that long since Roz was rescued in the nick of time—by the man on the bed in front of them.

Lana turned her head, watching Adam's face. "I would be extremely angry if my bodyguard was not up to protecting me while I checked out that recent shipment."

Adam moved his head then winced. "You can't—"

"Oh, honey, you just watch me. They can't get away with this crap. This has gone too far." She flashed a confident smile, settling the persona of a ball-busting executive around herself like a familiar coat.

"Dominatrix Lana?"

"Amazon Lana?"

Roz's voice cut through the comments. "How much would his loss affect you?"

Lana lifted her head abruptly. "I have not needed a man to fulfill my life." But the words sounded hollow, and she looked down at their linked hands.

A smile flickered across his dry lips under the covering of healing salve.

"Shit," she whispered, knowing everything was different now. His smile spread, though he winced from the pain of dry lips stretching. She felt the tears she'd suppressed filling her eyes and tried to turn away.

His fingers tightened. "No more hiding," he whispered, his voice harsh. No doubt from his dry throat. But there was the hint of a sheen in his green eyes.

"For either one of us?" she whispered back.

He nodded then took a deep breath, coughing again on the exhale.

The doctor stepped forward. "We need to move this meeting out of the room so my patient can rest."

Ty looked over. "Can you—"

"Play some conspiracy game to keep him safe? As long as it doesn't harm the patient or impinge on professional ethics."

"You served," Adam said after a large drink of water.

"Several tours. Couldn't deal with big hospitals once I got out, but this place works out just right."

"Our actual goal is keeping him alive."

The doctor's attention diverted to Adam's face. He nodded at what he saw there. "I wondered if some dissembling would be necessary," he said, escorting them from the room. "But for now, he does need to rest." He turned off the overhead light as he closed the door.

In the sudden gloom, Lana peered down at Adam. "Are you going to be okay?"

"So the doctor says. Hold on." He fumbled for the bed buttons and raised his head. "That's better. Come sit."

"Should I?"

"Can't keep the patient from getting better, can we?" He edged himself over far enough in the narrow bed for her to rest against his hip.

She looked at the wall above him, the machines offering relief, everywhere but at his face. Until his fingers pressed against hers another time.

"I'm down here."

She nodded, glanced at him, then away. Then she let herself collapse against his shoulder, bearing most of her weight on her elbow. Until he reached around her back and pulled her closer. Silent sobs wracked her body while she hid her face against his neck.

"I probably need a shower, but you don't need to supply the water," he rasped but did not let her pull away. "I dreamed of this, you know? Or maybe hallucinated. Or maybe it was that damned ugly horse."

At this, she did manage to raise her head, this time not looking away, not hiding her distress. "Horse?"

"Woke me up. Damnedest thing, when I saw all that blonde hair, I thought for a minute you'd found me. But your lips just never felt that..." He paused suggestively, grinned when her eyebrows raised. "...rubbery."

This brought a watery chuckle, and she began to straighten. At first, he resisted then let his hand slide along her back. Touching, soothing, no longer restraining. He ended with his fingers stroking along her chin. She turned her head enough to press her lips into his palm without breaking eye contact.

A voice came through the slightly opened door. "The ambulance is here. Looks like Major Powers came with it."

"No time."

"No time, now."

∾≫∾

"You were supposed to take care of him." Lana's voice cut through the early morning chill like a crystal knife. "You assured me you could protect us without compromising the mission. *Look* at what your protection did."

Secured in the dark of a body bag, Adam let himself grin. Lana played the outraged queen to perfection, scorn dripping off her voice. He could almost see her—head up, shoulders thrown back—while she tossed invectives at Powers's face.

"I should have known you wouldn't bother to go out of your way to keep him safe. All you care about are your stupid projects, your convoluted games. I hope you're proud of yourself."

Powers rumbled in perfect counterpoint. "Come now, Ms. Greene. You certainly could not expect us to protect Captain Roberts when he was on a separate mission."

"I would expect you to attempt to live up to your vaunted reputation of protecting your people. Or did your publicity department make that up?"

The gurney moved Adam away from their argument, and he felt the legs fold under his head, lifting him into the back of a closed vehicle. Ambulance, no doubt. Someone settled in next to him, and footsteps moved to the driver's seat.

"Phew, that's some woman you have there," the man sitting next to him said. In spite of the admiring words, something about the tone suggested caution, and Adam didn't respond. "It's okay, buddy, we're out of sight now. You don't need to keep playing possum."

Faint sounds, an impression of movement, led to only one conclusion. In spite of the friendly words, danger rode in the back of this ambulance.

Adam tensed, trying to gather strength in limbs that were entirely too weak. After all the planning, all the effort, to end up like this.

The vehicle slammed to a stop, and he heard a drawling voice from the front, "Yeah, I don't think so, buddy," Then the sound of a scuffle, over his head.

Ty Randolph. Shit, who was with Lana? Now Adam struggled seriously against the restraints.

"Take it easy, dammit." Hands grabbed at the straps around his chest, his knees, then an arm slid behind his shoulders. Someone unzipped the bag, slipped a pillow behind his shoulders, and pulled the covering off his face. Ty's tanned face came into view, scowl fully occupying his expression.

"Lana," Adam managed to gasp. "Who's—"

Ty dealt with the oxygen support as he answered. "Who's with her? Your team, of course. The only way they would not guard her was if they were guarding you. Since you were supposed to be dead..."

Adam nodded, then another worry moved in him, and he opened his mouth.

"Roz is off to a book meeting. Library, I think. Powers has a team on her. He knows what will happen if she or Lana is hurt. Or you, for that matter." Ty looked up at the driver, who had continued along the rough road at a suitable speed for non-emergency transport.

"Got that right," the driver said over his shoulder. "Powers slips up, Sydney's coming. Which means Starke. None of us want that."

"Damned straight." Ty nodded. "So you, Captain, just concern yourself with getting better so you can get back into the game." He sat back then looked over to the side of the ambulance, where a crumpled figure didn't look like he'd be moving for a while.

∽∾∽

Motorcycle engines grumbled, the sound magnified

in the underground parking structure until the four inside sounded like an entire pack. Lana took a step toward Adam's team as they prepared to pull out. She'd stripped out of the pink leathers, but she still felt the need to be out going and doing.

"You cannot go with them," Powers said, his voice sliding under the rumble.

Lana frowned at the bland man. "Why not?"

"Your cover story is that you're emotionally distressed. You have to be seen here or in the city. Not searching through the desert. Otherwise, the agents will be suspicious and move the girls."

"You don't think they've already been moved?"

"We haven't observed unusual activity in the area. In particular, not vehicular traffic."

"What about digital traffic? Internet noises?"

He nodded as if approving her question. "That's a concern, and, yes, we're monitoring that traffic."

"I hate just sitting around doing nothing."

"Doing—being directly involved—led to your kidnapping in Utah."

"Syd's ex-husband is dead."

"Yes, one monster is gone. There are many more to take his place."

"I could ask why you're helping, but I think you despise these people as much as I do."

"Quite possibly more." He led her to the elevator where an agent held the door open. "We need to be inside." He paused as the door slid shut. "I was not aware, or completely aware, of your reason for being in Utah. You concealed your intent excellently."

She nodded, acknowledging his implied praise. "Acting that way, making them believe I was soulless, at times in the past I was able to get closer to the victims. I said I needed to examine the merchandise."

She felt her mouth draw tight in disgust.

The elevator opened onto a bland hallway, directly across from another guarded doorway. Powers produced an identity card, which the guard studied. Lana patted at her pockets then shrugged. The guard pulled a tablet from his cargo pants, thumbed up a picture, and compared it to her. Then he nodded. She had the feeling he was suppressing a comment.

Powers settled on a couch, reached for a cup on a nearby table, noticed it was empty, and set it down. One of the collection of waiting men came over with a teapot to fill the cup and leave the pot. "You were able to convince them of your avarice for much longer than I would have ever thought you could."

"People see what they want to believe. In this case, I played the part of a soulless individual, more interested in the bottom line. I made sure none of the girls were hurt further so the merchandise didn't lose value."

He nodded. "A reasonable excuse. Were you able to move any of the 'merchandise' yourself?"

"A couple times, then I think someone got wise to me and started to pay more attention. When possible, I added an identifier—maybe a scarf, or a piece of jewelry, or a hair ornament. It would show up in some of the on line notices, and I could on occasion identify where the girl had been. Even if the girls traded off between them. Then—" She looked away, took a breath. "Then I met these ever-so-helpful agents. At first, they said they were suspicious since I had been around or close to or connected to several potential trafficking cases. I was able to convince them I'd been helping the girls as much as I could. So they asked me to help them."

"Asked you, or blackmailed you?"

The mellow voice came from behind her.

Lana turned her head as far as possible, which wasn't

much. "Sydney's right, you are scary smart."

Roz stepped into the seating area, holding out a mug of hot water for Lana, then settled on one of the chairs with her own cup of coffee.

"You're supposed to be—"

"Book thing, library, blah, blah." Roz waved a hand then pushed her long fingers through her cap of dark hair. "Someone set Adam up. Possibly someone in his old team, sad to say. Ty wanted me safe—and a possibility of sussing out the traitor, or traitors."

"You've got people watching the library," Lana mused. "Brilliant!"

Roz nodded graciously. "Thank you."

Powers cleared his throat. "Yes, well. Getting back to the former discussion, when the evidence is so blatant, there is not a lot of need for deduction."

Lana nodded and looked down at her lap, where her fingers stroked a thick silver bracelet she'd pushed up her arm. "Blackmail. At first, trying to connect me with the abduction and trafficking, though I kept proof of the opposite. I thought the whole maneuver was over the top since I was already working to help the girls. But too many projects went sour. Too few girls made it out to safe houses. I got suspicious. When I started checking into the agents, the more overt threats began."

"The so-called murder."

She nodded. "The death of the pedophile son of a powerful business/crime person. Dee Dee disappearing at the same time seemed to be an afterthought, as if she was just collateral damage. A promising life cut short by a monster. The young man's family had hidden his proclivities, turned a blind eye to his actions, for years. Finding him the way I did, they couldn't deny what he'd become. Professionally, I was in the clear."

"Privately?"

"Personally, emotionally, I was trashed. Privately, too much went wrong after that to be coincidence. I thought I could get away, but it seemed they were watching me too closely, so I tried to blend in with the largest group in town."

"The rodeo?" Roz leaned forward, while Powers took a sip of his tea and settled back as if observing an inconsequential discussion.

"Right. I knew there could be some problems with runaways or maybe just confused kids at any large event so I checked them out when I could. After a while, certain characteristics stand out—maybe some bruising, a way of looking around them. Once in a while, I could help someone get home—or get somewhere else safe." She jerked her head, tossing the stray hair off her face. "We've been through this already."

"Yes, we have, but right now we have time, and you need to relax."

"I am relaxed."

Roz snorted, a strange sound coming from such an elegant woman. "Lana, you're on the verge of shattering. If you do not let yourself come down from time to time, you'll burn out."

Lana felt her mouth twist in a wry almost smile. "Too late for that."

Aleksei spoke from where he leaned against the wall. "I believe there was also a purpose for me to hear this story." He stepped forward. "What I had known before was what those agents told me, and some short statements from Ms. Greene, which I now realize were intentionally spoken. Hearing more detail makes it easier for me to understand how she has worked, what she has done to present herself as corrupt while helping behind the scenes." He nodded briefly in Lana's direction. "It seems I owe you an apology."

Lana nodded in return, but Roz snorted, her face creasing into a frown. "You might owe her more than a simple apology. You do realize those goons you brought into the country killed Adam Roberts."

Lana let herself believe these words and brought up the emotions she would have felt.

His expression tightened. "Yes, Ms. Summerton, I do realize this. And I am trying my best to mitigate the results of their actions."

Lana reached out to the taller woman, rested a hand on her arm. "Roz, right now we have to move on. Later?"

Roz nodded. "Later. Maybe we can invite Mr. Novakov to Stormhaven for a trail ride." And she offered a wide, insincere smile.

"The both of you…" Aleksei frowned, seeming to search for words. "…neither one of you is what you seem to be. At first, I believed you flighty and shallow, as most Americans seem. But you use that as a weapon."

"Your prejudices—your narrow-minded unfounded misconceptions—have put a good man—" Lana hesitated, looking over at Roz. "—good men at risk."

"I realize this and hope to be able to overcome my misconceptions."

Roz stood, strode across the room, turned back to confront Aleksei. "My fiancé, my partner, my lover, is out there without his usual back up. He is trusting people he met not long ago because he did not allow himself to be restrained in his judgments."

Aleksei's strident cell phone ring intruded.

Lana managed a small smile. "Saved by the bell."

"Or the military march."

"This is Novakov." He nodded. "Yes, I wish to see them before payment. As I told you several times before." Another nod. "And the woman? She will be there?" He frowned. "I believe I made it very clear that you will have the woman there. I have a particular reason." His eyebrows pulled together as he listened. "You will fill my requests, or we will have no more reason to do business." He swiped his thumb across the phone, breaking the connection. Then he looked up to meet the eyes of those watching, an obvious question on his face.

"You've decided to believe the truth," Roz said dryly.

"As your Major Powers pointed out, when the evidence is so overwhelming, one must believe."

"Are you willing to help find real answers?" Lana posed the question as if the response had little meaning for her, though she could feel her heart stutter while she waited for his reply.

The room was silent, all attention on the frowning man. He nodded slowly. "I believe I could do no less for the memory of my sister."

$\infty$

The door closed quietly behind Aleksei as he left, and the tension in the room reduced with an almost audible sigh. One of the guards stepped out from the shadows, looking up from his phone. "Done. They took out the driver before he got in, and Randolph got the EMT. Both are under guard." He glanced at Lana. "Captain Roberts is fine, ma'am. Angry he couldn't participate."

Lana nodded, pushing away the emotions she'd allowed to show. "Good." She turned to Powers, who continued to sit in the comfortable chair, sipping his tea. "You will take better care of him this time?"

Before Powers could speak, the guard did. "Ma'am, Captain Roberts can take care of himself, but Randolph is worth a whole unit. Since we've weeded out the plants, they'll be fine."

She nodded then grabbed a breath, and straightened her back, throwing back her shoulders, and reached for the mantle of—

The guard spoke into her concentration. "You have the leg?"

She reached behind her and raised her arm, showing the prosthetic leg firmly embedded in her clenched fist. Then she felt her control slip into unexpected humor. "Where else could you say something like that?"

"Truth be told, ma'am, I've been waiting to say that ever since Roberts lost his leg."

"That's…" She struggled to find the right word.

"Pretty sick, yeah." He flashed a grin in her direction before continuing. "Glad to be sharing it with you."

Powers cleared his throat and stepped between them. "Yes, amusing. Now that Captain Roberts is secured, we need to understand the purpose behind the kidnapping and disposing of him without first killing him."

Lana moved toward a table. "Could it be dividing forces and eliminating the support of any of Adam's team?"

"Perhaps it was meant as a distraction for Ms. Greene?"

Lana shrugged. "Maybe." She set the prosthesis on the table with a quiet thunk and sat in one of the folding chairs. "Along with that so-called discovery of the holding facility?"

"Precisely. You were meant to think there was no reason to concern yourself with the missing young women. This would leave Captain Roberts free to respond to his call for aid."

The guard took his own seat. "That doesn't completely track, Major. Our entire team was called in, which doesn't fit into your scenario."

Powers nodded, reaching for a mug. "Which brings

up another concern. What was Mr. Thompson's role? He appeared to be working for or with the people who kidnapped the captain."

"Yes, the same people, it seems, who called in the entire team then left before we all arrived."

"Where is Mike Thompson?" Lana asked, looking around at the assembled team. "Has anyone seen or heard from him?"

Heads shook in the negative. "Not since he left with the captain and that bunch of thugs."

"It's almost like he was hustling them onto the chopper before we could get there."

"Protecting your team? Keeping you from harm?"

"Might be."

"Strange way for someone to act if he's gone to the dark side," Lana mused.

"I did not realize you were a fellow geek."

"It's the most descriptive phrasing, whatever the source."

"Possibly the most accurate. We don't have a location for Mr. Thompson, nor do we have a clear history or motive."

"He was always kind of a jerk—a glory hound," one of the men in the background muttered.

"For the most part, we could depend on him in a fire fight."

"For the most part?" Lana asked.

"He'd get odd ideas about how to proceed that might or might not interfere with orders."

She raised both eyebrows. "Did that cause problems for him with command?"

"It could, but he was usually good at avoiding censure."

"And he got out before some of his shenanigans came to light," the other team member said.

Lana shook her head. "Shenanigans? Really?"

"Trying to expand my vocabulary, been reading to my niece." His smile spoke of how much he appreciated being around to be able to read to her.

"Right. Is there something significant about Mr. Thompson's actions?" Powers interjected, sounding impatient.

One of the team members leaned forward. "That's the issue, isn't it? What's significant? What made him do what he did when he did it?"

"Take it a step sideways" another member suggested. "What sent Aleksei's goons off at that time?"

"You mean what did we do to set them off?" Lana asked.

Powers scowled. "Possibly. If that's interconnected somehow."

"I think it's all connected somehow." Lana allowed herself to express confusion, knowing she could trust this company with her true reactions.

One of the team members stood up to start pacing. "So what's the timeline?"

"Adam—Captain Roberts—and I went off the radar to a remote cabin for training. And, honestly, to get away from the surveillance."

Answers came in from around the room.

"At which point, the cockroaches started stirring up. Seriously, we started seeing a lot of what now seems like fake disturbances, putting everyone on edge."

"Then the so-called discovery."

"Right, and then the call in, separating you and the captain."

"Which he would answer since, in theory, there was no more need to search for kidnapped girls."

Lana tilted her head, looking for something that had drawn her attention. "You were reading to your niece?"

"Yeah. I spend time with the kids, give my sis a break." He grinned, happy to reveal this soft side.

"How many of you have pretty much moved on from active duty? From direct conflict?"

They looked around at each other, shrugged, then back to her.

"I think most of us. We put in our time, then more of our time. And at some point realized we were fighting the wrong battles for the wrong people and the wrong reasons."

"That same sort of thinking is why my father..." Lana trailed off then shook her head decisively. "No, I don't think there's a connection. Can't be."

"Care to elaborate?"

"I don't think my connection to who my father was has any influence on what's been happening."

"As a mercenary, or as a man of honor?" Powers asked.

"Good point. I had thought more the first. Not mercenary so much as someone who completed his contracts."

"Someone who watched out for those who could not watch out for themselves?" the team leader asked.

"That might be putting too much glory where it doesn't belong," Powers said.

"My father never worked for glory."

"Nor have you."

That silenced her while she thought a little longer. "Ah, but most people don't realize why I work, beyond what I let them think."

Powers nodded, acknowledging her statement. "Most people did not know your father. Or your sister."

She heard the muttering in the room as the team searched for clarification. "My father was a soldier, first, then became a soldier for hire, mainly so he could choose his own battles. My sister Sydney worked with him."

"Starke's wife?"

Lana felt a grin spreading. "You better never let her hear you say that."

"I'm no fool."

"To get us back on topic," Powers said, as though he didn't expect much cooperation.

"Sorry. Since I distanced myself from my father and his work, I don't think it has any bearing."

"Perhaps not. But I'm not sure we can completely dismiss the idea."

"Perhaps shelve it for now," the team leader suggested.

"As you said, to get back on topic," Powers said with his usual dry voice. "It seems the goal was to keep us off balance by taking Captain Roberts out of the operation then presenting us with a cataclysmic event that should have made it difficult for us to work, at least temporarily."

Lana nodded. "At least temporarily. During that time, move the real victims to a more secure location."

"Which we have no sure idea where." The team leader scowled. "We can spend all day playing guessing games."

"Why there?" Roz asked the room at large.

"Why where?"

"Why was Captain Robert's leg dropped in one place when he was miles away?"

"And why was he in that particular place? Good question." Lana stood, reaching for the prosthesis.

"Gentlemen, let's go see a man about a horse."

c∕∂c∕∂

They found the rancher by the horse pens, tending to

a Palomino mare with more mane than body. Hipbones protruded, almost clearly enough to see the joint between her pelvis and upper femur. Her coat was in patches of dull gold, and she lipped at the feed in her tub instead of actually eating it.

"Like I said, it was the damnedest thing, finding your man like that, with this mare."

Lana tried not to stare at the near skeletal horse. "She was out loose?"

He snorted in disgust. "Not intentionally. That damned whirly-bird spooked the stock and some of them took down the fence out that way." He pointed east, toward an area of rough terrain.

"Whirly bird?" Lana repeated. "Helicopter?"

"Chopper?" the guard added at the same time.

The old rancher shrugged. "Whichever. It buzzed the pens, got the horses all riled up, and they crashed out."

"Had the fence been damaged prior?"

"Yup. We checked that first thing. It's amazing how some people think it's a real hoot to cut up fences. That area was scheduled for some new wire when we got the time. Problem is, some of those horses were Mustangs, and they've been hunted from the air before. It made them extra nervous, 'specially as low as that jerk was flying."

"Why buzz the horses?" Lana muttered. "It doesn't make sense."

"To get someone's attention? Sir, even if you hadn't had horses get loose, would you have gone out to check the chopper or where the chopper flew?"

"No doubt, eventually. It got really low a few miles out then took off again." He turned when someone called from the end of the line of pens. "Be back in a minute."

The skinny mare lifted her head, looking their direction with dull eyes.

Lana offered her hand as a scratching post, and the mare took a partial step toward her. "Did you know about the copter buzzing the horses before this?" she asked the team leader.

"He might have said something to the others in that diner before we got there, but I'd think they'd tell me. They might've thought it was a part of taking the captain where we found him."

The mare had come close enough for Lana to stroke her rough coat. "The drop site?"

"I'd say. It could've been a day or two before anyone found him."

"Too late for the Adam. He was out there almost too long as it was."

The guard shook his head, looking out beyond the shelter's shade. "But they dropped his prosthesis miles from here."

"Either causing confusion or disrupting investigations? By dropping the prosthesis so far away, they could have had us concentrating a search there. We would have found him eventually…"

"But it would have been too late," the guard finished for her. "In the meantime, we would have used up resources better spent elsewhere."

"And those girls…" She drew a breath. "…we might have put off looking for them."

The rancher's harsh voice intruded. "What girls?"

They turned to find him entirely too close.

The guard automatically stepped between.

"Sorry, sir. We were—"

"We were discussing the reason Captain Roberts and I were in the area. I track and try to aid human-trafficking victims. The captain was helping keep me safe."

"Sex slaves?"

Lana nodded, waited for the scorn too many people

used to distance themselves from the uglier situations.

"That's worse than buzzing horses to push them over a cliff." The old man shook his head, obviously disgusted. "People make all this noise about how we're a civilized society. Maybe on the surface but underneath..." His voice trailed off, attention shifting to the horses, but Lana doubted he saw them.

"That's why we have to find the people who dropped the captain then find their bosses. Somewhere out there young women, maybe little girls, are being held. I'm afraid, in preparation to auction them off."

"You need to get there before that happens."

"Yes, sir."

"Well, why the hell are you hanging around here?"

# Chapter 20

Lana should not have felt strange, walking into the casino without Adam at her shoulder. After all, she'd only known him for…how long? Less than a month? Had it even been two weeks? She pushed the thought away as she stepped through the entrance and her heels struck the casino floor in perfect cadence. The view was the same as always: slots, hostesses, desperation, overlaid with false cheer. She still saw the secret transactions, the exchanges of currency for product, the setting up of meetings elsewhere. Most of the time, quiet men in plain suits stepped in to interfere with the arrangements and escort the groups to a more official location. And to be replaced by others ready to take advantage of fools. She shook her head, one quick toss to the side, and told herself to get down to business. Someone should be here soon. Probably Agents Short and Temple, to convince her she needed to come with them.

She wore black, of course. A more-conservative-than-usual-for-her dress, with enough width of skirt to allow a range of stride while still hugging her curves. Subtle but enticing and far more practical if—when—she needed to move. Loose sleeves fell to below her elbow, concealing the armband that helped remind her how critical her every move was and helped keep her connected to the man who had come to mean so much.

Special Agent Short's flat tones broke into her black mood. "Back at work already? You must not have missed your lover much."

"You asked to meet with me. I'm here. What do you want?" Her staccato delivery appeared to take Short by surprise. Too bad.

"They told me you would be angry."

"They? That's a convenient way to avoid the truth. You're damned right I'm angry."

"It would make you angry to lose your profit."

"My profit? You still believe that?" She poked a manicured nail into his chest. "Let me tell you. While your toy soldiers were out playing war games and…abducting…Captain Roberts—"

"They are not my 'toy soldiers.'"

"You're working with Novakov. Don't even try to deny it. He brought over those Slavic Rent-A-Thugs. While they were interfering with my work, a group of girls I'd been searching for dropped out of sight."

"You lost them? How careless."

Lana caught herself before her fist reached his stomach. "You narrow-minded asshole son of a bitch, didn't you listen to a damned thing I said?"

"Come now, Lana. You really expect us to believe you, after all the evidence we've gathered?"

"You mean the evidence you've invented?"

"It's all a matter of record. "

"Then I guess you're going to have to make up your own mind on how to proceed. For now, get the hell out of my way. This meeting has already wasted too much of my time."

She pivoted, preparing to stride out of the casino, nearly running into Special Agent Temple. His expression was nowhere near as pleasant as he usually pretended, as he reached out to grab her arm just above the elbow, pulling her to a stop. She turned into him, raising her fist to plant in his stomach, just below the ribs.

"You. Do. Not. Touch. Me."

Agent Short grabbed that arm before she could make contact. "We have a warrant that says otherwise." He smirked as he said this and reached into his coat to display his badge to the Security Guard who rushed over.

"Any problem here, miss?"

"Nothing we can't handle, thank you. Ms. Greene is late for an appointment." He shoved her toward the exit.

Lana heard footsteps behind her and, from the corner of her eye, saw her team, getting ready to shadow them. She struggled against the hold, not wanting to seem willing to go with the agents. Short shook her arm, no doubt adding to her bruise collection.

"You've already wasted enough of our time."

"I could say the same about you." She allowed them to push her toward the service hall.

"What makes you say that?" Temple asked in his fake pleasant voice.

"I know you've gotten in my way once too often. I know you have been complicit in what has been happening with the missing girls. As far as I'm concerned, you are as dirty as Aleksei Novakov or Ralph Hoffman."

"Yeah, yeah, yeah. Problem is, you have to prove what you're saying. And, sweet cheeks, in case you can't figure it out, we're in charge." He pushed her toward the parking garage, where an innocuous mid-level sedan waited. Before she could resist any further, she felt a pinprick in her arm.

"Sweet dreams, bitch."

# Chapter 21

A confusion of voices dragged Lana out of the dark void where she seemed to have fallen. Fallen, and apparently landed hard. She ached from her sore toes to the roots of her hair, possibly worse than she had after running away from Aleksei's goons the first time. Keeping her breathing shallow, she concentrated on the voices, soon sorting them into Short's nasal whine, Temple's false calm, and, yes, the heavily accented English of Aleksei Novakov. Words clarified as Aleksei raised his voice. "Your careless handling has reduced her value." Aleksei's cold voice showed only irritation.

Whose value? Were the other girls in this cold room? She hoped they weren't on what seemed to be a concrete floor covered with cheap carpet.

"Don't worry, Novakov. She's tough, she'll get over it."

"Yeah, not like she isn't accustomed to rough handling."

Rough handling, huh? Were they talking about her? And why was the carpet so harsh against her…skin? Damn them, they'd pulled off her dress. Did Aleksei throw out his words as a statement of scorn or of warning? She concentrated more on what she felt. Carpeting on her shoulder, her hip, her…she was completely nude in front of these men.

Time for her to wake up. She took a deep breath then another one, searching for clarity. Although her immediate desire was to curl in on herself, attempting to establish at least a modicum of modesty, she did not want the agents to think they had in any way shamed her. She allowed herself a small groan while she tightened her core and tried to pull herself into a sitting position, putting out a hand to control the wavering. *Ow, ow, ow.* When she got out of here, she promised to hit the gym more than once a year. When. Not if.

Head down, eyes still closed, she rolled up onto one hip, bracing a hand against the floor, resting her other arm across her thighs. Once she managed to squint her eyes open, she took a quick glance at her forearm. Huh, the armlet was still there. Now why would they leave that and take the clothing?

"Do you realize how long it will take for her back to heal? She will have to be displayed in a concealing garment." Aleksei's voice came closer, then a coarse cloth settled over her shoulders. "We also do not need for her to become chilled."

Lana opened her mouth then closed it again, trying to draw up enough saliva to talk. Best she could manage was a croak. "Yeah, red eyes and snotty noses don't do much for those glamour shots."

Hard footsteps pounded her direction, then sophisticated European shoes moved into her line of sight. "Really, Agent Short, you must not let her bait you."

"You're right. She's nothing but an amoral money-grubbing slut who thought she could scam us." From the sound of his voice, he moved away as he talked.

Lana suppressed the snort she so dearly wanted to share then raised her head to peer through bleary eyes. Swollen, bleary eyes with something holding the lashes together. Given how hot and tight her face felt, she bet she was bloated like a pre-cycle teenager. No pain yet, until she surreptitiously tried to wiggle her jaw, and pain exploded in her head. Against her will, a whimper escaped.

"You hit her in the face? Do you know how long it takes for that swelling to go down?" Aleksei still sounded more concerned with profit than damage.

"She ran into a door." The smirk was clear in Temple's voice.

"The mantra of cowardly abusers everywhere," she managed to say without wincing too much. This time both agents stepped toward her.

"You are wasting time," Aleksei said, his voice clipped, cold. "Time we do not have time to waste. Thanks to your foolish games, I need to avoid the authorities. Show me the merchandise now, or I will have to leave."

She felt the air displace as the door slammed behind the three men, leaving…silence? Certainly no breathing, no foot shuffling. Although her immediate inclination was to close her eyes, to sink back down into the welcoming dark, she knew this was probably her only chance to get out. So she'd do that. She'd get up on her feet and out the door. Right—her world went to gray, then to black, and she didn't feel the floor against her face.

*഑ഇ഑*

"Damn. Damn. Damn."

The works were probably whispered, but they hit her ears like a stadium crowd shouting. She squeezed her eyes shut, and, inside her head, she told that voice to go away.

"No can do, ma'am."

Had she said that out loud? She didn't dare raise or shake her head, so she tried to pry her eyes open and let in a sliver of light. It would also help to identify the owner of that trying-to-be-quiet voice.

"Nope, don't pass out again. We need to get you up and—" He reached for her shoulder and pulled at the scratchy blanket that had somehow stayed over her. "Oh, man, the captain is not going to be happy when he sees this."

She attempted to swallow, hoping to clear her throat. "You are possibly not aware. Captain Roberts is dead."

"I've heard that before, several times. Somehow he's still around." Large fingers grasped her bare shoulder, pushing and pulling and helping her straighten up. She heard scraping on the carpet, and a chair appeared in front of her. "You brace yourself on here. It's probably easier than me pulling you up."

Clever man, whoever he was. Between them, she managed to crawl into the hard plastic seat, the rough blanket coming with her.

By degrees, she straightened her back, and when a paper cup of water appeared in front of her face, she even tried drinking. The cup moved away, held in a large man's hand, then a somewhat familiar face appeared within her range of vision.

"You?"

"Yeah, me. Sorry, it's not one of your team."

"But you're—" *Mike Thompson, the man we'd thought had—*

"Right now I'm your best chance of getting out of here in one piece. No, don't try talking. Just concentrate on getting strong enough to stand up. Those damned agents want you ready to show off."

She lifted a corner of the blanket. "In this high-fashion ensemble."

"They sent some stuff for you to put on." He indicated a jumble of material on a bench. A memory flashed of falling onto that bench, propelled by hard hands. No doubt the "door" she'd "walked into." She shook her head.

"Nothing there looks like something I'd wear." It mostly looked diaphanous and skimpy. She shivered from more than cold. Those pink motorcycle leathers sounded pretty good right about now.

"Hold on." He stepped back, pulling his hand away from her shoulder slowly as if ready to step back in and steady her in the plastic chair. She braced herself. Time to grow a spine, or at least inject stiffener in the spine she had, sore or not. "Here." He offered a small sealed packet of pain killers. When she tried to lift her hand to take it but couldn't close her swollen fingers over the packet, he ripped it open where she could watch then pushed the edges to free the pills inside. "Can you open your mouth?"

She managed, bemused by his care as well as his business-like demeanor. With the pills in her mouth, washed down by more water, she could almost feel pain relief sliding through her body. Even if it didn't work that fast. She tried again to talk. "Why—"

"Why am I here?" His voice was muffled as he turned away to sort through the clothing. "Kind of a long story, starting out with some dumb-ass decisions."

"What changed your mind?"

"Lots of little things. Like those agents telling me you were a dealer who sampled your own stock, the person behind girls going missing. Not above hooking up for your own benefit. I didn't see that in you, and I couldn't see the captain helping out someone like that. Not to mention Ty Randolph." He turned back toward her, his hands full of draping cloth in a dark purple.

"But we were—"

"Yeah, I know. We all make mistakes. You should meet my ex-wives. Thing is, ex or not, he never bad mouthed you. Here, pick up your feet." He knelt to help ease a dress up her legs, under the blanket. "I've got my eyes shut, can you lift up?"

"It's not like I wasn't just on display for the world to see." She rested her hands on his shoulders, wincing when she leaned forward onto them. The dress slid over her hips, material barely touching her skin, and she sat down once she felt it bunch under her thighs.

"Eyes still closed, ma'am, can you help with the arms?"

Had this been Adam whispering instructions while he slid a dress up her body—

As it was, Lana complied, woodenly. Not thinking about what he might see or not see while wide straps slid over her shoulders and the blanket fell away.

"One more thing, ma'am."

"Lana."

"Nope. Sorry, ma'am." She looked down, to see his eyes tightly shut, his mouth in a grim line. "Worth my life to disrespect you. Problem is, this dress zipper is here on the side. And I don't think your fingers are up to working it. So if you could help show me where? Maybe turn a little? Ma'am?"

Sighing, she stood again, shuffled around, and lifted her arm. *Ow, ow, ow, ow.* And an itch on that place under her arm. She guided his hand toward the gaping zipper, even that much contact making her fingers ache. The dress tightened as the zipper snugged up, offering minimal support to her breasts.

Looking down, she realized there was no way to wear a bra—if she could have managed to put one on.

He stepped away, reaching behind him for a sheer shawl in the same dark purple.

"This should help a little. Hurry. They're not going to be patient for long. And those girls—"

His expression, and obvious distress, galvanized her into motion. She stepped into the low-heeled shoes he placed in front of her feet and moved into her best shuffle. Out the door, down the hall—toward the increasingly louder voices.

Before they came near the open door, Thompson muttered, "Sorry, ma'am," while he moved his hand from supporting her to restraining her. She drew in a deep breath and nodded.

*Showtime.*

The hand encircling her upper arm went from restraint to pain as low-voiced curses came from the man next to her. In keeping with her supposed drugged state, she spoke while barely opening her lips. "You want to ease up a little on the reality?" His fingers loosened but the cursing remained, his attention on the other end of the room, where a group of young girls in pretty dresses huddled together on a raised platform, arms raised against the lights. The rest of the room had just enough light for them to see the men: Aleksei's height made him stand out next to the agents, as well as some unknown men leaning forward to watch the girls. Lana leaned forward herself, squinting her swollen eyes. There was something familiar about—

She hissed a few curses of her own. Definitely not all strangers.

"What?"

"I know some of them, a little too well."

"The girls?" Horror laced through his hissed words.

"The men."

"You're not surprised about any of this, are you? How could you condone—"

"Careful with the judgment, hot stuff." She drew another deep breath, braced herself. "Okay, yell at me, shake my arm. Get their attention off those little girls."

He didn't need any more encouragement, raising his voice with a growl. "Get up here, bitch." He dragged her forward. "You've already wasted too much time."

The group of men turned as the room lights went up. "Ah, Ms. Greene, so nice of you to join us." Ralph Hoffman still had that genial expression on his fat face. "I was afraid you wouldn't make it in time."

"Mr. Hoffman, why am I not surprised to see you here? Stiffed any more contractors recently?" She looked around to include the rest of the men in her comments. "Beware, if Mr. Hoffman has any financial arrangements with you, I would strongly advise you take your money in cash, immediately."

"That won't be a problem, honey. These men are giving the money to me."

"I'm betting the agents are planning to cash in on your little project." She raised her head, tossing back her hair, though the motion hurt. So much. "How about it, Temple? Short?" She imbued their names with scorn. "You think you're getting enough to retire? You ever think you might end up like Tony B?"

The affability left Hoffman's face. "Johnson, shut that bitch up." He looked over at the agents, who were frowning. "Don't listen to her. For crap's sake, you know how she lies. She's just mad because I've horned in on her profits."

Lana let Mike push her forward, leaning on his hold, until they were close enough to be able to talk in a quieter voice. "I wouldn't count my profits just yet if I were you, Ralphie."

"Delusional as always," Steve Short said, with a derisive laugh. "It's not like you'll be walking out of here under your own power."

"Yesss." Hoffman drew the word out, nearly hissing his satisfaction. "We have such plans for you. Don't we, Aleksei?" He turned to the tall Russian, who had stepped toward the young girls. Several guards had also moved toward the stage. "Let's not be too hasty, gentlemen. We need to stick to the original program. Which starts with the lovely Lana Greene."

Thompson pretended to shove Lana into a circle of light, staying at her side but slightly behind her. In the light, her bruising was more obvious, as was her clothing.

"This was not the garment I chose for her."

She could feel Thompson's shrug. "Didn't fit," he explained.

"It does not matter." Aleksei's voice was as good as a shrug.

"I agree. It's not as if she'll be wearing it for long." Agent Temple no longer even tried to sound polite.

"Stupid-stupid," Mike breathed in her ear.

She lifted one shoulder, most of her attention on the young girls.

"Now, now," Hoffman chided in his overly cheerful voice. "Mr. Novakov specifically asked to have Ms. Greene here. It seems he has some unfinished business with our Lana."

"He's not the only one," Agent Temple muttered.

Hoffman let out a short laugh. "I'm sure you will have plenty of time to 'discuss' business with your former colleague."

"No colleague of ours. She's as much a part of the trafficking as—well, as Novakov is."

Aleksei merely turned, raising an eyebrow, then looked over at Lana.

"Yeah, you kind of got that wrong, guys. I pretty much had nothing to do with trafficking."

"What are you talking about? You were a big part of it. You helped obtain the girls and sell the girls. Hell, you brought us into it."

"Did I really?"

"You said you did."

"Yeah, here's the thing. I lied. Yep, I lied about bringing in the girls. I lied about selling the girls. I pretty much lied about everything I said to you ever since I found out you were the ones behind too much of the trafficking. You and your buddy Ralph." She nodded at Hoffman, who stood with his mouth hanging open.

"You don't know what you're talking about," Agent Short spluttered.

"Actually, I do. I've been collecting a lot of information about your little empire. Enough to get an investigation going."

"We go down, you go down. We have our own proof. We have you on tape"

"Hate to let you down. I lied on that tape."

"You'll have a hard time proving it," Hoffman blustered, reaching into his coat.

The lights flared then went out as bodies exploded into the room from the ceiling and doors and what seemed to be through the walls. Confusion and noise reigned for what felt like an interminable time, but no doubt was less than a minute before the lights came up again. Dark-clad men stood in front of the girls, while the guards were on the floor being secured by more of the same.

A new voice, deadly, spoke from the behind her directly to the agents, who had reached for their own weapons. "I don't think you want to do that."

"And Adam Roberts dying? Yeah, I lied about that too." Lana managed to pull her mouth into a mocking smile before the floor tilted and the room grew dark again. She barely felt the arms around her, catching her before she hit the floor.

# Chapter 22

"Well, that was pretty damned stupid."

Adam felt his upper arms grabbed on both sides, helping him ease to his knees, supporting Lana as well as he could with his leg screaming at him from hip to socket. He held her limp body against his chest, ignoring the voices around him while he searched for a pulse. When hands reached for her, he pulled her back.

"It's okay, sir. Here, we have a gurney for her. See? You need to let her go so you can take care of yourself."

As he reluctantly allowed the young medic to lift Lana from his arms, Adam pulled in a deep breath, trying to strengthen himself against his own body-wide ache.

"Your turn, sir."

Adam felt a horizontal rod push against his back while hard hands pulled him up and supported his legs until he could straighten them out on another gurney. His head was cranked up until he could see Lana, swollen eyes closed, filthy hair against her bruised face. But alive. She'd never looked more beautiful to him.

*೭∽೭∽*

"You picked a hell of a time to show your faces." A voice that sounded an awful lot like Roz drilled into Lana's head.

When Lana tried to raise her hand, she could only lift it a few inches. Before she could even tense her muscles, gloved fingers covered her wrist.

"Relax, ma'am. You need your fluids. We don't want you to pull out the needles."

"Don't want—" She tried to speak with force but only managed a half whisper.

"You need it. Whatever they used on you has to flush from your system. Looks like you were pretty dehydrated to start."

She swallowed, processing this slowly. Why dehydrated? No stranger to deserts and controlled inside atmospheres, she always made sure to drink a lot. Except—

"The girls?"

"They're fine. Well, as fine as their situation allows." Again, Roz. Where was…

Adam's voice rumbled from a few feet away. "Seems we had more help than we realized."

She turned toward the sound. At least her head wasn't restrained, but her eyelids felt glued together. Wheels creaked against the floor, then strong fingers interlinked with her free hand. A warm moist cloth passed over her eyes then across her face until she could blink and see long fingers holding a limp cloth moving away from her. Roz again. Another face, craggy, lined, shadowed with exhaustion, came into view. Worry shone from the bright green eyes.

"Hey, Goldilocks." His raspy whisper was deep, intimate. "How you holding up?"

She opened her mouth to answer then tried to swallow away the dryness. A straw touched the side of her mouth, angled so she could suck down moisture without moving her head. A good thing, since dwarves were pounding away inside her brain.

"Who?"

"Captain Adam Roberts, Retired." His mouth moved in a real smile, not just a quirky grin. She tried to scowl but had to be satisfied with a nose wrinkle. "Okay, who? Ty's around somewhere, along with Powers's support team. And it seems like we've acquired a new set of agents. No, don't sit up."

A flash of pain stopped her even before his warning, then she felt Roz press her fingers lightly on her shoulder. "I don't think either one of you is up to much dialogue. How about I talk, you add what I don't know?"

Lana nodded carefully and saw Adam do the same.

"Let's start by cranking this gurney up a little to get you off the floor, raise your head. And, you agents? Why not stand where they can see you instead of looming in the corners?"

"We really can't—" one of the agents started to protest but acceded to moving, along with his partner.

Lana saw someone taller behind them—Ty, urging them into the light like a tour guide. A giggle started to form in the back of her throat at the thought. She sobered soon enough when she could see the faces clearly. "You?" she croaked.

The men, innocuously dressed in casual slacks and loose shirts, stood at the end of the gurney as if uncomfortable to be on display. Hands in pockets, they tipped their faces away and looked down. Lana swallowed the offered sip of water without looking away from them.

"I think she's asking who you are. Or maybe she's asking why you're here."

"They didn't—"

"Gotcha. I'm betting these are the agents you tried to report Tweedledum and Tweedledummer to."

Grateful she didn't need to talk—to explain—Lana nodded.

"And they blew you off, didn't they?"

Adam's raspy voice wasn't loud, but she felt the support, the anger, almost as much as she felt the strength in the fingers intertwined with hers.

"We can't talk about it—" one of the agents started to say.

"Yeah, I think you can." That was Ty, looming behind them physically as much as his voice lashed out at them.

"We can explain, but not here. Ms. Randolph—"

"Greene," chorused four voices.

The agent took a step back. "Okay, Ms. Greene." He looked at his partner, who shrugged. "We can explain, but not here. We need to find someplace less public."

"And more like a hospital," one of the medics pointed out. "We've got her stabilized, but she needs a serious going over. Both of them do."

"No hospitals," Lana managed.

"Hospital," Adam insisted.

"No." She closed her eyes, trying to conserve strength. "Secrets—"

The other agent spoke into the tension surrounding them. "We need to get you somewhere more private, so we can start moving these girls."

Lana felt the surface beneath her shift, and Adam's fingers slid away from hers. *No!* She made a grab for him.

"Right behind you, Goldilocks. Just a short trip, and we'll finally get some answers."

❧❧❧

She hurt. Everywhere. She didn't feel like she was

going to dry up and blow away on the desert wind any longer, but there wasn't much else positive to say about her body, her head.

It was quiet here, only hushed voices intruding on her thoughts.

Hushed voices. Whose? Identifying them pushed her through the fog seeming to be between her and being completely awake. She took a deep breath and let it out, bracing herself for the increase in pain she knew would come with lifting her head.

"Easy there. Don't sit up. Let me push a couple buttons. You let me know when it's too much." A new voice, male, accompanied a large hand on her chest. She felt her head raise until she was almost sitting. When the shifting caused her aches to intensify, she gasped and the raising stopped. She concentrated on opening her eyes, identifying the lined face of the taciturn doctor they'd met in the small clinic. Sommers, that was it. Dr. Sommers.

"You wanted privacy," Roz reminded her from somewhere off to the side. "And you needed—need care."

"Don't turn your head. You people want to not talk behind her? I don't know what they did to her, but her neck is one solid bruise."

She heard feet shuffle, and the area at the end of her bed filled with shapes that resolved into identifiable people. Except—

"Hey, Goldilocks," Adam rasped as he slipped his fingers into hers and leaned his body against the bed frame.

"Were you cleared to get out of bed?"

"Sorry, Doctor." Adam didn't sound contrite. "How's this?"

The bed shifted as he lifted his hip to rest near hers,

holding their linked hands on his thigh. His truncated thigh. He'd left off the prosthesis.

"Not quite what I had in mind." The doctor's voice was as dry as the desert outside, but he pulled a stool to the other side of Lana's bed, seating himself close enough to monitor her.

"This is highly confidential," one of the new agents began.

"Tough," Adam growled.

Lana squeezed his fingers as much as she could. From the sound of it, he was not in much better shape than she was.

"Same deal," Ty said. "You will make free with your information and answer our questions. Neither Ms. Greene nor Captain Roberts are in great condition— thanks to you. We'll talk for them as well as we can."

"Now, wait just a minute—"

"Nope." For once, there was no humor in Roz's voice. "We've had time to think about what's been happening, and it's been pretty obvious someone else was trying to pull strings behind the scene."

"That was necessary."

"Maybe in your mind. Let's start with some ID."

The agents glanced at each other, glared at Adam, then seemed to shrug and dug into inner pockets.

"Agents Roger Kelley and George Robinson. How are we to know you are any different from Short and Temple?"

"Ms. Ran—Greene knows who we are."

Lana nodded, feeling the pull as her brow furrowed. The agents seemed intent on Adam's falling off pant leg. Good, the distraction was working.

"Here's a bit of irony. These are the agents who blew you off when you tried to report Short and Temple?" Adam said, with a grimace. "And now they want you to vouch for them?"

"Now see here, Captain—"

"At least you got that right. I think it's time for some explanations."

Lana drew a breath, bracing herself to not hide whatever pain she might feel, in spite of the drugs bolstering her body. "These are the agents I tried to tell about what Temple and Short were doing. They told me they didn't take advice from a tramp who obviously wanted to get back at her pimps." She turned her head enough to watch Adam's face, but it was Ty who stepped forward to grab one of the agents by the shoulder. Both agents turned as if they had fought together before, standing so they could keep everyone in their field of vision.

"Don't." Lana managed to push some strength behind the word. "They were simply reacting to my cover story. I didn't realize I was so good."

"Ms. Greene, we need—we want—to apologize for that. We did not dig deep enough into your file."

"In fact, a lot of the file had disappeared before we arrived in Nevada."

The agents stood where they could see her and Ty and remained balanced to move if necessary.

"Because of your short sightedness, both Captain Roberts and Ms. Greene were put at serious risk," Ty said.

"No need to be dramatic."

"Captain Roberts was overpowered, taken captive, and dropped out of a helicopter after his prosthesis was removed by force," Dr. Sommers interjected, his voice brimming with anger. "He suffered a partial dislocation of his hip, extreme exposure, and dehydration nearly to the point of irrevocable kidney damage."

"Adam?" Lana whispered, feeling her throat seize up from the news.

He stroked her fingers, murmuring nonsense to soothe her.

"Ms. Greene was drugged, taken captive, dehydrated, beaten, kicked, and has possible spinal injuries," the doctor continued. "Her hand was obviously stepped on, either before or after it was pulled behind her back in tight restraints. She was not raped, if you were wondering."

Lana tried to draw into herself during this bare recital, wanting to be anywhere but under the scrutiny of so many eyes. She felt Adam's fingers caress hers again, and his thigh pressing against her side, and turned her head in his direction to see only support and concern in his eyes.

"Aleksei?" he asked quietly.

She nodded. "He saved me from that, at least."

"Novakov? What does he have to do with any of this besides interfering in the investigation?"

"Or being a potential buyer for the girls?"

"Oh, let me answer that," Roz purred. "Due to the influence of Agents Temple and Short, Aleksei Novakov believed Lana was responsible for his sister's death. With their encouragement, he entered the US with a group of 'bodyguards' borrowed from some members of the Russian Mafia." She looked over at Lana, who nodded in agreement. "Lana was threatened after seeing one of the girls injured or dead in a suite rented for a meeting of pedophiles," Roz continued. "That's right, gentlemen, Lana was there trying to protect the girls, in spite of her treatment by the people who were supposed to be doing that very thing—that would be you two agents. She called the only person she knew would help, no matter what they thought of her personally."

"That would be me," Ty interjected.

"We got her to the ranch where she could tell us what was going on," Roz added.

"Amazingly, we managed to believe what she was saying in spite of our past history," Ty said. "Because we listened to her instead of blowing her off."

Roz nodded. "And because of that, we set up a team to take down this international nest of snakes, headed by men who were supposed to be protecting, not procuring. When they realized Adam would stand between Lana and trouble, they tried to eliminate him."

"Tried and failed," Lana managed before her voice faded out.

"Damn near managed it." Adam slid the water straw into her mouth. "If it wasn't for that mare, I wouldn't have made it." He looked over at Ty. "You have room on the ranch for a broke-down old mare?"

"Always room for one more old nag." Ty grinned and avoided Roz's affectionate nudge.

"All fascinating, I'm sure, but can you get to the point?" one of the agents asked.

"The point is, Special Agent Robinson, because you did not respond when Lana asked you to help those girls in danger, you are directly responsible for everything that has happened since then. Up to and including the girl who was found in a dumpster after she was killed at that so-called party."

"That seems a bit extreme. We needed evidence to take down agents under suspicion."

"Which Lana handed you on a silver platter."

They looked over at Lana. It almost seemed like they felt ashamed, then the moment passed. "The evidence had to be from a reliable source. For all we knew at the time, you were working with Temple and Short, not against them."

Lana managed to nod. "Then I was successful." She grabbed a breath. "For me to stay as close as possible to the girls, and the people involved in their situation, they had to keep believing I'd do anything if there was enough profit."

When she paused, Roz spoke up. "Before you open your mouth, Special Agent Robinson, that was a part she played—has, in fact, been playing for many years."

*But no more*, Lana thought. She was done with role playing. Adam's hand, warm on hers, bolstered her resolve.

"The question is not what you will attempt to do with Ms. Greene. The real question is what she can do to you," Adam's voice grated out, and there must have been something in his expression to make the agents pay attention.

Lana saw both Ty and Roz nod, a grim expression on their faces.

"How do you mean?"

"In the past—when Temple and Short were making her life miserable, when her business partner cheated her and set her up, when you threw her to the wolves—Ms. Greene was alone. She's not alone anymore."

Special Agent Robinson raised an eyebrow, looking around at their small group with what could only be a smirk. "Admirable, but I sincerely doubt you can stand against the US Government."

Adam chuckled. "You'd be surprised what we can do, by ourselves. But it's not just us."

"You ever meet Major Powers?" Ty asked, his voice bland, then he smirked when the agents reacted.

"He's not re—"

"He's real. Very real. And he hates trafficking, even more than Ms. Greene, if that's possible. He also doesn't have much time for people who get in the way of stopping said trafficking."

"We're not here to stop Ms. Greene." Special Agent Robinson offered what he might have considered a conciliatory smile. "Now that we understand who she is, and what she's done, we want to offer her a job."

Lana felt the bubble of anger rise out of her, but it ended up a harsh laugh which became a cough, leading to a spike of pain in her neck.

"Out," the doctor ordered. She heard the stool pushed back to crash into the wall as the he stood. "Now."

Without waiting to ensure obedience, he turned to Lana, easing her down against the bed. She felt Adam's calloused fingers burrowing into her hair as the room dimmed around her.

# Chapter 23

"They're gone." Dr. Sommer's voice was still crisp but not as strident.

Lana waited to straighten in the bed until his hand no longer pressed her back against the pillows. Carefully, watching for any new twinges, she toggled the bed adjustment until she was more upright.

"This passing out stuff has got to stop," she muttered. Easing her eyes open, she noticed Ty and Roz at the end of her bed, confusion on their faces.

"So this—" Roz indicated the room with a sweep of her graceful hand, ending with fingers pointing at Lana, "—this was all an act?"

"Not quite," Adam said, in a much healthier-sounding voice. "Lana was hurt, and I'm still nowhere near fighting strength. We needed to get those agents out of the way as quickly as possible. Convincing them Lana was badly injured seemed the most efficient way."

"She is injured," the doctor insisted. "Don't let her tell you otherwise. With rest—serious rest, not just dozing in the car on the way back into the city—" He sent a scowl her direction. "She'll be better in a couple of days."

"That last squeak was real," Lana admitted. "My neck is seriously sore. And my arm. And my stomach where Temple kicked me."

"Why are you avoiding these agents?" Roz sounded more puzzled than anything else. "Granted they seem a bit too *Men in Black*ish, but I thought they were more or less the good guys who could help clear your name."

"Why? Because I'm done with role playing. Done with working for people who would as soon throw me to the wolves as back me up. I told myself when Temple and Short were taken care of, I could—" She took a cautious breath, looking at the wall instead of the people around her. "—I could stop for a while and find myself."

"Just Lana," Adam murmured.

"Just Lana."

⌘

If she lay completely still, nothing hurt too much. But laying completely still did not take advantage of the wiry hair decorating smooth skin over hard flexing muscles. Nor did it caress her face against his chest or stroke her body against his. When she did dare move, when she attempted to nestle even closer, her body protested strongly, and a whimper escaped through her bruised lips.

"Shhh, Goldilocks." The chest under her cheek vibrated with his sleepy whisper. You're supposed to be sleeping. At least resting. Getting your energy back."

"It's not fair," she managed to mumble then paused to clear her throat. His chest shifted, then she felt a straw at her lips. Much better.

"What's not fair?" Was that a laugh in his voice?

"Super heroes and hot spy babes can get all beat up and jump into bed for another four hours of activity."

A chuckle rippled through his body, vibrating his

chest under her cheek. "Am I not living up to your expectations?"

She raised one hand far enough to tap against his stomach. "Down payment for a later slap." Idly, as if of their own volition, her fingers trailed through the narrowing band of hair until she reached loose, light-weight shorts hanging off his lean hips. Only to be stopped by a large hand. She managed a small pout while flattening her hand against the muscles in his stomach, letting her palm caress the powerful ridges.

"Sorry, Goldilocks, the spirit is very willing, but I think the flesh is weak for both of us. Those super heroes and hot spy chicks have people to keep them looking fresh. We just have each other."

She sighed then nodded. "Pretty sure you're right. Dammit."

"No problem. We have time. Lots of time."

"Don't forget we have to see a man about a horse," she murmured and managed a small smile when the chest under her cheek vibrated with a silent chuckle. She felt the sinfully comfortable bed under their bodies, the expensive soft sheets surrounding them. Took a deep breath, savoring his clean skin and the impersonal smell of a hotel room. Upper-end hotel room, considering the quality of the bedding. "Where—"

"Kyle Jorden—" He hesitated as if waiting for her to make the connection.

"Ty's rich neighbor. He helped you get to Vegas the first time."

"You got it. We're in an apartment of his. Not sure if it's a lease or what, but it's secure and no one knows where we are."

The promise of security and privacy was impossible to resist. Lana let her automatic wariness slide away as her body grew heavier until she let herself slide back into sleep. In another room, the phone rang. Before she could jolt up, Adam's arms closed around her, holding her still.

"Where's my—can't be mine, that's probably with the police," she mused.

Then she heard an unfamiliar masculine voice answer with a Southwestern drawl that sharpened immediately. The voice came closer until there was a soft knock on the door.

"You awake in there?"

"Yeah," Adam responded without moving, his arms continuing to hold her still.

"Sydney's gone into labor. They're on their way to the hospital."

Lana wrenched herself out of Adam's hold, bracing for the all-over soreness but, for now, ignoring it. She pushed the covers away, looking down long enough to ensure she was covered, then grabbed a robe draped across a chair.

By the time she was at the door, Adam was next to her, his arms slipped through the forearm braces of metal crutches, one of the crutches raised across the door to stop her.

"Jorden?" Adam eased the door open enough to talk through but kept Lana out of sight.

"Yeah." The rancher stepped back, looking down at the tablet in his hand. "Get yourselves ready, I'll find you a flight." He glanced up, and a smile of pure mischief flashed across his handsome face. "You have time for a shower but only a shower. No hijinks."

Adam pushed the door shut, growling through Lana's giggles.

∽∾∽∾

"I did some shuffling around," Kyle explained as he

turned into the lane leading to his Nevada ranch. "So we have the Baron instead of the Cirrus."

Lana sat up as much as she could. "You have a Baron? I'm impressed." Her voice held more mockery than approval, but she obviously knew more about the planes than Adam did. Kyle glanced in the rear view mirror, eyes narrowed. Seeing his lack of approval, Lana smiled as serenely as she could manage. "I really appreciate you doing this. A commercial flight would have taken so much longer."

"Doing it for Devin. And Sydney."

"I realize you like my sister, Mr. Jorden, and I'm merely reaping the benefit of your admiration for her and her husband."

Adam started to speak up, to defend this woman who had come to mean so much to him. A small hand landed on his forearm, settling the warrior inside him. Lana could take care of herself, and he granted her that privilege.

Kyle faced forward, not saying anything until he had parked near a grouping of small planes. He opened his door but didn't get out, instead turning in his seat to look directly at Lana. She looked back, seeming serene, though Adam could see the pulse pounding in her delicate throat.

"Ma'am." He nodded in her direction as if acknowledging who she was as well as what she'd said. "I do believe it will be a pleasure to get to know Sydney's sister better." He turned to exit the car, settling a battered Western hat on his head. "Now let's go see another generation of hard-headed Starke men being born."

℘℘℘

Her sister looked small, dozing against propped-up

pillows, her hair the only significant color against hospital white sheets. The strong bones in her face, so similar yet so different. Spare and stripped down to reality while Lana had opted for the veneer of sophistication, Sydney seemed more at ease with herself than she had ever been. The obvious reason lounged next to the hospital bed in a padded chair, one hand snaked through the bed bars, connecting to her sister with strong calloused fingers. The other arm cradled a bundle of blankets in the secure crook of his arm. Blankets topped by an impossible tiny pink knit cap. Pink. No wonder Devin looked both ecstatic and scared senseless.

"Kind of a game changer, isn't it?" Lana asked in a voice low enough not to alert her sister.

"A girl?"

"A baby. You think you're ready for them, that you've made all your plans. Then you hold them for the first time and realize you know nothing."

"You had a baby?" His keen golden eyes narrowed in her direction.

"Not me. Some of my friends. Took them down in a second. They ended up great parents, but that first day they either gibbered or cried."

A slight smile twisted his normally hard mouth. "I got the crying out of the way already."

"Don't kid yourself, those tears will be hanging around for a long time—thirty or forty years. Our dad could tear up at the oddest times."

"It didn't bother him, having girls instead of boys?"

She tamped down the flash of anger. "Is it bothering you?"

"Nope. We didn't check in advance. We didn't care. We just wanted a healthy baby." He looked down again, his face softening in a way she bet only Sydney had seen before. "Yeah, I had thoughts of fishing and hunting."

"No reason she can't do those if she wants. It never stopped us. You just have to be ready for the daddy-daughter days at school."

"Did your dad—" He hesitated as if wondering how that memory would affect her.

"When our mother let him," came a soft voice from the bed. Sydney's eyes slitted open, taking in the scene in one well-trained glance. Her fingers tightened, and she smiled at the tiny bundle in the big man's arm.

"Water?" Lana asked, easing to the other side of the bed. At the nod, she reached for the cup, holding the straw where it could be reached without effort.

Sydney sipped, gulped, sipped again, then nodded. "Thanks." Her voice was a little more clear but still tired. "Our mother didn't want us to spend too much time with Dad. She implied he would be a bad influence."

"But their separation agreement allowed us to spend time with him, and she didn't want to lose the child support. So she had to let us go. Didn't stop her from trying to cast aspersions on him when we came back." Lana forced calm into her voice, then a stray memory jumped up, and she smiled. "When Syd first heard that phrase, she thought it was 'cast asparagus,' and wondered why we were throwing vegetables around."

"You would remember that," Sydney muttered through a snorted giggle. "Oops, don't make me laugh."

Lana immediately moved in to apologize but not before Devin was there, worry on his face.

Syd managed a weak smile. "Totally worth it, babe. Such a great memory. Now, gimme our baby girl." She reached up to snuggle the baby against her chest, Devin's hand dark and large and comforting against the tiny back.

The intimacy pulled at something deep within Lana, and she turned away, not wanting to intrude.

Until a large hand clamped around her wrist, strength

tempered to hold her without pressure. "Get back here," Devin growled. "Might as well start right away with being the favorite auntie."

Lana let herself be pulled into position on the other side of the bed and dared to rest her hand against that tiny promise of together. Of family born and made. Speaking of which... "Where's Roz and Ty?"

"On their way. They got hung up." Devin's answer was terse, his tone non-cooperative.

Syd offered a small apologetic smile. Lana felt the door open behind her, and the energy of the new person in the room.

Adam slipped into the room, a half smile pulling at his mouth as he took in the group around the bed. "Pink, huh? Looking forward to eighteen years of keeping rowdy, young males away from her?"

"Thirty. She won't date until then, and only boys we approve."

Lana snorted a laugh. "Good luck on that one." She turned, not being able to twist her neck yet. Adam had the same taciturn expression, but she saw more of a shadow. "What's wrong? Are your men okay?"

"Everybody's fine. I finally got hold of that horse rescue rancher. The mare's gone." He stepped farther into the room when a sound of distress slipped out of her mouth. "Not that way—someone adopted her."

"I didn't think he was going to let her go until she was in better condition."

"You guys want a pet horse, we have plenty of spares." Devin's voice sounded caustic, but a near smile twisted his mouth.

Adam managed a small chuckle. "That's okay. She was just kind of special."

"You can sort it out later. If you're using the cane, your leg is probably hurting you. The cabin's all set up.

You should got back to the ranch and get some rest."

Something in his voice, something in the bland expression on Sydney's face, caught Lana's attention just before a huge yawn took over. Rest, in a bed she didn't have to leave for hours, maybe even days, sounded like a great idea.

சுஒஒ

Rest didn't happen right away.

They first checked in with Powers concerning the activity in Nevada, to learn, to their satisfaction, that Special Agents Temple and Short faced multiple charges and years of punishment. Aleksei Novakov was politely thanked for his help, such as it was, and escorted to the airport, his bodyguards evicted under guard even before he left. Mike Thompson had faded back into his shadow world. Powers shared this information himself, allowing his voice to reveal satisfaction over the culmination of their work. And also over the information shared about the new baby.

"Think he'll send an application for future employment?" Lana asked as the call ended.

Adam smirked. "I'd like to see him try. I'm betting that little girl will be winding a lot of strong men around her little fingers." He slipped his arm around her, pulling her gently against his chest. "Right now I'm more concerned with taking care of my own woman."

She nestled, completely agreeing with his agenda.

First a shower, appropriately conserving water. Then the intimate touches in the dark, relearning each other. Finding the places that hurt and soothing them. Growing passion and setting it free until hearts healed and muscles eased. Until they could fall together into a deep and blissful sleep.

In the darkest part of the night, the rumble of a powerful engine called them out of their sleep, along with hushed voices, muffled hoof beats, welcoming nickers.

Lana raised her head against the hold of strong fingers in her hair. "It's a ranch," she whispered, holding back the suspicion of a giggle. "They're just coming in late."

She let him snuggle her face against his shoulder and eased back to sleep with a smile pulling at her lips.

ℰↂℰↂ

"You're drinking coffee?" Adam followed his voice out through the screen door.

"Seemed like the right thing to help blow away some cobwebs." She raised her face into the stroke of the new day's sun, quickly replaced by strong fingers, then a cheek bristling with several days' whiskers. "Hmmm, interesting sensation. You planning on growing a beard?"

"You want me to grow a beard?"

That gave her pause, with a flash of how that beard could feel against—oh, yeah. "It could have its uses." She allowed the comfort she felt to show in her voice. Through the pine trees, she could just see the large pens where special horses paced, looking over to the barn for attention. Except for one horse that stood very still, as if soaking up the sensations of a high-country morning.

Adam set his coffee cup down on the side table, leaning over to surround her with his warmth, his scent. "You been out here long?"

"Long enough." She took another sip of the rich brew, raising her chin just enough to direct his attention to that one horse, coat showing almost golden in the growing light, stretched over such a thin body. From the stiffening of his arms around her, she knew when he noticed.

"What the—how did she—is that—"

"I do believe that mare followed you home. I bet you can keep her."

"I bet *we* can keep her." He emphasized the critical word, stepping away and turning back to look at her, the jewel-like green of his eyes brighter than usual, not letting go of her hand. "If that's what you want?"

She stood, setting down her own cup and stretching on her toes to touch her lips to his mouth—a gentle, seeking touch. "I can't think of anyone else I would allow to see me in ratty old yoga pants and fuzzy slippers. Much less have me drinking coffee. Let's go pet our horse."

He looked at the mare then back at her. "Later."

## THE END…AND THE BEGINNING

## About the Author

Mona Karel became convinced at an early age that her life would not really begin until she was about thirty five. She has no idea what precipitated that thought, but she claims she was a strange child. Until reaching that age, she led a peripatetic existence for many years, criss-crossing the country, working with horses and dogs—and waiting tables to support her other jobs. At thirty five, when many people are well into raising their families, Karel settled down to "real" work as a buyer and expediter. She married a high school teacher, which led to over twenty years in Southern California.

Karel can't remember a time she wasn't reading, though she doesn't remember much fun with Dick and Jane. Her preferred stories involved dogs and horses, and once she had gone through every horse book in the high school library, she started in on Civil War stories. They rode horses, didn't they? At that time romance was swash-bucklers and Gothic, and many preferred the stronger heroines of Mary Stewart and Victoria Holt. Then Karel discovered romance in the form of Silhouette, Candle-light, and RWA, and her life was complete. Karel has since retired to New Mexico, where she lives in the wind at 6,500 feet with her Salukis. When not writing or going to dog shows, Karel works at a solar related firm.

www.ingramcontent.com/pod-product-compliance
Lightning Source LLC
Chambersburg PA
CBHW072203170626
46813CB00003B/775